About th

My dad is Paul Holbrook and he is the author of whatever book this may be. I haven't read it.

Paul Holbrook lives in a small house in North Yorkshire with his wife, two amazing daughters, his father-in-law and of course his dog Lucy, who he loves with all his heart. I am his youngest daughter and he didn't realise what he had done by asking *me* to write his biography – love you Dad! Anyway, he has been doing some work with Ryedale Special Families for quite some time now, along with his job as a teaching assistant at the local secondary school. He has been into horror stories and Jack the Ripper for a long time now and he directed his passion for horror into a group of thrilling books, all of which I have not read, but will in the future. He was overjoyed at finally finishing this book, and finding Unbound to publish his book. I really hope you enjoy this book.

– Eve Holbrook

DOMINI MORTUM

DOMINI MORTUM

THE GHASTLY INVESTIGATIONS OF SAMUEL WEAVER

PAUL HOLBROOK

Unbound Digital

This edition first published in 2018

Unbound

6th Floor Mutual House, 70 Conduit Street, London W1S 2GF

www.unbound.com

ISBN (eBook): 978-1-912618-15-6
ISBN (Paperback): 978-1-912618-14-9

Design by Mecob

Printed in Great Britain by Clays Ltd, Elcograf S.p.A.

Thank you to my test readers Ian J Williams, Rob Townsend, Louise Moore, Debbie Thompson, and of course Kathryn Holbrook, whose combined support, guidance, and belief have helped me through from the first draft to making this book a reality.

I would like to dedicate this book to my uncle, Bob Thorpe, for his generous support, and once again to Kathryn, for believing in me and being there always. xx

Dear Reader,

The book you are holding came about in a rather different way to most others. It was funded directly by readers through a new website: Unbound.

Unbound is the creation of three writers. We started the company because we believed there had to be a better deal for both writers and readers. On the Unbound website, authors share the ideas for the books they want to write directly with readers. If enough of you support the book by pledging for it in advance, we produce a beautifully bound special subscribers' edition and distribute a regular edition and e-book wherever books are sold, in shops and online.

This new way of publishing is actually a very old idea (Samuel Johnson funded his dictionary this way). We're just using the internet to build each writer a network of patrons. Here, at the back of this book, you'll find the names of all the people who made it happen.

Publishing in this way means readers are no longer just passive consumers of the books they buy, and authors are free to write the books they really want. They get a much fairer return too – half the profits their books generate, rather than a tiny percentage of the cover price.

If you're not yet a subscriber, we hope that you'll want to join our publishing revolution and have your name listed in one of our books in the future. To get you started, here is a £5 discount on your first pledge. Just visit unbound.com, make your pledge and type DARKE18 in the promo code box when you check out.

Thank you for your support,

Dan, Justin and John
Founders, Unbound

Super Patrons

Mark Alexander
Andrew Arnell
Beverley Barf
Fliss Barker
Stephen Begg
Helen Binks
Angie Bowers
Kevin Bragg
Linda Bramley
Richard W H Bray
Dawn Briston
Tanvir Bush
Joanna Chambers
Renee Chambers
William Chambers
GMark Cole
Dom Conlon
Hilary Corton
Maureen Cresswell
Catherine Davies
Jessica Duchen
Corey Eastwood
Micheal Elliott
John Ellson
David Fairclough
Jane Gascoyne
Frances Hakkak
E O Higgins
Justin Hill
Bernard Hill
Emily Holbrook
Kenneth Holbrook

Eve Holbrook
Simon Holden
Claire Marie Jackson
Eunice Jaquez
Julie Jones
Dan Kieran
Patrick Kincaid
Ewan Lawrie
Aimee Lawson
Milcah Marcelo
Jessica Martin
Chloe Martin-Owen
Philip Middleton
Emma & David Milbourn
John Mitchinson
Virginia Moffatt
John Moloney
Tommy Moore
Louise Moore
Adrian Mules
Karen O'Sullivan
Tiarnan OCleirigh
Andy Park
Gary Parker
Julia Parker
Lorraine Phippen
Justin Pollard
Charlie Ridgewell
Stephanie Segal
Janice Staines
Tabatha Stirling
Diana Tanaka
Tot Taylor
George Thomas
Stacey Thorne
Bob Thorpe

Rob Townsend
Mark Vent
Prakash Vyas
Dale Walters
Wendy Wardell
Pete White
Ian J Williams
Graham Worth
Diana Worth

1

Beginnings

Death is not the end.

There is no eternal silence when one passes from the world of the living. There are also no such places as heaven or hell. I know this now.

I was raised with a firm belief in heaven and God's greater glory. An unbending confidence in the existence of a better place, safe within the arms of our creator; a place towards which all those who have faith, and who lead a pure and simple life, are taken when their time upon this earth has ended. A place that does not exist.

But death is not the end.

***

'It is a truly evil thing that has been done here today.' The man in the dark brown suit looked down at the body by his feet. His voice sounded dry – impassive, even, but I knew the man well and I knew how much scenes like this disturbed him.

He removed his scuffed bowler hat, scratching at his nest of red hair. His ruddy, stubbled cheeks puffed out as he looked upon her body. He was a large man; someone whom I would imagine was powerful and dangerous in his youth. Now, however, he looked beaten.

The child's eyes were cold and blank; there was no soul in her body, just stillness. Her long, blonde hair was dirty and matted, stuck roughly across her forehead like some ill-fitting wig. She was almost naked, for not even in death had she been afforded dignity. The remnants of a tattered grey dress showed upon her shoulders and, at the other end of her pale, skinny body, she wore a solitary shoe, well worn with the beginnings of a hole. I only dared imagine what terrible ordeal she had been subjected to before her life was finally taken.

Had she been alive, afforded a bath and a set of new clothes, she would have been a sweet child to see, happy and smiling, eyes full of joy and wonder. I was familiar with this area. I had been in rooms like this before and I had seen countless others – different ages, different genders but they all shared the same things: poverty, hunger and murderous death. I would have shed a tear at her demise, but to me she was the source of my living and my tears did not freely fall.

'How long has she been dead?' I asked, not taking my eyes from her face.

'I'm no doctor, but I would say within the last day, five hours, no more than that. The smell of death has not set in yet to this room.' He nudged the girl's shoulder with his boot, flaking off some dried blood.

I crouched down and looked closely at the large splits which ran down from her chest to her tiny waist. The weapon that had done this to her had not been sharp and, as such, the force needed to create such large wounds must have been great indeed. The knife had not yet been found and I doubted that it ever would be. To the experienced eye, though, everything you wished to know about the weapon could be read from the wound. I counted myself as relatively inexperienced, but it was possibly a large kitchen chopping knife, with a blade which was chipped through use, causing tears to the skin. I looked up at the Inspector; he would have thought this through already and noted it upon his first sight of the body.

'Are you sure it was the mother?' I asked, pressing her skin lightly and noting how cold the girl was to the touch.

'That's where I would put my money,' he muttered. 'The father ain't been on the scene for years. Mary Pershaw, the mother, has been falling foul of the law lately, trying to roll her marks, even getting the girl in on the act, as bait. I've pulled her into the station three times this last month alone. Sweet girl, really. I felt sorry for her. I even set her up with a new agency in Marylebone, temporary service work in some of the well-to-do houses. She should have started with them last week.' He shook his head. As much as he was good at his job, he had far too much heart. He would not last much longer. 'She must have just lost it. Neighbour says she heard screaming in here first thing this morning, both Mary and the girl; he banged on the door telling them to shut up. Mary came to the door covered in claret and told him to leave her be, slammed the door in his face. By the time the local police arrived they found Mum gone and the kid ripped to shreds; it doesn't take a great mind to work out what happened.' He walked to the window, wiping his fingers across the glass and making a clear gap in the dust and grease. 'Mary won't get far before she's picked up... poor sod.'

'You speak like you have sympathy for her. The woman's obviously an hysteric. She needs the noose, not a bleeding heart.' I had misread the level of pity in him, however, and he flew at me, pushing me from where I crouched, leaving me sprawled on the blood-covered floor.

'Watch your mouth, Sam Weaver!' His gravelled voice cracked in anger. 'You know nothing of what goes on behind these doors and you are only here because of my friendships with those above you! Get on with your business and take your leave, before I lose my good temper and throw you from this here window!' His burst of anger shocked me. I would never have imagined that someone so large could move at such speed. I had forgotten his reputation for sudden violence.

'I beg your pardon, Abe. I did not mean any offence to you. I was just speaking my mind.' I picked myself up from the floor and withdrew my materials from the leather satchel. It would not take me long to create a rough draft for my image, for I had already taken in the sights of the room. This first drawing would be concerned with the shape of the body upon the floor. I prided myself on being as realistic as possible, as brutal and horrific as you like; that's what made me so good, that's what sold newspapers.

My initial drawing would be taken back to my rooms, where I would spend time embellishing and completing the sketch-work, before delivering it to the offices of *The Illustrated Police News*. It would then be passed on to one of the engravers employed by Mr Purkess, the proprietor. These engravers would finely carve my work into blocks of box wood. There are some who think that these engravers are artists in their own right; some who think the engravers are responsible for the quality of the pictures adorning the covers of the newspaper. They were merely workhorses, dull and mindless transcribers of a greater art.

As I pencilled the outline of the child's body, I sensed the presence of the police inspector behind me, looking down at the paper as the girl's image slowly appeared. I heard the slight pop of a stopper, closely followed by the small slosh of liquid. It was a sound that I was used to when with him; whisky was probably the only thing that kept him going through the day.

'I apologise, Weaver,' he grumbled. 'I should learn to control myself better. It is hard, though, when you know the victims. It's a terrible thing when a child dies. There have been at least half a dozen like this in the last couple of weeks: child dead, mother missing. A cynical man would think that there was something funny going on, but there's nothing that I can see to link the deaths.'

I did not reply – my mind was elsewhere, thinking of the words that I would use to describe the scene, words which I would submit along with the finished picture.

'Do you know the child's name?' I asked, adding a picture of a wild-haired, screaming woman wielding a knife.

'No. Does it matter?'

I did not reply and continued to draw.

He paced the room, waiting for me to finish. There would be others arriving soon, men to take the body off to be examined by doctors so that they could decide what the Inspector and I already knew.

'I'll be finished in a whisker, Abraham,' I said, putting the final touches to my initial sketches. 'Maybe we can adjourn to the pub at the end of the street, catch a couple of quick ones before we have to go about our business. What do you say?'

I knew that the Inspector would never turn down a drink and I had other, more pressing matters in mind, matters that only he could assist me with.

***

Over the past few months I had nurtured my professional but friendly relationship with the good Inspector Thomas, which included offering him the opportunity for drinks when possible. We visited various taverns across the west side of London and I always spent the time teasing out information from him whenever I could; always with subtlety, always in a friendly and caring manner. Deep within, however, this information fed my obsession.

We entered the pub and approached the bar. Those that stood in our way parted before us like a tide, making a clear path for myself and my large companion to avail ourselves of the liquid delights held therein.

The barman, who, like everyone else in the pub, knew the good Inspector, began to pour our drinks before either of us had said a word.

Abe reached for the inside pocket of his coat, a gesture of sorts, and one which received the expected outcome. The barman shook his head.

'Have that one on me, Inspector Thomas, as thanks for all your assistance in the past.' The other customers lowered their eyes and stayed quiet.

I made a point of nodding slightly to the barman, a prearranged sign that he was to keep sending drinks and I would settle any debts.

'Shall we sit awhile, Inspector?' I said, motioning towards a booth to our left.

He grumbled in reply and made his way to the seat, pushing his generous frame along the bench.

'Days like these weigh heavy upon the soul, Abe.' I took a small sip of my beer. 'I find that a gentle drink helps to mask the horror of what our eyes have seen, does it not?'

He shook his head and lifted the tankard to his lips, draining half of the contents and leaving a line of froth on his broad red moustaches. He was in a drinking mood and I smelled my quarry.

'You are correct, Sam, most correct. It is a small mercy in this job, a small, but blessed, mercy. Today is nothing, though. You would not believe the things that I have seen in my time.' His eyes cast towards the soot-caked windows. 'Did I ever tell you that I used to work on the other side of London? The East End?'

'I think you may have mentioned it before, Abe,' I said, motioning to the barman to start pouring another drink for the Inspector. 'Where was it you were stationed?'

'It was Whitechapel,' he said. 'H Division, the back end of the world, policing the worst that the world has to offer. I was a sergeant under Inspector Frederick Draper.'

'Ah, Whitechapel.' I winced. 'A horror of a place. I had even heard of it before I came to London.' I took another sip of my drink and eyed him carefully; he had lost himself in that place. The tension within me rose; I was so close to my goal now that it was hard to contain my excitement. 'You must have seen some horrible sights. There have been some big cases in Whitechapel in the past.'

The Inspector drained his drink and a new one appeared at the table just in time. He immediately reached for it – this was too easy.

'I knew Darke,' he said between gulps.

'Who?'

'The killer, Sibelius Darke, the Pale Demon. Surely do not tell me you have never heard of him? I met him a few times, and had him down for it from the start. I had him within my grasp – but I was foiled by my betters and forces out of my control. I even had him the night before his most terrible act.' His faced flushed at the memory.

'The Pale Demon,' I said. 'I had not heard of him before last year. Even in York, a city where we pride ourselves on knowing the nation's events, the name of Sibelius Darke is not one which I had heard mentioned.'

This was of course an extreme lie; I had known of the name Sibelius Darke since the first stories of him appeared on the front pages of every newspaper worth its salt six years earlier.

An immigrant of Finnish descent, Darke (born Dhakrot) had brutally carved a name out for himself in Whitechapel during the late autumn of 1877. He was a portrait photographer who had a studio on Osborn Street, a short walk away from his family's undertaking business. Despite not following in his father's footsteps in the funeral trade, he did have a peculiarly morbid speciality regarding the photographs that he made his business from. It was from family portraits of the recently deceased that he made his name, creating what had become known as memento mori: reminders of the loved ones lost and of the fleeting nature of our time in this world.

Following a series of deaths in the area involving young street children, Sibelius Darke had come to the attention of the police and the investigating Inspector Frederick Draper, on the discovery of Darke's father and brother, who were murdered in their home and suffering from similar injuries to those suffered by the urchins. He was questioned on more than one occasion, but never arrested for the string of murders, which eventually came to a crescendo following the terrible murder one night of several boys in St Mark's Orphanage, just yards from Inspector Draper's police station.

Strangely he was not arrested, despite being seen outside the orphanage on the night of the killings. The following day, Darke visited the Dolorian Club, his gentlemen's club in Pall Mall, shooting many members at random and setting fire to the building. His guilt could no longer be denied; but, before he could be taken in by the police, he committed suicide by taking poison and setting his own studio ablaze.

The case of Sibelius Darke had been an obsession of mine since I first heard the name, and when I moved to London I began to collect as much information about him as I could, in the hope of bringing it all together by writing a book on his terrible crimes. The fact that I was now sitting drinking with Abraham Thomas, who knew both Inspector Draper and Sibelius Darke, was no lucky coincidence; I am a man who always succeeds in getting what he wants, whatever the price.

I looked at Thomas now and drummed my fingers upon the table. 'Tell me,' I said innocently. 'Is it true that he was a child killer and a cannibal?'

'He was, and more besides. Do you know that he killed his own father and brother? Strung up by their ankles from the staircase like sides of beef, they were. The things that he did to them do not bear belief. His brother Nikolas's head was torn clear of his shoulders, separated by nothing more than a madman's hands. That poor boy was spared, though, when compared to the treatment meted out to their father. Tortured he was, slowly ripped and shredded with no weapons other than teeth and nails – his tongue was even taken from him whilst he lived. The doctor said that it was probably bitten out. You can only wonder at the depths of depravity and bloodlust that Darke sank to in his murderous frenzies.'

He pushed some more of the drink down his throat, before placing the now empty tankard on the table.

The barman came over with another and I asked for a whisky for the pair of us, a small tot to push the big man over the edge.

'I had him, you know, Sam. Just before he did his worst,' he continued.

'The orphanage? I heard it was a terrible scene.'

'Poor little bleeders. Darke was in the station and being held on both sides by my officers on the night it happened. I shall never forgive myself for not keeping him, but I knew that I would be for the chop if I held him.'

'What do you mean, Abe?' I asked. This was new to me.

'I had been told that he was not to be held, not to be locked up; my hands were tied. We were told to follow him, to watch him, but that he was in no way a suspect and was not to be treated as such. We were told that our killer had been found the previous night, a man named Arthur Downing, found hanged from his rafters on Love Lane.'

The Inspector paused for a moment. 'He came to us, though! He came through our very doors at Leman Street and taunted us with what he was about to do! I bade the men hold him for a while, but I was just playing with him, having some sport. Nobody believed that he would actually do it. When he made to escape from the hands of my men I told them to leave him be. He was crazed and harmless, I told them. Those boys, those poor, poor boys.' He drifted away from me. 'I saw their remains, Sam. I walked among their broken and torn bodies, saw what was left of them, what he had done.'

'How did it end? How was he caught?'

'He wasn't caught. He died and got away with it all. Burned to ashes at his rooms he was, two days after the orphanage. I remember a young constable, Townsend I think his name was, ran into the station calling out that the Darke place was alight, so we ran to it thinking that the mob had burned him for a child killer.

'When I got to Osborn Street, the place was on fire. Crowds had gathered; most had come to see it and to help to try to put it out before it spread, but there was some fighting an' all. Some of the crowd had started shouting out to let the place burn to the ground, let the flames take Darke back to hell. They tried to stop the people carrying water; they knocked the pails out of their hands. That was when the woman ran out of the building and into my arms.'

'A woman? There was a woman in the building with him?' I had not heard this before either.

'Yes, young thing she was, little more than a child herself. God only knows what horrors he had put her through; she was crying and raving, as crazed as I have ever seen someone.' He shivered, and took another drink, knocking back the whisky and starting on the next beer. 'The words coming out of her mouth didn't make no sense; demons and spirits, hell and death.' He paused for a cold second, before adding, 'I believed her.'

I let out the slightest of laughs and immediately cursed myself, as the large man lunged across the table at me, knocking its contents onto the floor. Huge hands found my collar, pulling it tight, and his damp, red face came within an inch of my own, the stench of stale whisky and sweat overpowering.

'Laugh at me?' he growled. 'Laugh at old Abe Thomas! Stupid old drunk am I? Is that what you think? Someone to be laughed at?'

Around the room, all other movement and sound had stopped, every face turned towards us.

'I... I'm sorry, Abe,' I wheezed; each word carried pain and effort as it was forced out through my constricted throat.

'I know what I saw, Weaver! I am not a madman and I know what I saw!' He suddenly noted the silence around him and, seeing that we were the focus of attention, released his grip, his voice dropping to a tight whisper. 'As I held that poor girl into my chest and listened to her ramblings, I looked towards the fire and saw something that I shall never forget.'

'What was it?' I croaked. 'What did you see?'

'I saw the beast that was Darke, rising up in the smoke as it poured from the building. Large and white he was, unearthly and cold – a pale demon. He rose into the air, above that blazing building, dragging with him the souls of his victims. She was right, the girl was right. Darke was from hell itself, returning from where he came. And I could see them, God help me, I could see them dead boys being dragged off to hell with him.'

He let go of me with a push that sent me tumbling onto the floor. Standing up on unsteady legs, he made his way towards the doors, snarling and snapping at those who came in his way, causing them to jump backwards in fright.

'The girl, Abe?' I called after him, in desperation. 'What was her name?'

He stopped in his tracks.

'She was called Beth, Beth Finnan,' he said, his voice a low rumble. 'She was the fiancée of Darke's brother, Nikolas; her father, Tom, owned the Princess Alice.' His hands shot forwards, hitting the doors hard, sending them crashing outwards, a sudden and final noise signalling his departure, as he disappeared into the bright street beyond.

The noise echoed through the bar as the dust slowly settled once more.

I allowed myself a smile and, pushing myself to my feet, made my way outside, throwing money onto the bar as I went. My investigations and eventual road to fortune could now begin in earnest.

2

The Twelve

Over the next week I threw myself into discovering more about the girl, Beth Finnan. I travelled across the city to Whitechapel at the first opportunity, taking with me a small binding of sketch paper, a couple of pencils and a portion of my spare ready, to use for the procurement of useful information.

I decided to take the most direct route to the Princess Alice, which I found, as prominent as ever, on the corner of Wentworth Street and Commercial Street. I knew from my previous enquiries that this place was a regular haunt of Sibelius Darke from his childhood, required as he was to regularly visit public houses in order to recruit hired mourners for his father's funeral business.

As I stepped through the doors into the bar, I wondered how many times the Pale Demon himself had walked through these doors with murder in mind. Within the bar, light was a precious commodity, despite the fact that it was midday outside; the only sign of such were the dulled white beams which fought their way into the room and did little more than highlight the dust, smoke and flies which thickened the air.

I approached the bar, ignoring the staring eyes of the other customers. In places like these, any new person could easily attract attention through the cut of his clothes or simply by being a new face. I knew that someone as square rigged as myself would be under scrutiny as soon as I entered the door and I would quickly be taken for a mark.

I had, of course, visited the area many times in the six years since my arrival in London. My sharp interest in Darke had made that a necessary pilgrimage. I had visited the shop front where his photographic studio once stood, long since gutted by fire; it was now a bakery. I had also journeyed around the corner onto Whitechapel Road to the undertaking parlour once owned by his family. It was now under the ownership of George Woodrow, a one-time friend of the family who would not, despite my best appeals, talk of Darke.

'What will it be?' asked the young woman behind the bar, a pale-looking, plain thing with a sullen expression upon her face.

'I'm after some information actually. Is the landlord around?'

'No drink then?' Her dull eyes showed little in the way of any willingness to engage in conversation.

'I'll have a small beer and the landlord, thank you. That is all.'

She did not respond and lifted a glass from the shelf above the bar. With the numb demeanour shown only by the most ignorant of society, she poured my drink before placing it on the bar before me. She then turned away and started towards the other end of the bar. As I raised my hand to further attract her attention, she barked over her shoulder, cutting short my reminder, 'I'm getting him!'

'Thank you, my dear,' I called, in a tone that she would not have recognised as sarcasm.

The landlord appeared presently, an overweight man with a pock-marked, unshaven face, who bustled over to me, squeezing his frame past his dour employee.

'Selling something? I'm not interested, so there's no need for any patter,' he grumbled as he approached, his eyes flicking over me.

'I am not selling anything, sir,' I said, raising my palms. 'Merely wishing to find someone, a client of my employers, Hodgson, Hathaway and Head.'

'Debt collectors are they?'

'No, nothing so brutal. They are solicitors. I have been tasked with finding their client regarding the sale of a business within which he has a stake.'

'Money due, eh?' He scanned the room as he settled his broad arms on the bar in front of me, leaning forwards. His voice lowered to a whisper. 'Is there a fee to be paid to those that can help?'

'I have expenses at my disposal.' I gained his interest immediately. 'The man in question is the previous owner of this establishment, a Mr Tom Finnan. Do you know of him?'

'I met the man on one occasion a few years ago. He lived here with his sister and daughter. They left in a bit of a hurry – it was a quick sale.'

'Excellent, and do you know of his whereabouts now?'

His eyes narrowed and he remained silent. I reached into my coat for my wallet, which I placed on the bar in front of me.

'Pluckley, I think he moved to Pluckley in Kent. I heard he took on a pub there, the Black something, it could be Swan or maybe Horse. I can't remember too clearly.'

I pushed some coins across the counter towards him.

'Horse, it was, definitely Horse. He left something behind as well.' A spark lit and I added more coins to the pot.

'Did he? Well then perhaps I could deliver it. Is it a large package?'

He said nothing and, snatching the coins up from the bar, walked off to the doorway which led upstairs. He returned holding a large black tin.

'It's locked,' he said. 'I never tried to open it of course.' I examined the tin. It was old and dented in places and the paint had been scratched off around the lock and rim.

I lifted the tin from the bar; there was a little weight to it and, upon shaking it, there was a rattling sound.

'I shall make sure that it is delivered to him. Tell me, you say that he left in some haste. Was there a reason for this?'

The landlord folded his arms and set his face in stone. 'Family business. His daughter was… unwell.' His head lowered and turned away; it was clear that our conversation was over.

With the location of Tom Finnan established and my battered package in hand, I left the Princess Alice with a broad smile across my face and headed back to the offices of my employer.

***

'This fixation with Sibelius Darke will lead you to trouble, Weaver. You drive idle curiosity to the limits of obsession!'

'But it is a good story, sir – possibly the greatest. I am uncovering new, important information every day, information which you would be the first to publish, enough for a special edition all of its own. I could fill eight pages with the information and pictures that I have already; people will buy it, you know they will. It would sell more copies than Calcraft.'

'I admire your spirit, you have a lot to offer. You are superior with a pencil and ink and I have seen no other who can quite recreate a scene the way you do.' The warmth in George Purkess's smile was sincere and I felt a surge of confidence within me. 'However, you are one of seventy artists that I have at my disposal. Others are begging for the kind of attention you demand, and it would be easy for me to cast you aside if you continue to press me with these matters.' He reached onto his desk and picked up a piece of notepaper. 'If it's murder you want then this city is producing it afresh every day. Nobody wants to hear old news; I cannot sell it. Go to this address in St John's Wood. There has been some kind of incident at a house in Boston Place. My man in the police has been a little touchy about the details, but go and see all the same – for me.'

I looked at him in hope for a change of heart but there would be none. For a day that had promised so much and provided me with such excitement, the spark of exhilaration ignited by the news of Tom Finnan's whereabouts was quickly being extinguished by my normally malleable patron.

Mr Purkess was a man large in both size and in presence; he had the ability to walk into a room and immediately draw all eyes towards him like moths towards gaslight. His frame was round, although not so stretched as to make him seem fat; he was more solid, like an oaken barrel, immovable and well formed.

As he sat behind his desk now, idly rubbing his fingers over his pocket watch, which was attached to his waistcoat by a heavy gold chain, I could see that his immovability stretched to stubbornness in this matter. I would have to work further on the man to turn him to my path.

I sighed in temporary defeat, a sign to Mr Purkess that I was, for now, beaten. His little victory made him straighten himself somewhat and he once again pushed forwards the piece of paper with the address on it.

'Take this job, Samuel. They are expecting you and it is on your way home. You are dear to me, boy, but I cannot allow you to disappear off hunting for things that no one wants to hear of any more.'

I forced a smile and took the note. 'I will not give in, you know, Mr Purkess,' I said, the overfamiliarity of my tone fully intentional and aimed at annoying him. I misjudged his response, however, as he laughed out loud and stood, guiding me to the door.

'Get out of my office before I lose my humour and retire you early! Go to Boston Place and do not come back until you have drawn for me a grisly murder set to shock and disgust everyone who sees it!'

I joined in his laughter and set off. Despite my need to carry on my investigation, I could not deny him.

***

I had first come to Mr Purkess's establishment in the Strand a little more than six years earlier, fresh from King's Cross. I had travelled down from York carrying only a small suitcase containing a set of clothes, a toilet bag and some examples of my illustrations.

I presented myself at the offices of *The Illustrated Police News* and found myself quickly embroiled in an altercation with an older gentleman named Mr Henry Cope, the current editor.

'You cannot just walk in off the street and demand to see Mr Purkess; he is a busy man!' Mr Cope snapped, as long grey wisps of hair, normally drawn across his pate, became loosened and waved in the air in his agitation.

'I wrote to him over a week ago, he will be expecting me. If you could just be so kind as to check his diary you will see my name there.'

'I read all of Mr Purkess's mail and I have no memory of your letter,' Cope stormed, and I noticed with interest a thick blue vein drawing a line down the middle of his high forehead.

I looked around the room at the other gentlemen sat before their desks, preparing the next edition. Most continued with their work; however, more than a couple were observing the exchange between Mr Cope and myself with some amusement.

'If you will not leave these offices immediately I will be forced to resort to other measures.'

'And what would those measures entail?' I asked calmly. 'Fetching the owner of your newspaper downstairs to eject me? Do not allow me to delay you any longer.'

'What I meant was that I would bring in an officer of law to remove you!' he barked, pushing his way past me towards the entrance to the offices and reaching for the handle of the door. His exit was halted, however, as the door opened inwards and the large figure of Mr George Purkess himself bustled through. The other men within the office rose from their seats immediately.

'Good Lord, Mr Cope, we are in a hurry!' Purkess boomed. 'What is the emergency that you should leave my offices in such a fluster?'

'I was fetching a policeman, Mr Purkess. We have an intruder on the premises who has refused all reasonable demands to leave.'

I stepped between them, offering my hand. 'Allow me to introduce myself, Mr Purkess. My name is Mr Samuel Weaver; you were expecting me, of course.'

Mr Purkess took my hand and met my gaze and, for the briefest of moments, there was an uneasy silence. The other workers remained standing, awaiting his response.

'Weaver, you say? I can't fully recall the name,' he said, my hand held within his own firm grip. 'Humour an old man with a poor memory and remind me of the nature of our business together?'

'I am here to take employment with you,' I responded. 'There was an article in the *Pall Mall Gazette*, in which you stated that you only employed the best artists and writers. You want the best in word and picture – I am both and at your service.'

His eyes flicked from mine to Cope's and I saw the eruption of a smile within him.

'Do you mean to say that you have travelled across the country in search of a job based on a passing boastful aside to a hack writer from a rival paper?' He laughed. 'You must have something, boy, if only a misjudged sense of worth. Let us go upstairs to my office and you can continue to amuse and blind me with tales of your wonderful work.' He released my hand, only to place his arm firmly around my shoulders to lead me to the stairs. 'Mr Cope, have one of the lads sent out for coffee from Verrey's for myself and this promising young gentleman.'

As I passed the now puce Cope, I allowed myself a sly smirk and
made a vow to myself to engage in the sport of baiting this fine gentleman at every opportunity.

***

I thought of this first meeting as I made my way to Boston Place and
the supposed murder scene. I was aggrieved to have taken on this job.
I knew that it would be worth attending – every murder scene was
– but I was angry at my incompetence in persuading Mr Purkess to
allow me to indulge my obsessions. I had spent long years nurturing
our relationship, but had not yet reached the point where he would
fully bend to my will. This assignment almost felt like a punishment as
a result, a punishment for daring to believe that I had the man under
my control.

As I turned the corner of the street I immediately spied the house.
There were two policemen stationed outside, rocking on their heels
and looking for all the world as if they would rather be elsewhere.

'Good afternoon, gentlemen!' I called as I approached them. I
immediately recognised the older of the two as he had been in attendance at many of my jobs over the past six years. 'I hear there is some
nastiness inside this fine house. Is it a sea of blood in there?'

Normally I would have expected a darkly comical response from
the men, as they witnessed every imaginable horror on a daily basis.
Today, however, there was no such reaction. They simply looked to
each other nervously before opening the door and standing aside.

'No jokes today, lad,' the older policeman muttered as I passed, his
mouth twitching edgily under his moustaches. 'This is not one to
make light of.'

I entered the gloom of the house, a silence blanketing my ears the
moment I crossed the scarred stone of the threshold. The household
itself was a three-storey tenement much the same as every other in the
street. It had a foreboding edge to it though, which stroked the back
of my neck with cold steel pins, as I walked through the dim light of
the entrance hall.

A staircase ran up the left side of the hallway, each stair bare and wooden, worn and split in places. I took a glance upwards but saw only blackness in the upper landing.

'This way,' the policeman said, the sound of his voice shaking me from my thoughts. He gestured farther down the hallway towards a large wooden door ahead, closed and forbidding. My eyes shot from the door to the constable's face and I could see that he would not be going any farther forward unless forced.

A surge of nervous energy erupted within my stomach. I always felt an edge of excitement when entering the scene of a killing. It was not necessarily bad; it was a necessary energy boost, a force to drive me on. This time, however, in this house, in this place of murder and death, the feeling was different somehow, not necessarily stronger but more urgent. I somehow knew that whatever lay within this room would not be a fit sight for human eyes.

'Am I to enter alone?' I asked, more in desperate hope than expectation.

'The Inspector said you have twenty minutes,' he replied, shaking his head. 'I have been in once and I will not return unless ordered.' He removed his helmet and drew his handkerchief across his forehead. 'It is not... a good place. It is not for lingering.'

I ran my tongue around the inside of my dry mouth and forced myself to swallow, hoping to push downwards the ball of fear which had become lodged within my throat.

'Very well,' I murmured and walked slowly down the hall. As I reached the door I noticed that the dark green paint upon it had blistered and bubbled as if it had withstood a dangerous heat from within, creating a web of cracks and fine splits in the woodwork. I took a brief moment to brush my hand over the door lightly, almost expecting to feel the sting of heat upon it. It was cold.

I reached down towards the door handle, my hand touching cold brass, and I flinched as I felt a tremor in the metal. I thought it to be a vibration from within the room but soon realised that the tremor came from my own hand. I gripped the handle hard and pushed downwards, opening the door.

As it opened the first sensation which struck me was an acrid metallic odour. The sheer weight and force of the emanation filled my nostrils and barged its way to the back of my throat, its thickness causing me to retch somewhat. I instinctively withdrew my handkerchief from my coat pocket and covered my mouth and nose to prevent further assault. A noise from behind caused me to turn; the constable was exiting through the front door. I caught a final glimpse of his back as he scurried away. The door slammed behind him. I was alone.

I had been to many places of death and horror, and each had a similar feel, a silence that I had become almost inured to. This house, however, placed within me a sense of true terror. Stepping through the doorway and into the stench, I took in the scene before me.

There were few lights in the room, no more than a couple of candles of various sizes and colours lighted along the skirting and upon the mantelpiece. The small yellow flames struggled to survive, flickering in the darkness and giving off a dim smoky light. The mantelpiece itself sat above a large and dominating fireplace of once-white marble. The wax from the candles, red and cream coloured, had run down onto the shelf and begun to drip onto the hearth, creating stalactites which resembled teeth surrounding the maw of a cold, black opening.

It was to the far side of the room that my eyes were drawn, for that was where the bodies lay, the bodies of twelve young women, the soles of their feet pointing at me.

The women were placed in a line across the bare-boarded floor. Each one had been carefully positioned, their arms lying at their sides, hands outstretched, palms upturned. I noticed then that through their wrists and ankles were struck large nails, the type used in railways, each one driven hard through sinew and bone. Each thick spike sealed its victim to the wooden floor beneath and I wondered whether the women had been alive and conscious when the spikes were hammered home.

Their expressions were impassive and unemotional; one would almost think them merely sleeping, the lids of their eyes being closed in rest. It was clear, however, that this was not the case, for the rest of their poor bodies told a different tale. Each wore roughly sewn, grey cotton skirts, coarse to the touch, yet their upper halves, although unclothed, were decorated in a fashion. The bare arms of each of the bodies carried upon them patterned carvings.

The blade used had been sharp beyond compare; each cut upon their bodies was intricate and clinical, creating symbols and patterns upon their pale canvas. Beautiful lines of red painted their soft skin, and I wondered at the time it had taken to create them and whether the girls had watched as their torturer had made his mark upon them.

I did not rest my gaze upon these pictures for too long, for of all parts of these poor young women that attracted my eyes, it was their torsos which were most gruesomely entrancing.

The same sharp blade, used to such dramatic effect upon their arms, had delivered to each a long and deep incision from the base of their pale throats to the navel. I prayed that these cuts were made after death; anyone enduring such butchery whilst living would have suffered unimaginable pain.

I stepped closer to the bodies, edging nearer to those poor souls. The skin of their chests had been peeled back to the edges of the body on each girl. The precision of the cuts showed that this had been done with the utmost care, love even. Within each chest cavity I saw that the breastbone had been sawn neatly down the middle, the ribs pulled apart exposing the vital organs of each woman.

The flicker of the candles brushed light across the wall which rose behind their heads and it was then that I saw the picture painted upon its surface. It was the head of a stag. I moved closer still, admiring the simplicity of the work, despite the expression within the stag's eyes, one of vehemence and dark brutality.

It was as I studied the stag's face that I realised with horror that it was the women, laid eviscerated upon the floor, who had provided the 'paint' for this creation.

The head, although large in itself, was given the appearance of greater size by the outgrowing antlers which sprouted from the upper sides above the ears and stretched like long fingers out towards the outer walls and ceiling. It gave the stag the appearance of a tree, its branches reaching desperately out to heaven.

My eyes followed the branches and it is with the greatest of terror that I reached the end point of one of these tendrils. For upon the wall at the tip of this painted antler was a heart, a human heart nailed to the wall with a large spike like those which had impaled the hands and feet of the young women upon the dusty wooden floor.

I stepped back in shock, and it was only then that my eyes took in a full view of the painting upon the wall. For there was not just one but twelve hearts nailed to this grotesquerie, twelve human hearts, each belonging to one of the poor women lying at my feet.

I stood for what seemed like an age, trying to take in all that was before me. This was partly because of the pure cold horror of it all, but also so that I could memorise it fully.

Whatever brief sketches I made at this stage would never be the final product delivered to the offices in the Strand. Often the pictures that made their way onto the covers were different. I did not dramatically change anything that I saw; however, there would be some degree of artistic licence to enhance and where possible make clearer that which my eye had observed. I prided myself on truth and loyalty within my work, but I was also aware of the need for clarity and the expression of feeling which I wished to draw from the reader. If I could inspire horror, fear, anger or loathing, then this was success in my eyes; more importantly it was success in the eyes of Mr Purkess, who knew the impact I was able to strike upon those who had paid their penny for a gruesome story.

Almost panicked, I pulled my sketchbook from the satchel at my side and immediately scribbled as much as I could, as if it were liable to disappear from my gaze at any moment. I became lost, my mind becoming one with the paper as the fine tip of my pencil began sketching all before me.

At most scenes that I attended I would make maybe a dozen different sketches; varying angles of the bodies, close-ups to show particularly grievous wounds and even, when provided with such information by the attending police, a vision from my own imagination of the situation which had brought about the death. This could be in the form of a cruel, violent man plunging his knife towards his cowering wife, or perhaps a group of children's arms outstretched from a window and surrounded by the flames of their home as their desperate parents attempted to re-enter the building.

For this room, however, this place of abject terror and unimaginable suffering, I found myself almost crazed by the images in front of me and the machinations that they created within my mind.

I was so immersed within my task that I did not notice a presence in the room behind me; in fact, I had no notion of how long it had been there.

The large hand, which fell suddenly upon my shoulder, caused me to jump in such alarm that I tumbled from my crouched position and fell forwards onto the bloodied floor.

As I hit the ground, I rolled over to look up to the owner of the hand, seeing a face illuminated briefly before the candles blew out in the room.

I was plunged into a terrible darkness.

3

The Ghost Village

During my fifteenth year I saw my first man die.

This may, of course, not be such a shocking revelation to the average person; people die in their thousands every day. However, the nature of my experience and its effect upon me would perhaps not sit lightly upon the minds of normal men. I feel, though, that a knowledge of the nature of this event will afford a better understanding of the type of man that I am and of the elements which make up the more complex areas of my personality.

I had always had a love of drawing and of creating illustrations primarily for myself to enjoy. My interests and aspirations, however, were not in the fine arts, in painting and suchlike; it was not for me to spend long hours in a studio, delicately using oil paints to create beautiful images of the world from a distance. No, it was about documenting the brutalities and realities of life as they happened before me. This may not be thought of by those in respectable society as art, but for me it was art in its purest form, showing the world in all of its ugly splendour.

Aligned with this skill in graphic depiction was my burning interest in the macabre – those dark areas of life which are feared, so often ignored, but which live in the most shadowy recesses of the minds of us all.

My father, a liberally minded man by most accounts despite his age, supported my interest, supplied me with the materials required and allowed me time away from my studies to venture into the city from the rectory where we lived on the outskirts of York.

I became a common if unusual sight on the streets, often sitting upon the cobbles at the side of the road, pencil in hand and drawing life as it unfolded around me. It was in these days that I loved my art; I was quickly able to capture the world, be it an altercation between two street traders or the poor and crippled begging for alms from a passing gentleman or lady.

On the aforementioned day, when I had not long reached the age of fourteen, I had been filled with a sense of foolish bravery and had strayed from Stonegate and St Peter's – the main streets that I normally frequented – and walked towards the River Ouse, hoping to see the boats which ferried goods in and out of the city.

It was a fresh November morning and, as I reached Lendal Bridge to look out across the river, I espied the large factory on the other side. All thoughts of river men now forgotten, I strode across the bridge with purpose and straight through the wrought-iron gates towards the main building. I had not thought of what I would say if challenged regarding my trespass, but it was of no matter to me. I wished to see what lay within and perhaps even sketch the men at work in the factory. To my surprise I was not challenged in the slightest and managed to wander freely into a great room where men and women carried out their labour, packing boxes ready to be loaded onto the boats on the river; it was a relative hive of action and I found their sense of purpose almost entrancing to observe. It was only when a voice came from behind me that I shook myself from my awe.

'You'll be delivering a message will you, lad?' I turned to see a broad man standing over me, his arms folded resolutely, his eye accusing.

'Why, yes, sir,' I answered, finding that the lie fell smoothly from my mouth. 'I have a note regarding an order. I was told to give it to the store's manager. Could you tell me where I might find him?'

He looked me up and down, his gaze finally resting upon the satchel at my side. It could have passed for a delivery boy's bag.

'You want to go up those stairs,' he said, pointing to the other side of the room. 'Follow the gangway into the boiling room and keep going. The stores are through the door at the end.'

It seemed best at this time to continue with the ruse and I turned to run towards the iron steps.

I touched the brim of my cap as I started ascending the stairs to the metal walkway which ran near the roof of the room and along its length. I continued on to the end of the gangway to the door marked Boiling Room.

It was the heat of the room which affected me the most as I walked in. My clothes immediately stuck to my skin and I felt a cloying nausea within me as the mixture of moist warmth and the choking sweetness of the room assailed my body. The room itself was large, although not as huge as the main factory floor that I had just left. There were three enormous metal drums, each over twenty feet in height, which dominated the room, and from each of these vats ran pipes which led off out of the room. Each drum was full of hot melted chocolate. It was only then that I realised the purpose of the factory. Standing on the walkway just ahead of me was a man armed with a long wooden pole, which he used to stir each vat in turn.

The man was tall, thin and of older years. He wore a set of blue, loose-fitting canvas overalls with a bib top which attached over his shoulders. Under these he wore a linen shirt which, although once white, was now covered in brown stains and the dampness of sweat. On his head a blue cloth cap did a poor job of covering a mop of wiry grey hair which protruded from the bottom, sticking out in all directions, and equally thick, grey whiskers adorned his cheeks. He toiled in his task and, as I studied him, I noted that his lips constantly moved as he muttered to himself under his breath.

He had not noticed me and, seeing an opportunity, I took my sketchbook and pencil from my satchel and began to sketch the man at work. He leaned as far as he could over the metal railing and waved his pole around in the thick, brown, creamy liquid. As he withdrew the pole to move on to the next vat, he looked up and saw me.

'What you doing, boy?' he shouted, his red, puffed face glistening with sweat. I didn't reply and hurriedly pushed the book back into my bag. Twenty yards past the chocolate stirrer was a set of metal steps leading down and I decided that my adventure in the factory should end and the best way of escape was forwards to floor level, where I could find a way out of the building. He called to me again but I continued to ignore him, lowering my head and walking towards the staircase behind him.

As I neared him I could hear him muttering to himself, cursing all born children and asking for a return to the days when a boy like me would have been forced into gainful employment. Hearing his grumbles, I sped up, pushing myself forwards towards my goal. As I reached him he suddenly turned towards me. His thin arms reached for my jacket, grabbing handfuls of cloth and pulling me towards him.

'Do you not answer when someone speaks to you?' he spat in my face. 'I asked you a simple question, boy!' There was a rattle in his voice as he pulled me closer to him; his face was just inches from my own now and the thick stench of the man and his breath overcame the sweetness of the chocolate. 'Where's your tongue, boy? What are you doing here?'

Fear hit me and I tried to wriggle free from his grasp; crying out, I threw my arms up in an attempt to dislodge his hands. I must have misjudged the strength required for the task, however, for he fell backwards, his lower back striking the gangway's railing.

The next few moments have lived clearly in my memory ever since. Whenever I close my eyes I am able to replay them within my mind, like a zoetrope at a funfair, each individual image shown to me with near-perfect clarity. My eyes did not leave his face, as his expression changed from anger to astonishment and finally to fear, as he realised what was happening to him. As he hit the barrier his feet must have slipped on the floor, flying forwards and upwards as he tipped over the top and began to fall. His hand reached out to grab at me again, not in anger or aggression but in pure fear for his life. As his fingers outstretched before me my first instinct was to grab at his hands. I resisted this urge.

The old man cried out as he disappeared over the edge and I lurched forward to watch him tumble into the vat of chocolate below. The brown liquid sucked him down and within seconds he disappeared completely from my view, the only sign of his impact being the outline of his body shape left upon the skin of the surface.

Suddenly panic hit me and I shook myself out of my torpor. I had to get away, run far away from this room before anyone realised what had happened.

As I turned to run, a sudden noise caught my attention and, like a sweet but deadly volcanic eruption, the old man burst to the surface, gasping for air. His arms reached desperately up to me and he tried to cry out for help. Whatever sound he tried to make from his mouth was lost in a morass of wet gurgling chocolate.

I reached for the long wooden pole and hauled it over the side. Images flooded through my mind: I would be a hero, the boy who saved the man from drowning. I would be in the papers, and everyone would know me. Thoughts of the future possibilities flashed in front of me and I made my decision.

With all of the strength I could muster in my young body, I swung the wooden pole as hard as I could, striking the drowning man on the side of the head with a sickening crack.

He sank for the final time.

I stood watching the gently bubbling surface of chocolate for a further minute, before turning to run for the stairs – and I did not stop running until I was clear of the factory gates.

***

The match flared, illuminating the broad, smiling face of Inspector Abe Thomas above me.

'Feeling a little jumpy today are we, Samuel?' he said as he began to relight the candles along the mantelpiece.

I pushed myself to my feet, looking down at the blood that now smeared my best woollen trousers.

'It is a scene from hell, is it not?' I replied, ignoring his attempt to unnerve me. 'I have nearly got all I need in terms of sketches. To be honest, it is not an image I will be forgetting any time in a hurry, and I will be able to complete my work at home. Are there any thoughts on who could be responsible for such an act?'

The candles lit, Thomas stared down at the women on the floor and spoke in a low rumble.

'None that I could tell you. There are spiritualist groups and occultists springing up all over London – it is hard to keep track of them all.' He walked slowly along the line of corpses before raising his head to gaze on the bloody stag upon the wall. 'This is a revelation. I've never seen the like.'

I retrieved my sketchbook from the floor and moved closer to one of the bodies to capture some of the detail of the carvings on the arms.

'There is something of the occult in these markings, Abe, and this hart must signify something; both the hart and indeed the hearts for that matter.' I tried to vanquish any trace of humour in my voice, failing as I made the quip. The look of disgust on Thomas's face was cold enough to make me lower my gaze.

'You may want to note these also, Samuel,' the Inspector said, pointing to the floor by the doorway, where two perfectly formed footprints were marked upon the floorboards. I had completely overlooked them when I had entered the room; I suppose I was too in awe of the spectacle that met me but, as I neared them and took a closer look, I noted that they were golden, as if someone had stood barefoot in a pot of gold paint and marked the floor. There was no trail leading from them – they stood alone and I wondered what their purpose had been, if indeed they had been part of whatever accursed ceremony had been performed in this room.

'Who does the house belong to?' I asked, running my fingers over the footprints.

'The previous owner left in a hurry two years ago, according to the neighbours. Six months ago, all of the properties in this street, and the next one over, were bought up by the Falconer estate. No change for the tenants, really; just a different person to pay rent to. This house has stood empty, though. There has been no attempt to fill it, although there have been some comings and goings in the past few weeks apparently. The neighbours reckoned they were just workmen coming to do the place up. I've got some descriptions but they were all a bit vague; people mind their own business around here.'

His words drifted over me somewhat, so intense were my attempts to capture the scene. 'Keep me informed if you hear anything more, will you, Abe?' I said. 'I'm sure Old Mr Purkess will be chomping at the bit to get the edge on the others for this.'

'Tell Purkess to hold off on putting it in this week's edition,' the Inspector said. 'I will need to make good headway with my investigations before I am ready to see this in print. Tell him it will be the usual arrangement: access to my files in return for the time required to catch the killer... or killers.'

I nodded in assent, finishing my work hastily. As I stood and turned to leave, the voice of Abe Thomas stopped me in my tracks.

'One more thing,' he said, pointing towards one of the bodies. 'Do you see that one on the end? It's Mary Pershaw, the woman suspected of killing her daughter last week. It looks like we have found her at last.'

I peered down at the sliced carcass and noted that my sketch of 'Mad Mary, the Crazed Child Killer on the loose in Paddington', which I had submitted to Henry Cope, and which would be appearing in this week's issue, was uncannily similar to her true looks.

'Unfortunate for her, Abe, although at least she won't kill again.'

'None of them will,' said the Inspector, his voice almost a whisper.

'What do you mean?'

He turned to face me, his cheeks glowing red.

'Do you remember I told you of the other women who'd killed their children and disappeared recently? Well, to the best of my knowledge, you're looking at them.'

I was silenced by this knowledge and, without another word, I left him in his room of hell.

***

Three days later I found myself seated upon a train bound for the Kent countryside. I had passed on the wishes of the Inspector to George Purkess, who had accepted his terms with the hint of a clenched fist. I knew that he was desperate to get the exclusive on this terrible incident, but Mr Purkess was nothing if not astute in keeping those within his pay, be they colleagues or police, within his grasp when required. Sensationalism and stealing the edge on his competitors was a keen hobby of his, but his enthusiasm was best kept in check in instances such as these.

With promises of sensationally graphic drawings and words dripping with horror and mystery to come, I then told Purkess that I would be unavailable for two days due to a family concern which required me to travel immediately to York.

Mr Purkess of course agreed to my terms. I had long since built up enough bounty with the man – although not enough yet to push for his support for my investigations into the murderer Darke. In truth, if he were to find out the actual destination and nature of my journey all of this hard-earned bounty would be lost immediately.

The journey was not a long one but I found the time to read *The Times* as well as the first proof of the coming weekend's edition of *The Illustrated Police News*. I had not, to my disappointment, made the front page with my sketch of a terrible fire which took place at a paper factory in Shoreditch, killing five men. The article, which I had also written, finally appeared on the third page and I read through it, noting at least two details with which I was unhappy but which now would be too late to change – even though this edition would not be on public sale until the coming Saturday.

I was not alone in the carriage and, over the top of my newspaper, I watched with interest the couple travelling in my car. The first, an older man, spent the entire journey staring out of the window. My second unknown companion was a broad-chested woman of middle age, who knitted with an angry temperament, her needles clicking with sharp and rhythmic stabs. Throughout the whole of the journey neither said a word, until they reached Tunbridge Wells, when the gentleman stood up and reached out his hand for the woman.

'This is our stop, my dear,' he said, motioning out of the window at the sign on the platform. She did not reply but, after roughly pushing her knitting into a carpet bag, took his hand and stood.

As they left the carriage I allowed myself a smile. There before my eyes and sitting within the same car as myself had been the perfect answer to those who asked me why I would never marry.

Within half an hour the train pulled into Pluckley and I withdrew my bag from the rack above my seat. I was the only passenger to disembark and, as I opened the door of the carriage and stepped down, I felt the eyes of the train's passengers upon me. I wondered whether there was a secret which I had not been let into, for the platform was deserted.

It was a summer's afternoon, the sun shining unashamedly, unrestrained by cloud, yet there was an unnatural feel about the place. The sun, which had been causing London to swelter and stink when I set off, seemed to give no heat here and the cold brought a shiver to me.

I thought to head straight through the exit gate but found myself walking towards the wooden building at the centre of the platform, my inquisitive nature urging me to discover if this place was as barren as it seemed. I peered through the filthy windows, wondering if there was any life here. There was none. Even in the ticket office, which I assumed would be manned throughout the day, there was no sign of habitation. Partially assured that there was no one to be found, I decided to walk into the village to find the Black Horse and its land-lord, Tom Finnan. As I approached the gate, however, I caught sight of the clock hanging over the platform; it struck me as quite odd. The clock ticked, I could hear it quite clearly; in fact, it was the only sound I could hear in this empty place. The time on it was quite wrong, however, stating that it was twenty past eight. I knew that this could not be correct as my train had left London Bridge at ten-thirty that morning.

I pulled out my watch but noted that it had also stopped at twenty past eight. I was sure that I had wound it; I always did as soon as I woke every day. No matter, I would correct it as soon as I could. I hazarded a guess that the time must be about one o'clock and altered my watch accordingly, winding it once more. As I did so, I sensed a movement ahead of me and glanced up to see a solitary figure stand-ing at the end of the platform. It looked to be an elderly man dressed in the livery of a railway guard. He had not been there moments before and I wondered how he had managed to appear at such speed. I reached down to pick up my bag, with the intention of speaking to him and asking for directions to the Black Horse, and in that briefest of moments when I took my eyes off him, he disappeared. I consid-ered that it perhaps had been a trick of the light but the day was so bright; I had clearly seen him.

I sighed, wondering if the village of Pluckley were conspiring against me. Bag in hand, I strolled through the gate, to find an inn called the Dering Arms before me.

The doors to the pub were closed and locked, although I could see that a fire was lit within and heard voices from inside. I rapped hard on the door and the voices quickly stopped, to be replaced by the scraping of bolts. The door opened, just enough for me to see a thin, hawkish-faced man who eyed me suspiciously.

'Are you not open?' I asked.

The man sniffed, his eyes darting around to see if I was accompanied.

'Not at this time, not on a Thursday!' he snapped and shut the door again.

The bolts were being fastened as I knocked on the door again. A curse came from within.

'We're shut, I said!' came the muffled voice within.

'I'm looking for the Black Horse,' I called. 'Is it near?'

'Mile an' arf up tha' road. Keep walkin' n' you'll fin' it!' came a distant cry.

I went to leave, but stopped sharply and shouted through the door a final time.

'One last thing.' I withdrew my watch from my pocket. 'Do you have the correct time?'

There was no reply.

I set off with the cold sun shining down upon me. There was not a breath of wind and the only sound came from my footsteps along the country track. How such bright daylight and stillness could be described as eerie was a mystery to me, but eerie it was. I had the feeling of eyes upon me, a malevolence of sorts that I could not shake, and I found myself repeatedly looking back over my shoulder, even though the lane was deserted.

I passed the odd house on my journey, but I saw neither man nor beast along the way. I thought to stop and call at one to enquire whether I was indeed on the right road but my stubborn will forced me to push on under my own initiative.

Eventually I came across a group of squat and dilapidated houses at a distance, which looked to be more of a village than what I had seen of Pluckley so far. I walked towards them and saw a sign that told me I had indeed found the Black Horse. The chimney was smoking and there were signs of light and movement inside the building.

As I stepped through the doors of the pub, all conversation ceased and I felt the eyes of every customer upon me. I stopped for a moment, meeting their glares and smiling. I went up to the bar, the tide of locals parting to create a path of sorts for me. The barman was deep in conversation with an older man but, noticing me, he cut off his discourse and strode over to where I stood.

He had red-coloured hair streaked with white. Although I could plainly see that he was over sixty years old, time had not dimmed the strength and power of the man. His skin was weathered and lined, each crease upon his face a deep and hard-earned crevice. It was his eyes which struck me the most, however: they were a shade of green and most friendly in manner. This was a man who exuded comfort and trust in those who met him, a most favourable requisite in the landlord of a public house. I guessed almost instinctively that this was Tom Finnan, the associate of Sibelius Darke. As he approached he did not speak to me; he merely placed the palms of his hands upon the bar and raised his eyebrows slightly.

'I am visiting the village for a couple of days and wished to find somewhere to stay,' I said. 'Have you rooms available?' As I spoke, the noise and hubbub of the room resumed and the locals continued with the conversations that I had interrupted by my entrance.

'There are rooms; they are charged at one shilling per night, break-fast included... drink?'

'I'll take a cider please,' I said, placing my bags on the floor. 'The walk from the station was longer than I thought it would be and it's been a long day.'

He didn't look up and started to pour my drink.

'Travelled down from London, did you?'

'Yes, just for two days. Some time away from work to indulge in my interests.'

'Which are?'

'Ghosts, sir. I have a keen interest in our visitors from the afterlife. It is little more than a hobby really, but I am a curious fellow and have a need to answer the unexplained.'

The look that he gave me would have stripped the paint from the walls, such was its intensity. I avoided his gaze and took a small sip of my drink.

'I would suppose you receive a great many visitors to Pluckley in search of ghosts?' I said.

'We have more than our share,' he muttered.

'I can assure you that, despite its being a hobby, I take the matter very seriously.'

'They are not things to be taken lightly; I have seen what they can do to a person.'

'You are a believer then?'

'I believe in so much as I have seen the damage that they are capable of.'

'You have witnessed a ghost?' I asked, pulling out my notebook in pretence.

'I have not seen for myself and I will not talk about it further!' he said, walking away.

I cursed myself for my failure to gain the confidence of the man on the first attempt. I had two days to work on him, however. Finnan disappeared through a door at the end of the bar, where I heard him talking to an unseen individual. Moments later the door reopened but it was not Finnan returning; in his place appeared an older woman. She held her nose in the air and made it obvious that she was not willing to engage in any conversation. I picked up my drink and bags and moved to a seat by the window.

I scratched my notes regarding the Black Horse and its landlord into the thick leather-bound book within which I kept all of my findings on the Darke case. The notebook, which I had started upon first hearing of the murders nearly six years ago, was now almost full, each page covered in discoveries, ideas and suppositions, statements from witnesses and, of course, drawings of important places, people and my own imaginings of Darke's murderous sprees.

Finnan did not reappear and so I was treated to the company of the miserable woman behind the bar, who displayed her terse nature to all who dared ask for her service. I eavesdropped on her interactions with the locals, discovering that her name was Miss Anne Finnan and that she was the sister of Tom Finnan.

After a while I left my seat to approach the bar again, gaining her reluctant attentions with difficulty.

'Good afternoon,' I said, employing my most endearing smile. 'I shall be staying here for the next two nights. I wondered if I might retire to my room, as I am tired from the journey.'

'I'll take you up now and have a boy come and bring your bags presently.' She glowered at me. 'I'll be wanting your two shillings first, though.'

'Please take this, it will cover my room and any refreshments,' I said, as I pulled out a handful of coins from my pocket and placed them on the bar.

She collected the money from the bar and bade me follow her through a door at the side of the bar. 'Doors are locked at midnight and breakfast is when I ring my bell,' she said as we ascended a thin staircase. 'There's also a knocking-up service if you wish to be woken early.'

'I do not think I shall need to be woken, thank you,' I replied. 'Would you be so kind as to tell me the time, though, as my watch appears to have stopped?' My request was ignored; the woman had already resumed her disregard of me and was walking down the stairs again.

I observed my room; it was practical and would suit my needs. Within minutes, after a gentle knock upon the door, my overnight bag was brought in. Alone again, I lay upon the bed, noting that the mattress had long since seen better days, and wondered what my next step might be. My plan was reliant on getting to Finnan but, as things stood, it was clear he would be difficult to question. Perseverance would be the key, I thought, as I fell into a light sleep.

I slept for longer than I had intended and was woken in the early evening by the noise from the pub below. After a quick change, I made my way downstairs. After ordering a drink and a small meal from the ever unhappy Miss Finnan, I took a seat on the far side of the room. It was as I ate that the door opened and almost immediately silence reigned over the room, as it did when anyone entered. All eyes shot towards the latest patron, who was obviously a regular as the pause in noise was brief.

The new arrival certainly knew how to make an extravagant entrance. He was older than I, probably by ten years, appearing to be in his mid to late thirties, and he carried himself with a frame similar to that of an actor. His chest swelled, each step taken with purpose and thought. He was, moreover, elegantly dressed, wearing a fine green tweed suit and carrying a long cane which was used more for ornamentation than as an aid to walking. His eyes roved around the bar, as if to attract the attentions of anyone who would bear him witness. Miss Finnan had taken a large and very individual tankard from a shelf at the bar and began to pour his drink. In a moment of pure theatre, it was filled to the brim and presented to him upon his final step.

'Any in tonight, Anne?' he asked, his voice rich in texture. He picked up the tankard and gulped the contents before placing it down with some force.

Miss Finnan kept the scowl on her face and nodded in my direction. The man made his way to my table, motioning to the seat opposite.

'May I?' he asked, already placing his drink upon the table.

'Do feel free,' I replied, returning my eyes to my notebook.

He took the seat and, pulling a newspaper from the inside pocket of his overcoat, opened it wide and started to read. We sat in silence for a short while.

'Ghosts, is it?' he said from behind his newspaper.

'Pardon?'

'Ghosts and spectres and visitors from the other side. The spirits of those who refuse to shuffle off this mortal coil. Are you in Pluckley hoping to find some? I could help with that.'

At first I thought to deny any interest but, in the absence of my prey at the bar, I was bored, so I decided to humour him. I closed my notebook.

'Well, yes, I am actually. I will be staying in Pluckley for two nights – a short break from work, you understand. I thought to carry out some investigations into the large degree of paranormal activity in the area. I am a writer and artist, you see, and I am keen to find the truths behind some of the stories that I have heard.' Parts of my admission were true enough.

A large, charming grin spread across his face and he reached across the table to slap me on the shoulder.

'Then you are a lucky man indeed, dear fellow, a lucky man. In fact I would dare to be so brave as to say that we are both lucky gentlemen this evening.' He reached into the pocket of his waistcoat and withdrew a printed calling card. 'Allow me to introduce myself: Higgins, Edward Higgins. I am known throughout the county, and in fact far beyond, as a ghost hunter and paranormal expert of professorial proportions!' He leaned forwards, the sheen of his face lit red by the small candle which sat upon the table. 'If you have the funds, I could provide an experience which would chill your bones but fill that little notebook of yours. What do you say? You, I and the many ghosts of old Pluckley – how does that take your fancy?'

'And how much would the pleasure of your company for a tour set me back, Mr Higgins?'

His grin shone wider. 'Ah, now there is the rub. Normally I would charge sixpence for my standard tour. However, for you, sir, and on a night like tonight, I think that two bob and a drink or two at your expense when we return would be ample – and it would be as great a pleasure for me as it would be for you. It would be the best bit of flash you ever invested, sir, I can guarantee it. The dark is descending on us, the moon has risen and I feel something in the air tonight. Do you scare easy, sir? I think we might see something this evening if you have the bravery to face it with me.'

'Oh, I think you will find that it takes a lot more than a chill wind and a ghost story to send me running, Mr Higgins. I would say that you have a deal.'

He drained his tankard and raised it high above his head, laughing.

'Anne, my dear, a refill for me and one for my fine friend here, Mr...?'

'Weaver,' I replied. 'Samuel Weaver.'

'A drink for Mr Weaver if you will, Miss Finnan, and a dash of the usual for us both. It is a bare cloudless night out there and we will need a warmer in us when we face the icy shiver of the spirits in the dark!'

To my surprise the barmaid made her way over to our table, where she took both my and Mr Higgins's empty vessels before returning shortly afterwards with replenished tankards and two glasses, which upon tasting I realised held brandy. We supped our drinks quickly and set off into the cold night air to hunt for ghosts.

'By the by,' I said as I followed Mr Higgins out of the door. 'I don't suppose you could tell me the time; my blasted watch has stopped again.'

'Time? Time? I do not bother with time, my dear boy,' he called over his shoulder. 'I look to the sky to see when it is the evening and I listen for the bell that tells me the bar is closed. That is the only time that I am governed by. Now follow on, follow on, we have lots to see, many stories to tell and I aim to have us back here in time for a couple before this night's chime of doom!'

4

Fright at Frith Corner

I had been quiet on my return to the rectory from the chocolate factory, taking myself to my room and causing my parents concern. Despite my independent streak, and regular jaunts into town, I was a conscientious son and an exemplary pupil. I realised early on the benefits of submitting a few short hours of my valuable time to school work, which gained me both the confidence of my schoolteachers and the respect of my father. These little victories ensured that I was given certain freedoms to pursue my own interests, which included both art and journalism. I was an avid reader of any of the newspapers which came into our house. I studied their form, the style and voice that the writers employed to inform their readers and, most of all, I learnt what worked and what did not in terms of good reportage.

On the evening of the incident at the chocolate factory, I told my mother that I was feeling unwell and wished to go straight to my bed without any dinner. She offered to call for Doctor Furnbridge, a friend and associate of Father's, but I told her that taking to my bed for a good night's sleep would be all the medical assistance I required.

Once in the confines of my room, however, I quickly set about translating the memories of the afternoon into the pages of my sketchbook. These images turned into graphic drawings of the terrible death that the chocolate stirrer had suffered. I must confess that my sketch was not a true representation of the incident as it actually happened, for I had taken the liberty of imagining and displaying the poor victim desperately crying and waving for help as he was caught in the act of drowning; a tragic accident.

I studied the papers intensely in the following days and, finally, four days after the incident, a short piece appeared in the *Yorkshire Post*:

Terrible Death at Rowntree's Factory

A most extraordinary discovery was made this week at the Tanner's Moat factory owned by Mr Rowntree. The discovery came following the disappearance of Hiram Osborne, a factory worker of some nine years. It would appear that Mr Osborne, a loyal worker and ex-army man, slipped and fell from a gantry whilst going about his work, landing in a large vat of heated, liquid chocolate.

Mr Osborne's body was found floating in the vat, quite unconscious, by his fellow workers. Pulling him out, they attempted to revive him but he had clearly been dead for some time. Mr Nathaniel Hubbard, store's manager at the plant, commented saying that Mr Osborne would be sorely missed in the factory.

I read the article with a morbid relish and, upon the newspaper's disposal, ensured I cut out the piece and kept it alongside my drawings of the man's death.

Three years later, I had the temerity to include this picture within my portfolio of sketches which I used to obtain my first journalistic position at the *York Herald*. At the time my appointment caused quite a stir, due to my age, and in those first few months of work I was the subject of many malicious rumours regarding the circumstances surrounding how the position was obtained. It is true that my father was involved with, and had donated funds in the past to, the newspaper. Both he and the publication's editor at the time were also members of the local Masonic lodge; however, Father disagreed strongly with my ambitions to pursue a career in journalism, having long since wished for me to follow him into a life in the clergy. I have always been stubborn with regard to the feelings of others and I would not be swayed, not even by Father.

Father was a learned man, well respected by all, and always willing to devote his time and energies to those who came to him in need. This, of course, meant that he was always terribly busy and as such had limited time to spend with either myself or my mother. I did not think too badly of Father for this at the time; his work was important.

Mother also displayed an inordinate amount of patience given the time that Father spent at his duties. She was a quiet, timid woman whom I adored without question and for whom I would have done anything. As a parent, she was as good a friend as one could wish for and, when I was not out in the world sketching and drawing, spending time in her company gave me some of my most cherished memories. Mother doted on me also, and provided me with everything that I needed to be happy and content. Although loving and generous towards me, she had moments during which she seemed somewhat distant, as if her mind were elsewhere. I often wondered what she was thinking as she sat quietly of an evening in front of the hearth, staring into the flames. Sometimes I asked her but her only reply would be, 'I just dream. I am always dreaming.'

Of what she dreamt I never knew. I suspected, during my most cynical moments, that she longed for a different life, one of excitement and incident, perhaps even of lost love. When in the company of Father, she would stare at him with such love and adoration, her eyes never leaving his face, constantly looking for approval and a return of her devotion. Yet Father was cold towards her, and directed all of his love towards me on the rare occasions when the three of us were together.

I am sure Mother felt a pang of jealousy in these times, with Father all but ignoring her as he lavished attention upon me, asking what I had been up to at school or what I had been drawing that day. He loved my drawings and constantly encouraged me to use my skill to document everything around me. I appreciated his allowing me to develop my skills, and would always take time to share my drawings with him.

'You have a rare gift, son,' he said to me one evening, as we shared supper together during one of his brief visits home from church. He would often stop by at home in between his duties, which included helping out at a soup kitchen or holding one of his many evening services. 'You have something handed to you by God himself. Gifts like this should not be ignored and left to fester and rot; they should be embraced and nurtured, they should be shared with the world.'

I would leave my day's drawings on the desk in his study, so that he could look over them when he returned late at night. When I saw him at breakfast, he would comment on them, telling me what he enjoyed about them and how I could develop them in the future. I would always take his advice in good humour and, when I thought that his views were valid, I would adapt and alter the picture. As I got older, however, I began to feel that I knew much better. I was the artist. It was my creation and any criticism given to my work, even if it be by my father, was taken badly, although I tried not to show this and would respond with a tight smile and few words. I was nevertheless grateful for the freedom and licence that Father gave me regarding my passion, and was careful not to let on to him how cutting I found the slightest hint of any criticism.

After the article regarding the death at the chocolate factory appeared in the newspaper, I decided to show Father my drawing of the scene and an accompanying article which I had written myself, and which gave the episode a more sensational and emotional edge. He found my work most disturbing in its realism, something which I saw as giving it merit, but immediately after this he began to take a little more seriously my aspirations for a life in journalism.

I often thought of my experience at the factory and of the sight of Hiram Osborne slowly sinking beneath the surface of the melted chocolate. However, my thoughts never included any guilt or regret. To me the man meant nothing – he was simply part of the key which I had used to help me to attain the life of which I had always dreamt. What point was there, I often thought, of sitting idly and dreaming of the moon, when through work, purposeful action and instances of hard-earned luck, the moon could be yours to own?

***

'The moon is the ally of the inquisitive ghost hunter, my dear Mr Weaver, a genuine ally indeed.' Mr Higgins strode ahead of me with purpose in the dimming light of the country lane. He had filled the evening air with his extensive knowledge of the supernatural since leaving the pub. 'It is the spirits, you see, they glisten in the silvery light. You are so fortunate to have visited on such a clear night, and a full moon also. Follow me, and we shall see what good form the dead of Pluckley are in tonight.'

His arms waved ceaselessly as he spoke, throwing himself enthusiastically into a well-practised repertoire of stories. Each one was steeped in supernatural history and as unbelievable as if he had thought them up on the spot. He told me of the Dering family and how they had resided at Surrenden Manor on the outskirts of the village for over five hundred years. The house itself held ghosts of its own but two members of the Dering family, ladies referred to as the 'Red Lady' and the 'White Lady', held special places for him as both of their stories told of love and sadness. '...and you can never get enough of love and sadness in a ghost story. Gold dust. I couldn't make it up, Mr Weaver, really I couldn't.'

I let him ply his trade and spin his tales. He was a born storyteller and I found that the escapism of it all was enjoyable to me. I became carried along on the tide of my guide's enthusiasm. I admit that the drinks imbibed before we left the inn helped in this regard. Higgins had also taken measures to ensure that liquid refreshment played a continuous part in the entertainment, pulling no less than three flasks of brandy from the pockets of his coat at various points in our journey. These shots held the evening chill at bay, as well as ensuring that we were kept merrily drunk throughout.

We had sallied forth from the pub at an alarming rate, walking down the road that I had trod earlier in the day, passing the Dering Arms, which remained locked and uninviting. Upon nearing the station he pointed out the woods in the distance. A still mist hung between us and the treeline and I thought to walk in its direction, but was stopped by my guide.

'We do not have time to enter the 'Screaming Woods' this evening, my friend, which is a terrible shame as it is an experience to be savoured,' he said, holding his arm across my chest. 'The eldritch howls of the long and recent dead can be heard throughout the night, and it is a brave man who dares enter. Few have tried and they left in such terrible states that they ended their days unable to speak of what they saw; most were placed in asylums, gibbering wrecks of men, hollow of mind and bereft of soul.'

'What did they see in there?' I asked, awaiting a terrible tale of murder, suffering and the afterlife.

'See? See? I don't know. Did you not hear me say that they never spoke of it?' He lowered his arm and strode away, muttering under his breath.

I rushed to catch up with him and found myself struggling to maintain his pace. As we levelled, I saw that he had again taken to his flask, which he passed to me.

'The landlord at the Black Horse… Tom?' I asked. 'Do you know him well?'

'I can't say that I do, Mr Weaver. He has not been in the village for that long, and places like this can be a little hard to crack if you're new – being a landlord helps, of course. I find him a charming man.' He smiled the smile of one who knows who butters his bread.

'But where did he come from? Did he run a pub before coming to Pluckley?'

Higgins glanced sideways at me.

'London, I think. He left under a cloud of some kind. I haven't liked to ask, don't want to ruffle feathers, if you know what I mean. He is a man with purpose, though; his move to Pluckley was entirely intentional.'

'What do you mean?'

'He goes out a lot, he spends a lot of time in and around the church – and he seems to be doing something. I've not worked out what it is yet. He has become close to the verger, Mr Williams.' He paused for a moment as he walked, giving thought to a memory. 'He asked a lot of questions about Surrenden when he arrived, very interested in the big house for some reason. Idle curiosity maybe.' Higgins looked at me intently and grinned. 'Some people have a propensity for it.' His pace quickened.

'Tell me,' I enquired, feeling the need to change the subject somewhat, 'have you ever met with the spirits yourself?'

'But of course,' he blustered. 'On many occasions – come on, keep up, lots to see and the pub awaits us.'

'And these ghosts,' I pressed. 'Have you spoken to them?'

'That has been my misfortune, I am afraid,' he growled. 'It would seem that I attract them in some way.'

'What do they say to you, Mr Higgins?' I could tell that I had found a place of aggravation within his nerves, which I decided to settle upon for sport.

'Say to me?' His tone gave the impression of mild annoyance. 'Well, they have said a lot of things: messages for family members, unresolved matters, sometimes they are just stuck between worlds.'

'So you are a clairvoyant of some kind, a medium?'

'Why yes, you could say that I have a gift,' he said, lowering his eyes and pressing onwards. 'Finnan once asked me to hold a sitting in the pub, after hours. I refused him, though, despite the lure of free drink. It is not an experience I enjoy or would recommend. To me the gift is a burden that I bear with an unhappy heart and avoid at all costs. I prefer telling the tales rather than allowing my body to be taken over by some ungodly wretch from the afterlife. One does not like to feel used.'

Suddenly he halted and thrust an arm outwards across me.

'And here we are at the legendary Frith Corner!'

We had come to a stop at an unspectacular crossroads. The moon seemed less apparent here, fighting to be seen through the tall trees which seemed to press upon the intrusion of the byway. Between the trees stood bushes which merged into the hedgerows, creating the impression of a wall about the junction. I found it otherwise quite unremarkable.

'Legendary?' I coughed.

'I wouldn't say it if it wasn't true, Mr Weaver. There are few places in the world more linked to the spirit world than Frith Corner. There is something about the place that creates a particularly close doorway into the other world.'

'The other world? That sounds interesting, can we visit?' I asked, partly in humour and heavily influenced by the alcohol that I had consumed.

'It sounds funny, I know it does, but terrible things have happened here.' He pointed dramatically towards a large, dead oak tree at the side of the road. Its empty, broken branches reached up into the night sky above our heads, as if clawing for the life that had been lost from it. 'This tree is the site of a most grisly and terrible death. It was a murder so foul that it caused the spirit of its victim to roam without cease in the afterlife, that same spirit now being condemned to haunt the place of his death, bringing fear and terror to the descendants of those that carried out the deed.'

'You say "descendants",' I interrupted. 'Does this mean that the family of a murderer live on in the village?'

'Not just one killer, Mr Weaver, many killers; in fact it is unknown who dealt the final death blow, but we will come to that. Let me tell you the whole story.' His chest puffed out and I decided that I would let him continue without further interjection.

Before speaking, Higgins produced a hip flask from his coat pocket and took a large swig. He brushed his hand over the top of a tree stump at the side of the road, which I am sure he used as a perch quite regularly, and settled himself down.

'The year was 1752 and the road through Pluckley was damned and dangerous. This was, of course, before the days of the railway; carriages and coaches travelled through Pluckley by road, carrying goods to and from Folkestone and Dover. In the early part of that year a pair of highwaymen had taken the road as their own. The identity of these bandits was a mystery, although there were rumours that they were local to the area. They would appear out of nowhere, rob their poor victims and disappear as quickly as they came; there was even talk that they used magic to remain invisible at the side of the road, appearing suddenly with loud cries and violent threats to shock their prey into handing over their valuables.

'These were violent men too, not afraid of bringing harm upon those who refused to hand over their goods. But it was this brutal behaviour that started the chain of events which brought about their downfall. Their names were Thomas Flynn and Robert du Bois and they were indeed local men. Flynn was an ex-soldier injured whilst serving under Clive at the siege of Arcot, and returned home to Pluckley a war hero. He soon found, however, that local fame would not buy him food or provide a roof over his head, and so he began to scrape a living as a farmhand and occasional builder.

'Du Bois on the other hand was a born criminal, in and out of trouble since his youth. He was born to a respectable enough family. His father, the village baker, was well loved and respected by all who knew him. Young Robert, on the contrary, was born bad – a thief and a liar, known for his wild and cruel temperament. It was only his father's good name that prevented the village from delivering their own brand of justice to him. At the age of seventeen, he was caught in the act of stealing horses from the Dering estate. He was taken before the local magistrate and spent the next two years in Newgate.

'His time in prison did not cure him of his criminal sensibilities and it was the first of two instances in which he was gaoled. In 1750, he was released for the final time from Newgate and, claiming to have found religion, he returned to Pluckley, begging forgiveness and taking a humble position as a gravedigger at St Nicholas's Church. There he toiled for the next two years, head bowed low; a changed man.

'All was not as it seemed, however. Du Bois had met many rotten types whilst inside gaol; he had listened to tales of the great Jack Sheppard, and had even spent time in the company of none other than James MacLaine, the notorious masked bandit. He had marvelled at MacLaine's stories of daring adventure and the glamorous life led by a highwayman, and set out for a similar life of his own. He returned to Pluckley searching for a willing accomplice and met Flynn, who shared his vision of notoriety and riches.

'They used a well-known oak tree, this very tree standing before us, for their dastardly deeds. It is hollow, you see, and as such was a perfect hiding place where they could wait for the passing carriages and travellers. When their prey approached they would leap out onto the road, shocking their quarry and striking fear into the hearts of their victims.

'Their takings were regular and if it had not been for the greed and propensity for violence of du Bois, they would have evaded the notice of the law-keepers of the area. During one ill-fated robbery of a carriage bound for London, du Bois pulled one of the guards from inside the coach and set about him, beating the poor man relentlessly before the eyes of his fellow passengers.

'"This is what happens to those who dare to travel our road with no willing to pay the toll!" du Bois shouted, before throwing the body of the man back into the coach. The guardsman died of his injuries before reaching the capital.

'Men of the King's guard were immediately deployed to Pluckley and heavy-handed law arrived in the village. Flynn was arrested almost immediately; he had a loud and loose mouth when drunk, but could not talk his way out of a trip to the Tyburn noose. Yet he would not speak of his accomplice. It would seem that his military code of honour prevented him from giving du Bois up to the authorities. In fact, it is doubtful whether he would have been believed even if he had, such was the fine but false character that du Bois had built for himself within the community during the two years after his release from prison.

'Nevertheless, it was a visitor to Newgate whom Flynn received the day before his hanging which sealed the fate of du Bois. The visitor was the village baker, du Bois' father, who, unlike everyone else in the village, had not been fooled by his son. In his final hours before facing the noose, Flynn gave up his partner and told of the hollow oak at Frith Corner. A group of locals, loyal to the baker, gathered outside the Black Horse pub with murder in mind. Du Bois was hauled screaming from his bed, dragged by horse down the very same road which he had ruled for so long. He was tied to the very oak tree that you see before you now and, once secure, he was stabbed countless times by the mob with sword, spear, pike and fork. No one knows who dealt the killing blow – some say that it was his father who did it, tears in his eyes as he impaled his son's body to the tree.

'The body was left for all passing travellers to see...' Higgins paused for dramatic effect, '...and it is said that on moonlit nights, the ghost of du Bois will still leap from the hollow tree, to scare the unsuspecting traveller. The figure of the highwayman's ghost has even been seen by some, staked to the tree and screaming in pain.'

I looked at the old oak; there was nothing there. No hint of ghostly apparition, no crazed, dead highwayman leaping from the undergrowth, nothing.

After a few moments' silence I could not help but let out a small giggle.

'Do you still have enough in your flask to share, Mr Higgins?' I asked. 'I would hate to face the dead sober.'

'You are a fine audience, Weaver, although not easily shocked and scared by what Pluckley has to offer. No matter, I have enjoyed your company and shall enjoy it some more back at the Black Horse. I was going to show you 'the Devil's Bush' but fear it might be time wasted.'

'Oh please, dear Mr Higgins,' I laughed, taking the flask from him. 'The Devil's Bush? How can I return to London after visiting this village without saying that I have seen the Devil's Bush?'

He sighed and pointed to a large bush which seemed to stand apart from the rest of the undergrowth.

'This is the Devil's Bush! A bush said to have grown from an enchanted seed sent from the Judean desert, where Jesus himself met with Satan. It was transported by dark forces and planted by witches during a ritual in which the blood of a sacrificed child was used to water and feed the earth in which it was placed.' He took a small drink before continuing. 'Stories are told of how acolytes of witchcraft come to this site to perform their dark sacraments. It is said that, if a person is of cruel mind and black of heart, they should dance around the bush three times, calling upon Satan to appear to them! Once upon the earth, he will bring about the end of days, destroying God's world and heralding an age of darkness.' His voice had risen to a bellow and he raised his arms into the air as he finished. I struggled to contain my laughter.

'Come now, Mr Higgins, are you really trying to say that if I dance around a bush, the devil in all of his demonic glory will appear before me?'

'Well, of course that is the tale,' he answered. 'No one has ever been so far out of their right mind to try it, naturally – and I should imagine that the devil will only appear to those whom he wishes to visit.'

A nervous sheen had crossed his face now as he saw that I had started to circle the bush slowly. He let out a stuttering laugh.

'I wouldn't bother, you know, Weaver. Trust me, I know about these things. The wind is not right, the moon too bright, he'll not be appearing, you should stop.' He pulled his everlasting flask of cherry brandy from his coat pocket and took a lengthy swig.

I was not to be dissuaded and began to dance around the bush, arms raised in the air.

'Come forth, oh Satan!' I called in mock reverential tones. 'Show yourself to me and my good friend here!'

Once around.

'Where are you, Dark Lord? Stir yourself from your pit in hell and come to this magic bush in Kent!'

'Stop it, Mr Weaver!' Higgins snapped. 'You are wasting your time and mocking the spirits. I shall have to call a halt to the tour if you continue.'

Twice around.

I did not care; the tales of my esteemed tour guide were nonsense anyway. Stupid lies, created to scare the ignorant and infatuate the gullible.

'Where are you, Beelzebub? Is the cold night air not to your liking?' I had begun to laugh hysterically now, a combination of the alcohol that I had consumed with such relish, and the preposterous nature of my actions.

Three times around.

Nothing.

Not a hint of the devil appeared. Not a scent of brimstone, no eternal flames of damnation, nothing. I slumped giggling to the ground at Higgins's feet, laughing maniacally.

'There you are, Higgins old boy.' I pointed. 'There is your magic bush in all of its stupendous glory.'

'Well, I warned you that the night was not right,' he said, but his eyes did not move from the bush and the metal flask remained close to his lips. 'Come on, Mr Weaver, to your feet. We should return before it is too late to order more booze.'

I had started to right myself, pushing up onto my elbows, when a sudden breeze blew through the branches of the trees above our heads and an evening fog appeared and began to shift and swirl in the air.

Immediately my laughter stopped and I felt a coldness within me.

We froze in silence as we watched the grey mist collect and converge, sculpting itself before us. To our horror, it took shape from the base up, the contour of a man slowly being created. First the feet, then legs, torso and finally head. Although still ethereal in nature, the mist appeared to solidify further and detail was created on the form. He was well dressed in smart formal clothing, with tailored trousers, a waistcoat complete with a chain leading to a pocket watch and an overcoat. As the head slowly formed, I saw that the features were those of a relatively young man with shoulder-length, white hair, a clean-shaven, angular face and sharp searing eyes which stared directly at me. Was this the true face of the devil?

To my terror his lips began to move, although at first there seemed to be no sound.

'Are you seeing this, Higgins?' I stammered. 'Tell me that you are *actually* seeing this?' My guide did not reply but I heard a soft gurgle as he took another drink from his flask.

A sound came from the figure. It was like a distant noise at first, slowly growing in volume until I could understand the words that were coming from the mouth, although they faded in and out of my hearing.

'... unfinished... rising... Louhi... Pohjola... end... death.'

I felt a strong hand gripping the scruff of my collar, pulling me to my feet.

'I do not know about you, Mr Weaver,' Higgins hissed, 'but I have heard enough from the devil, and we should make our departure. Run!' He pulled at me and I did not need any further encouragement.

We fled the scene with all the pace that our drunken legs could muster, while the wind continued to blow behind us, creating a rush of noise in the trees as loud as a steam locomotive. I did not dare to glance behind me; I looked only ahead at my tour guide, who seemed to have gained incredible speed through pure cold terror. We did not slow or stop until we saw the lights of the village in the distance. As we paused, bent over with hands on knees, we looked at each other for a moment. We did not speak but it was clear that we had seen something unimaginable. Something which I am sure, despite Higgins's earlier talk of supernatural experiences, was quite unusual and new to him too.

We fell through the doors of the Black Horse a little shaken. However, the shock that we both felt soon turned itself into an excited energy and we found ourselves alternating from drunken laughter and incessant giggling to sudden periods of silence and deep thought. We had shared something that evening and I was sure that the experience would feature heavily in all of Higgins's future tours.

The rest of the evening in the bar was blurred to my memory; my only later recollections were brief and included brandy and laughter. What I did know was that my new acquaintance was fine company and I cannot recall any occasion previous to this night when I had enjoyed myself as much. By the end of the evening, the entertaining Mr Higgins and myself were on first-name terms and had arranged to meet once more, on the morrow, for another drink or two. Eventually, as the last of the customers left the pub, Miss Finnan let us know in no uncertain terms that she would be closing up for the night and that it was time for Mr Higgins to make his way home. This was despite our best efforts to charm 'just one more cherry brandy' from her.

I stumbled upstairs, following Miss Finnan's directions towards my room, where I eventually found my bed, which sat underneath a low eave that I caught my head on twice. Despite the room initially spinning at a relentless rate, I found myself shortly asleep and dreaming of bushes, demons and the voice of the white-haired man.

5

The Devil in the Dream

I woke sharply to the sound of a bell ringing. I wondered why there was a bell as I had never been woken in this way before at my rooms in Paddington. As it rang on and the fog of my mind cleared, I remembered that I was not at home at all and it was the call to breakfast.

I tried to sit up but found that I had precious little in the way of physical control over my body. My first attempt was met by an involuntary groan which would usually only have been heard coming from someone at least thirty years my senior. I gave up on the task momentarily and, spying my waistcoat pocket watch on the floor not two feet from my bed, I tried reaching out; but the exertion of the act was immense. I sighed and reached again, spilling myself completely out of bed and rolling helplessly to the floor, my head finding a remarkably true aim on the floorboards below. I groaned again and, after pulling the watch free from the waistcoat pocket, found only that it had once again halted in its function and read twenty minutes past eight o'clock.

The bell rang again from downstairs, wielded with relish by Miss Finnan, no doubt in full awareness of the pain that it was causing to my fragile skull; it would not stop until I appeared at the breakfast table. I dressed as hastily as I could, taking a moment to gaze in horror at my reflection in the mirror: my eyes were as blank as a corpse's, my skin pallid and soft. I promised myself that I would not imbibe any more drink until my return to London, and made my sorry way downstairs towards the dreadful ringing noise.

Miss Finnan stood with her hands on her waist, watching me as I entered the bar. She still held the bell, and I detected the hint of a smile on her usually glowering face. A place had been set for me at one of the tables and I pushed myself onto the bench behind it.

'We have tea or we have coffee, which do you prefer?' Miss Finnan had not removed her hands from her hips or her eyes from me since I had entered.

'A coffee would be most gratefully received, thank you,' I croaked, forcing a smile. This time her grin was evident.

'I'll return with it, and your breakfast.' She swung round briskly, placing the bell upon the bar top with a final clang. The thought of food twisted my guts and made my mouth watery and bitter. I am sure that I had previously felt worse (I had had scarlet fever as a child from which I recovered slowly, being confined to my room for nearly two months); however, I suspected that even cholera would be preferable to the dry ache which permeated my head and body on that terrible morning.

The plate that Miss Finnan arrived with shortly afterwards could not have been fuller and, given my present state, less appetising: thick slices of toasted bread, fried tomatoes and mushrooms, pink and fatty bacon and two sausages which were cooked to bursting. This she slammed down in front of me with a large mug of coffee, before retreating behind the bar to watch with interest as I broke my fast.

The gaze of my torturer never left me, despite her attempting to give the impression of cleaning the other tables and polishing glasses and tankards. It would seem that she could not decide whether to be disapproving of my lack of appetite or pleased at my misfortune. With muscles tensed and a resignation that it may not be the last time that I saw this meal, I ploughed in and forced down the lot. The disappointment on her face was incalculable.

'Very nice, Miss Finnan,' I called to her. 'Very nice indeed. Tell me, is there the possibility of another coffee? I feel that a breakfast of that quality should be given the pedigree it deserves and be washed down well!'

'I'll get you another straight away,' she said, and at last the smile which appeared on her lips was not because of my suffering.

Despite my initial feint I still felt unwell inside. Another coffee and a wash followed by a walk in the fresh air would go a long way to returning me to normality.

At that moment Tom Finnan appeared through the door of the pub with a large wooden box full of vegetables and bread. He nodded in my direction.

'Good morning,' I called.

'Morning,' he replied. 'I trust that you are feeling a little more stable than you were last night. My sister tells me that you were in the company of Mr Higgins; it takes a strong constitution to manage a night with old Edward and be able to stand straight the following morning.' He placed the box on the bar and called to Miss Finnan, telling her that he was back.

'I'm fine,' I replied. 'I have had a wonderful breakfast and am looking forward to getting out for a walk.'

'That sounds like a good plan,' he said, coming over to my table and sitting opposite me. 'I feel I must apologise; I did not play the role of gracious host when you arrived last night. Talk of ghosts unsettles me – something that I am forced to tackle now that I am living in this village. My name is Tom Finnan.' He reached his hand over the table and I received it gratefully.

'I am Samuel Weaver, and there is no need for apologies. We all have our own beliefs and they should be respected. I promise to keep any of my conversations with spirits away from you for the remainder of my stay. For someone with an aversion to the spirit world, this does seem a strange place to make your living,' I added, and he smirked at my observation. 'Tell me, have you been here long?'

'Less than a year. We previously ran a place in Essex and before that in London. I wanted this pub, though, and negotiated with the previous landlord. I was able to persuade him, eventually.'

'But why Pluckley?'

'I have interests in the area. Nothing related to the supernatural, trust me.' He paused for a moment and sipped his coffee. 'And what do you do for a job? When you're not chasing things that don't exist.'

'I am an illustrator, of books; nothing interesting really – technical manuals, instructional material, the odd medical book.' The lie came fluidly to me; I had used it before.

As we continued talking, I found that I actually liked the man; there was an effortless charm about him which made for a perfect landlord. Eventually he finished his coffee and excused himself.

'I have a meeting later this morning and need to prepare for it,' he said, looking at his watch.

'Oh,' I remembered, retrieving my own watch from my pocket. 'What is the time now?'

'Twenty past eight,' he called over his shoulder, before disappearing into the kitchen.

An ironic grin spread across my face and I hurried upstairs to wash and freshen myself.

***

An hour later, from my vantage point at the window in my room, I saw Tom depart. I grabbed my jacket and satchel and hurried down the stairs, shouting my goodbyes to Miss Finnan and telling her that I would return later.

I kept a safe distance from Tom and saw that he had not walked far, only to St Nicholas's Church some fifty yards away. He was met by a short, thin man with wire-framed spectacles which sat upon his nose precariously. I assumed he was the verger, Mr Williams. The men shook hands and spoke for a few moments before stepping inside. On their disappearance I hurried up the path through the graveyard and made my way to the side of the church. Standing on a pile of yet-to-be-laid gravestones, I peered in through the window. Although the glass was stained, and my view of the inside of the church distorted, I could see that the men were alone inside and stood by the pulpit in discussion. Tom's arms waved in the air in an animated fashion and there was no way in which I could understand any part of their conversation. Eventually they stopped and Williams led him to the back of the church.

I ran to the front, tried the handle and found that it was unlocked. I needed to get closer to them as the content of their conversation intrigued me. The discovery of any knowledge at all could be of use when I finally broached the subject of Finnan's dealings with Sibelius Darke. I pushed at the large oaken door of the church and stepped inside.

The church was large, and my footsteps echoed around the walls despite my best efforts to remain quiet. I had decided that if they were to appear and confront me regarding my business in the church, I would say that I was a God-fearing man and visited churches on a daily basis wherever I found myself. This was not true, as I admit that this was the first time that I had stepped into a church building since leaving my father's guardianship in York. Being raised within a religious family and devout spiritual surroundings had done nothing but repulse me, and I railed against any form of religion.

I could hear the low murmur of voices from a door at the end of the church, voices which quietened to silence as I approached. I stood and waited for their conversation to begin again; however, it did not. After some time I grew weary of waiting any longer and gently knocked upon the door. There was no answer. I knocked again, a little more insistently this time, and called out for attention. Still there was no reply. My hand settled slowly on the handle of the door and, apologising for interrupting, I opened it and found that it was not a room at all but a steep stairway leading down to the crypt.

I stood for a moment and listened for any hint of sound. There was none, and so I stepped lightly down the stone stairs and into the darkness. I found neither Tom nor Mr Williams present and, as I walked around the tombs which lined the low-ceilinged room, I saw that there were no other exits.

Perhaps they had come out of the crypt when I had run to the front door? It was a mystery, to be sure. I hated mysteries. I noted the metal plates which lay upon the stone burial plinths and saw that the majority of them were members of the Dering family. Higgins had mentioned to me last night that both the Red and White Ladies were entombed within this crypt, their bodies held within oak-and-lead-lined coffins in an attempt to preserve their beauty forever. I felt a dark urge to pull the stone lids from one of the coffins. I was sure that, no matter how beautiful these ladies may have been in life, they would be nothing more than bones and dust now. I resisted the urge and walked towards the stairway again, noticing as I went a yellow shield with a black cross upon the wall of one of the arches. The same symbol was evident on each of the Dering coffins and I took this to be part of their coat of arms.

Angry at losing the men, I gave up on my search and left the church. I would return to the Black Horse later in the afternoon in the hope of seeing Finnan again.

I spent the rest of the morning and early afternoon revisiting the spots to which I had been introduced by Higgins the previous evening. At each of these I made a sketch of the area, sometimes inserting the ghosts which Higgins had assured me were often seen there. At Frith Corner I drew a few sketches of the Devil's Bush with the figure of the white-haired man floating on top of it. In daylight the bush seemed completely ordinary. I did not have anything near a rational explanation for what I had seen the previous evening; perhaps it was merely an illusion fuelled by cherry brandy and high spirits.

My image of the devil's appearance at the bush completed, I then moved on to the dead oak tree at the other side of the road. Here I drew a few pictures of the highwayman Robert du Bois, jumping out to terrorise travellers as they passed, then surrounded by an angry mob and pinned to the old oak tree which had been his hiding place, and finally returning as a spirit to haunt the descendants of those who murdered him. I knew for a fact that my employer, old Mr Purkess, had a particular fondness for tales of highwaymen; and the right pictures, combined with the words, would act as safely 'banked' pieces for the paper, which could be rolled out on quiet news weeks.

My drawings finished, I decided that before returning to the pub I would head east out of the village, in the direction in which Higgins had said the manor house, Surrenden, stood. It was not a long walk and I found the manor easily enough, as there was a large wall surrounding the grounds which obscured any view of the house itself. I followed the wall until it finally reached a large set of iron gates which stood between two pillars. Atop each of the pillars sat a large stag's head, carved in sandstone and staring out towards all who approached; I found myself thinking of the grotesque deer painted in blood upon the wall of the house in Paddington. Underneath each stag's head were the newly carved words 'Domini Mortum'; my Latin, although a little rusty, told me that the words meant something such as 'Lords over Death', an odd inscription for a country house indeed. I found myself thinking of Mary Pershaw laid upon the floor, her chest opened up and her heart staked to the wall. I would be returning to

London the following day and foremost in my mind was to find Abe Thomas to see if there had been any further developments.

I stepped up to the gates and stared through at the winding path, which I assumed led up to the big house, and thought back to my conversation with Higgins in the pub, during which he had told me that for years the manor had been owned by the Dering family. They were no longer in residence, however, and another titled family had taken ownership shortly before Higgins had arrived in Pluckley himself. Higgins was vague regarding their identity, merely saying that it was some toff from the city who had bought the country seat with winnings from a card game.

Hunger gently nudged me and I took a quick sketch of the gates, complete with their adornment and inscription, for no other reason than that they intrigued me, and set off back to the village and the Black Horse.

***

I was met, as I stepped through the doors, by the unnatural sight of Miss Finnan's smiling face.

'Is your head recovered enough to deal with a beer?' she asked. I paused for a moment, thinking about the time of day and the temptations ahead to continue drinking.

'I think it best if I forced myself, Miss Finnan. I always find that the best way to deal with fear of the unknown is to crash onwards and deal with the consequences later.'

She returned shortly with a full mug and, although the first few tentative sips sent shudders through my body, I found that it was not the painful experience that I had feared it would be.

When Miss Finnan offered me another drink, I politely declined and instead went upstairs, where I lay on my bed gently dozing for a time. I do not know for how long this was as I had long since given up on trying to ascertain the time and had instead decided to enjoy my break away from the deadlines and constraints of London life.

As the evening began and the noise grew in the bar downstairs, I decided to wash and return to my hosts. Tom had not been in the bar earlier, his sister letting slip that he would often go missing for the day to somewhere unknown to her. I still had hopes of breaking down his defences further to find out more of his involvement with the child murderer Sibelius Darke.

I was not disappointed when I entered the bar; Tom Finnan stood behind it busily serving drinks when I walked in. He saw me and nodded hello, shaking his cupped hand in my direction to offer a drink. I pulled up a stool at the bar and tried my hand at conversation with him whenever he was available. Over the course of the evening, I discovered little from him, yet found myself having to provide a glut of false biography to him; he was indeed the epitome of a good barman.

My efforts had just begun to grate a little with me when a hand slapped firmly upon my shoulder and I turned to see the ruddy, smiling face of Higgins.

'A large brandy with a beer to wash it down with, Tom, if you please,' he said. 'Samuel, we have business to discuss.'

I stood and followed Edward over to a table tucked away in a dark corner of the room.

'I've given some thought to our… experience last night at Frith Corner,' he said, his voice low. 'Something about what or who we saw has niggled at my mind.'

'I can assure you, Edward, it has not sat easy with me either,' I said. 'It is not every evening that the devil is conjured and tries to speak to you.'

'Well, that's just it, you see. That is it exactly, old man. I don't think the devil appeared to us at all.'

'Do you mean we imagined it?'

'No, we saw what we saw; I just don't think that he was the devil. In fact, I think that I've seen him before, somewhere else.'

'Where?'

'In a dream, Samuel. In a dream.'

I laughed loudly and all the eyes in the room drew to me.

'Higgins, you are a joy,' I hissed. 'A spirit appears before us after I called for Satan to come forth, and you claim that it is an old friend whom you met one night whilst asleep. What next? Are you going to tell me that you commune with Napoleon and Julius Caesar is a drinking companion?'

'There is more to it than that, Samuel,' he smiled. 'His face was familiar to me, what little I saw of it. I spent the night awake fighting my memory for where I could place him, and it was only when drifting off to sleep that it came to me.'

'Who is he then?'

'I'm afraid I do not know his name.'

I laughed aloud again.

'No, wait,' he said, beckoning me to stop. 'Remember when I told you last night that Tom Finnan had asked me to contact the spirits with him?'

'Yes,' I said, immediately interested.

'Well, initially I agreed. He offered me good money – and to do a favour for a man who owns a pub is worth a thousand good deeds for anyone else. He had arranged a room for us above the pub and I had given him instructions on how I needed it to be set out, and that I needed at least two others present. He told me that Anne would be one and that Mr Williams, the verger, would be the other.

'But the night before the sitting I was visited in a dream, by this man who you thought was the devil. He told me that he would be talking through me at the séance; that he would need to take control of my body in order to speak to Tom.'

'But you said that you knew this was how it worked. Surely you were aware of this when you agreed to hold the séance?'

'I did, Samuel. Of course I did. The thought of the money and the booze was payment enough to make me agree.'

'Then why did you change your mind?'

He stared hard into his drink, searching for the words.

'My gift has many facets. Things that I do not fully understand. One of these "parts" is a kind of knowing. It is a completely natural feeling, as easy as hearing a familiar sound or being able to recognise an object through touch with your eyes closed. I hope you can understand me, my friend. This is something that I rarely speak of.'

I nodded and bade him continue.

'Well, this man,' he whispered, 'he was steeped in death, soaked in a darkness that I have never felt before and never wish to experience again. This man has been linked to the darkest evil. He has been joined with something responsible for terrible atrocities, and I could not imagine opening myself up to him. I cancelled the sitting with Tom the following morning.'

I sat back in my chair and thought for a moment.

'I have also been giving our incident at the bush a lot of thought, Edward, and I think there are elements of delusion involved here,' I said, and reached over the table to grip his wrist in reassurance. 'I am not saying that we saw nothing – I am sure we did see something. I think, however, that what appears at the bush when a foolish drunkard such as I calls to the spirits is not the devil. What appeared to us was the image of what we think of as the devil, as it were. To you, a believer in such things, previously visited in a dream by something so dark and evil that you ran as far as you could from it – to you the same 'devil' appeared, summoned by the strength of your fear. I have heard, though, of instances of group madness where the fears and hallucinations of one spread to others through strength of belief – and not a little alcohol in our case.'

'But we both saw it,' he implored.

'I am quite sure that we did, Edward, I am not denying this. What I am saying is that we saw what you wanted us to see, what you truly believed to be there – I was drunk, Edward, you could have told me that Spring-heeled Jack himself was going to appear before us and I would have seen him.'

Higgins smiled. 'Spring-heeled Jack, now there is a legendary story worth telling. If only he had appeared near Pluckley, I could slip him into my tour.'

'This is exactly the point I am trying to make, Edward. You have a talent for imagination and storytelling, a gift stronger even than the clairvoyance which you so vehemently suppress.'

I withdrew my notepad from my pocket, scribbled a name and address upon a piece of paper and passed this over to Edward. 'If you ever wish to sell some of your ghost tales then contact this man; his name is George Purkess and he is a friend of mine. I will tell him that you might be in contact and that your stories are worth printing. He will listen to me.'

Higgins took the piece of paper from me.

'Perhaps you are right, Samuel.' His eyes glazed slightly as he paused for a moment of thought. 'I will take this address from you, but I warn you that I might not use it. I am happy here. I get to tell my tales, make enough money to eat and drink; I am content. However, I do travel to London on occasion. I have small business interests in the city and I would be glad to look you up when I visit.'

'Then we should have one more drink, a toast to your happiness and to future meetings.' I smiled. Raising my arm I turned to the bar, where Miss Finnan stood drying a tankard. 'Dear Miss Finnan, could I have a couple of large cherry brandies for myself and my very good friend here? Just the one, though; I do not want to miss my train tomorrow.'

It would have been easy to stay in the same spot all evening but urgency prevailed and I eventually excused myself so that I could return to the bar to talk to Tom some more.

'You are certainly a pair, the both of you,' the landlord said as I approached. 'It would do wonders for my profits if you were to stay on in Pluckley.'

'I would love to; Higgins is certainly a rare man. Tell me, has he lived in Pluckley for long?'

'He arrived a couple of years ago apparently; I'm not sure where he was before then. He has a small cottage on the edge of the village, but I get the impression that he has other abodes. He spends long periods away from the village. He is a fine man, though. He loves the area and has developed an incredible knowledge of the supposed spirits of Pluckley. He does the tours for fun, you know; I do not think he has need of the money. It must be nice to have the luxury of not having to work for a living.'

'Yes, unfortunately I too have work to return to. My employer only grudgingly allowed me these two days and I must return tomorrow. Edward tells me that you lived in London once before.'

'Yes, Whitechapel,' he said, the word slipping out of his mouth before he could prevent it. He appeared to roll his eyes a little at his openness before deciding to continue. 'I owned a pub called the Princess Alice on the corner of Wentworth Street and Commercial Street, a nice place; good people in Whitechapel – for the most part.'

'I have never been to the area myself,' I lied. 'I live to the west, Paddington way.' I shifted in my seat slightly, ready to play my riskiest card. 'I have heard of Whitechapel of course. Did you run the pub with Miss Finnan? You were never married? I am sorry if I seem to pry – it is just my nature.'

His face flushed a little, but he was mine.

'No apology needed. I do not talk about it enough. Yes, I was married once. She died a long time ago though, my wife. She left my daughter and me behind. My sister Anne came to live with us to help bring up Beth, acted as a mother to her.' There was a terrible sadness in his voice as he mentioned his daughter's name.

'Did she not come to Pluckley with you?'

His face immediately set firm.

'No. No, she didn't. Something happened to her, to all of us, something terrible. She lives away from us now, somewhere where she can forget about it all. Please excuse me. I don't wish to speak any more.' There was a snap in his voice. The conversation was over. Tom walked down the bar and whispered something in Miss Finnan's ear before taking his jacket and leaving the pub. She came over to where I sat.

'Tom has gone out for a while, for a breath of fresh air. He gets like this sometimes, I can see it in his face. Did he mention Beth?'

'Yes, he did. It must trouble him greatly. I am sorry for broaching the subject.'

'Beth was the only thing he lived for. Do not worry yourself. A brisk walk and some time to himself and he will soon be recovered. He will probably apologise to you in the morning.'

'Ah yes, the morning. I will be sad to leave here. Truly I will. If you will excuse me I will take to my bed and see you tomorrow, Miss Finnan.' I stood and gave a final wave to Higgins, who had found himself an audience to buy him drinks as he regaled them with a humorous tale involving a serving wench, a saucy ghost and a liaison in a cellar. The laughter of his audience rang in my ears as I made my way up the stairs.

I did not go to my room, however.

With the noise of the busy pub rumbling through the floorboards, I crept along the corridor to the rooms of Anne Finnan and her brother, Tom. The first door I opened was to Miss Finnan's quarters. I scouted around it quickly but found nothing of interest apart from a photograph of a young girl, who I assumed was Beth, the landlord's missing daughter. I thought of stealing the photograph to add to my collection, but it was placed by Miss Finnan's bedside and would be noticed if it were to go missing. I stepped out into the corridor and on to the next room, which would have to be Tom's.

The room was sparse, with little in the way of ornament. However, there was a desk in the corner, which had papers strewn across it and a wooden box at one side. I thought of the metal box given to me by the current owner of the Princess Alice, and which was to be returned to Tom. I never intended to bring it with me, but had not yet managed to unlock it to see what the contents were. I would take it to a locksmith upon my return to London.

I lightly touched the lid of the wooden box on the desk and found it to be unlocked. Inside were yet more papers and I took the risk of lighting a candle to be able to see what was written on them. The majority of the papers were letters of correspondence, legal papers relating to the deeds of the Black Horse, letters to gentlemen's clubs requesting information on how to attain membership and, finally, at the bottom of the box, was the evidence I had been seeking.

It was a letter from a medical superintendent, a Dr Octavius Jepson, regarding the internment and safe keeping of Bethany Finnan. From the details of the letter I could see that she had been a resident of the City of London Lunatic Asylum, at Stone near Dartford, for the past five years. Her committal was stated to be permanent due to 'prolonged and violent hysteria related to mental trauma'. Tom Finnan might have been cagey and unresponsive, but Bethany Finnan... mentally unbalanced and weak of mind, she would tell me everything.

I blew out the candle and folded the letter, putting it into my pocket. It was as I turned to leave the room, however, that I received my greatest shock.

For there, upon a cabinet on the other side of the room, was a cork board upon which were pinned many photographs. Yet it was not the group of photographs which was remarkable – they were of various gentlemen and people in whom I had no interest. At the centre of the board was a picture of Tom Finnan with his daughter and another man standing outside the photographic studio of Sibelius Darke on Osborne Street. I knew then that this man must be Darke himself, the child killer and cannibal of Whitechapel; for it was he who had tried to speak to me the previous evening at the Devil's Bush.

6

The Maiden in the Tower

The carriage took my mother away four days before my sixteenth birthday. I did not fully understand what was happening, although I knew that she had been prone to fits of hysteria in the weeks preceding her committal.

As time moved on I saw her less and less about the house, for she had begun to take to her bed for days at a time, shunning all but the smallest scraps of food and refusing to speak to anyone in the house, even the servants.

When I say that we had servants, I am not trying to pretend that we lived in a stately home with staff attending to our every need. All the same, our house was comfortably large and Father employed a cook, a maid and a gardener to assist Mother with the upkeep of the home as he was so rarely there. The cook, Mrs Coleman, was a sweet lady who fussed and cared for Mother and myself as if we were her own family. Mrs Coleman and her daughter were natives of York. She had come to our employment soon after I was born and her daughter, Victoria, had taken up the post of housemaid a few years later once old enough.

Five years older than me, Victoria was a plain but gentle thing. She loved to look at my drawings, often asking me to create sketches for her: flowers, landscapes and the like. I did this, of course; she was the closest thing I had as a friend in my youth and I found her innocent charm relaxing company. Victoria would also often act as an alibi for me when my wanderings about the city reached a late hour, for which I was always grateful.

I first seduced Victoria when I was fifteen. It was the beginning of an unfortunate chain of events that led to the final disagreement with Father and my move away from York.

On the day that Mother was taken, I had spent the morning in the house. I heard the carriage pull up outside the house and had assumed that it was a visitor for Father, who had decided to stay at home today rather than attend to his church duties. When I heard the screaming begin, I realised that something quite different was happening, and that my mother's sickness had finally come to some sort of turning point. I rushed out of the drawing room and into the hallway, where I was blocked by the broad frame of Mr Morgan, the gardener.

'Your father says you are to stay in the drawing room for this,' he said. 'It is not something for a young lad to see.'

'Get out of my way, you oaf!' I shouted and tried to push past.

He was a large man, though, much larger than I, wide enough to be a wall across the passageway. The screaming of my mother was coming from up the stairs and was interspersed with other voices, which I did not recognise.

The loud wails of my mother grew in volume as she was brought to the top of the staircase. I looked up and caught sight of her; she was being held by the arms by two large men, at whom she railed and swore.

Once again I threw myself helplessly against Morgan; I struck him with my fists but he was too large, too strong, and he wrapped his arms around me, restricting my movement.

Mother's cries continued outside, increasing to a violent crescendo, which I later realised was caused by seeing my father as he stood to see her off. The carriage thundered away from the house, heading towards the institution which would be her new home from that day forwards.

Morgan released me from his hold when the last sounds of the carriage's wheels upon the cobbles faded from our hearing, and I immediately rushed to my room.

Father came up later and sat on the edge of my bed as I lay sobbing into my pillow. He explained that Mother had been unwell for some time and had always suffered from fits of nervous hysteria. He told me that she would be going to stay in a place of safety for a period of treatment and that eventually she would return to us restored and happy once more. He told me that he had secured a future for our family; he had bought the deeds to the rectory from the Archbishop, and that even when he and Mother died, the house would be mine, a large and spacious home for me to live in with my family when I was older. Secure our future maybe – but bring Mother home again? I knew this to be a lie the moment he opened his mouth.

***

I thought of Mother as I travelled back to London from Pluckley. I had not written to her for two weeks and promised myself that I should compose a letter upon my return, something that could be read to her.

My return journey was uneventful. Anne had arranged for a local man to take me to the station in his cart and I enjoyed the view of the countryside on the way there. Soon I would be returning to the grey filth of the city and, although I loved the bustle and energy of London life, I felt a twinge of regret at leaving this strange village. I was the only person to board at Pluckley and found the train to be quite empty. I was alone within my car for most of the journey, only being joined for the final three stops by a loud and obnoxious man who filled the car with sickly, sweet-smelling smoke from his large bowled pipe. I kept all conversation with him to a minimum; my only comfort during the short time we spent together was that once the journey was over I would not have to spend another minute with the man.

I stopped by the offices in the Strand on my way back to my rooms to find Henry Cope in an unusually pleasant mood.

'Ah, Mr Weaver, what a pleasure it is to see you. I trust that your family in York are well?'

I stared at him for a moment, attempting to read the cause for this good humour before he took the pleasure of telling me himself.

'I am fine, Mr Cope, as are my family,' I said slowly. 'Did you miss me?'

'Oh, you were missed indeed, Weaver. You will not have heard the news, of course?'

'News, oh yes, we do get to hear the news in Yorkshire, you know. What story in particular were you referring to?'

'It is not a story which has appeared in the press as yet. It is murder, Weaver; a most terrible murder. It happened on the night that you went away and Mr Purkess was most aggrieved that you were not available to attend. He sent James Fairchild in your place, and a wonderful job he did too by all accounts. I have not seen the pictures yet myself, of course, but I am assured by those who have that they are of the highest quality – and I am sure they will be the main feature on the front cover of next week's edition. Such a good man is Fairchild, reliable and courteous to everyone he meets; you should try to be more like him.'

My smile was broad but I boiled inside. Fairchild had been Purkess's number one London artist for the last ten years, a position from which I had worked hard to remove him. In the last six months, Mr Purkess had offered me work that would have normally gone to Fairchild automatically. In terms of style and content, I had a massive advantage over him and knew that I could not be beaten when it came to providing the most sensational of pictures. In comparison to mine, his depictions were adequate but terribly dull.

'Mr Fairchild is someone whose qualities we can all aspire to, I am sure, Mr Cope,' I said. 'Perhaps you can send him my best regards when you see him next. I am glad that he was given the opportunity to briefly blow air into the dying coals of his career as a result of my absence.'

The hooded eyes of Cope studied me for a second and he bit the corner of his lip as he tried to judge the level of my sincerity.

'Who from the force attended the murder scenes?' I asked.

'Inspector Thomas, of course,' he replied. 'That man is never off duty, no matter what state he is in. There was only one scene, though: a young woman, by the name of Felicity Moore, brutalised and murdered in the most disgusting of manners. Nailed to a tree in St Peter's Park. I would not dare tell you of the atrocities that were done to her body. If you are interested you should speak to Inspector Thomas; he, like you, seems to revel in that sort of thing.'

The anger within me grew. Why could it not have been just a plain everyday stabbing? Why not a drunken brawl which led to an unfortunate death? This murder sounded exciting and I had missed it due to my obsession with Darke. It was, if nothing else, even more reason to hate him.

'Is Mr Purkess in, by any chance?' I asked, motioning towards the stairs which led to his offices.

'Why of course not, Weaver. Surely you must know his movements better than that. He is lunching and I do not expect him back today, any more than I do any other day when he has gone to lunch.'

I shrugged and said no more to Cope, taking a few minutes to wander the offices and look at the pieces being written for next week's edition. I found the writer putting the 'Tragedy of St Peter's Park' murder into words. It was sparse to say the least, full of vague assumptions, tawdry descriptions and lazy in its creativity. I had been gently pushing Purkess for some time to allow me regularly to put the words to my pictures, but he had, in the main, been resistant to my more explicit writing efforts.

'The world is not yet ready for the combined energies of your work, Mr Weaver,' he had said during one such heated discussion. 'The words, when combined with your pictures, will cause weakness and distress to any ladies who read them; society will not appreciate the reality and shock value that you bring.'

I disagreed, of course; I knew the hearts and minds of men, their darkest desires for the excitement that came from a brutal and base act, and the thrill that they felt when seeing the cruel suffering of others. I knew men – and I knew that they would happily soak themselves in all the gore and horror that I could offer them, if only they were given the chance.

As I left the offices to return home, I called out to all who would listen that I was now 'on duty' once more and would be available to work as and when needed.

***

Over the next week I was indeed called upon to attend some scenes of disarray and tragedy in the city. There were accidental deaths: a man run down by a dray as he returned home from work to see his wife, who had gone into labour that day. And there was the usual array of killings related to drink and its effects: a woman who cut the throat of her drunken and abusive husband as he slept, before preposterously turning herself into the police, claiming that she did it in self-defence.

None of the unfortunate events in the area showed any link to the murder of the servant girl in the park. This changed, however, six days after my return from Pluckley.

A police carriage pulled up outside my rooms and I was requested to join Inspector Thomas at a scene in Lancaster Gate, outside Christ Church.

When I arrived I found the Inspector standing at the end of the road.

'Morning, Abe,' I said. 'Another one?'

He did not answer but nodded, pointing up the street to a spot outside the church, where a number of police had gathered. I could tell that the Inspector was in no mood for banter today.

'Has there been any movement on Boston Place?' I asked, more in hope than expectation.

'Nothing official,' he grumbled. 'We have the names of most of the girls, to go with Mary Pershaw; but I have the feeling that there is actually a link between Boston Place and these murders.'

'How so?'

'The last scene – you will have heard of it. A partly clothed girl, Felicity Moore, arms aloft and nailed by her palms to an oak tree in the middle of St Peter's Park, her body ripped and her insides emptied onto the ground in front of her feet.'

'I did hear vague details; I understand that another artist attended the scene.'

'James Fairchild. Yes, he seemed a decent enough man. Not suited to these places, though. He did well not to lose the contents of his stomach.' He gave a smile but it was cold; there was no happiness in it.

'Some people are meant for this, Abe,' I said solemnly. 'What's the link?'

'The spikes that were used to nail her hands to the tree. They were cut spikes, like those used on railways and…'

'The same as those used at Boston Place,' I said, completing his sentence. 'To nail the bodies to the floor and the hearts to the wall.'

He looked grimly at me.

'I think that was the beginning,' he said. 'The root of these killings.

I know murder, Samuel, and that girl at the tree and this poor child are somehow connected to those deaths.'

'Is Boston Place still being kept out of the press?' I asked.

'Not for much longer,' he replied. 'People talk and sooner or later the story will come out, or a version of it.'

'We may not keep it to ourselves for much longer, Abe. Not if there's a link to these murders.'

'I know, I know. Just give me another week and I promise you that it's all yours. Tell Purkess that himself. Tell him I'll owe him one.'

I nodded in assent and we approached the newest victim.

'A milk cart found her, just as it was starting to get light this morning. The driver thought that someone had dumped a pile of rubbish in the road,' Thomas said as we neared the mound. 'He saw no sign of an assailant other than a tall, jaundiced woman in a light grey cloak. She couldn't have done it, of course – this isn't the work of a lady – but I would still like to find her. She may have seen the murderer.'

I could see why the mistake had been made; it did not seem like a body at all but a pile of rags.

'This is how he found her,' he continued. 'We haven't tried to move her yet as we were waiting for a doctor to arrive. I want to know if she's all here.' He breathed out hard and long. 'We wouldn't even know it was a girl if it wasn't for this.' He pointed down at one side of the bundle and the horror of what was at my feet began to be revealed to me.

The pile sat about two feet high, stacked into a neat pyramid of black, torn clothing and glimpses of pale flesh. Around this lay a moat of blood which had settled into the spaces between the cobbles. Although the cause of death was unclear, one thing was for certain. The girl had been jointed. Each cut section of her had been carefully placed on top of another in a bizarre tower of cut body parts. At the bottom was the torso, followed by the thighs and upper arms; on top of these had been placed the calves and forearms; and finally at its apex sat the hands and feet, reaching up to the heavens. The area where Thomas had pointed gave the positioning of the final piece of the puzzle. The head of a girl with long dark hair, tied into a plait and hanging from the tower, stared out of a cage made of her own limbs.

Her eyes were wide in terror and I could only imagine the agony that she felt when her end had come – or had it been relief?

I quickly set about sketching the bundle, knowing that the doctor could arrive at any time and the image, which the killer must have wanted to be witnessed by all, would be dismantled. I could not draw my eyes from her and completed my sketch without ever moving my gaze. Time seemed to stop as I lost myself in the grotesque beauty of this killer's work.

When the doctor arrived, two young policemen were given the task of taking each of the pieces of her and laying them out on a sheet which had been placed on the pavement. They did so with tears in their eyes and I knew that, however long they lived, they would each bear the memory of this day etched into their minds until their deathbeds. When they had completed their harrowing job, and the doctor set about examining the corpse, I drew her again.

She was a pretty girl, or had been. The milky white skin on her cheeks was flecked with blood, which gave the impression of a freckle-faced child. I could tell by what was left of her clothes, her calloused hands and her worn fingernails that she was a working girl of some description, perhaps in a kitchen somewhere. Her shoes were flat and sturdy enough, although the edges of the soles had started to wear more than would be tolerated by someone who could easily afford to buy new. Before her legs had been taken from her torso, she had been wearing long skirts; these now lay in a dirty heap at the side of the road.

'It was a large blade that done her; something long enough and sharp enough to take each piece from her in just one slice. There are no hack marks. There is no sign of a bag or anything to identify her, but someone must know who she is,' Abe said. He nudged the kneeling doctor in the back with his knee. 'Can we hurry this up, Doctor?' he barked. 'I just need to know. Is she all there?'

The doctor looked up from his grim work and nodded.

'There is nothing amiss as far as I can tell at this stage, Inspector,' he said. 'Not unless the killer took her organs and stitched her back up, which I doubt.'

I turned from the girl and, saying my goodbyes to Abe, I walked away. I had all the pictures that I needed to compose something shocking enough to make the front page of next week's edition, if given the nod by the Inspector. I would visit Abe later this evening to find out if there had been any developments. The sound of the doctor's voice stopped me in my tracks, however.

'There is nothing missing, Inspector, but there has certainly been something added.' I turned to see what he spoke of.

In his hand he held the iron cut spike that he had withdrawn from her.

***

It was a week after the discovery of the jointed girl that I finally had time to visit the asylum near Dartford. There had been no further killings, although both Inspector Thomas and all who knew of them expected another at any time. The only link between the dead girls was they were clearly in service of some kind. Thomas had sent his men to ask discreet questions at houses in both the St Peter's Park and Marylebone areas, but the owners and their staff were cagey and unhelpful, to say the least.

News of the two murders and the twelve bodies at Boston Place were hearsay only and the police refused to confirm or deny their existence. It would not be long before I would be forced to make this knowledge public, but in the meantime I kept my word to the Inspector. I knew that, if handled clumsily, telling all, although sensational and good for circulation, would cause irreparable long-term damage to the goodwill that we had carefully and methodically nurtured with the police.

It was mid-afternoon and the sun threw a dazzling blaze upon the asylum, seeming to bathe it in warmth and happiness. From my knowledge of such institutions, I knew that this would not be the case once inside the doors and this realisation made me pause for a while outside. I took this time to sketch the building, paying particular attention to the tall tower which rose above it. I had been informed, following a number of letters over the past two weeks, that Bethany Finnan resided within the tower itself, away from the other residents.

I had written claiming to be the cousin of Bethany Finnan, and explaining that I had come over from Dublin and wished to visit. This was a ploy filled with risk, as her father could have been contacted by the asylum at any stage to confirm my identity. My enquiries had taught me that Bethany had been committed to the asylum by Tom following a number of violent incidents where she put herself and others at risk of injury or death. Tom had asked that she be kept in separate quarters and paid a fee to the medical superintendent Dr Octavius Jepson. My prior knowledge of such places, both through my father's church activities with the York asylum and my own mother's care at The Retreat, led me to believe that the only place such funds went was into the pockets and accounts of those in charge of the asylum.

I swallowed hard before pushing open the large doors at the entrance to the building and, after introducing myself, was led into the tower and up a steep spiral staircase to the room at the top.

The room was a bright burning in my eyes as the warden unlocked and opened the door for me and I stepped inside. Every part of the room was white and reflected the light of the day shining in through the large windows which seemed to circle the room. There was a sparsely dressed bed in the centre of the room, the only bedding a soft white blanket which lay neatly stretched across the sheeted mattress.

As my eyes became accustomed to the blankness of the room, I saw her. She was sitting upon a painted window seat, her face turned away from me as she gazed out into the freedom of the countryside beyond. She wore a thin white dress, no more than a nightgown, which caused her to further blend in to her surroundings.

'I have come to visit with you, miss; I recently stayed with your father, Tom.'

She did not respond and I studied her frame, slight and poised. Her hands lay crossed upon her lap, their skin as pale and smooth as to almost appear translucent. Her hair was long, dark and brushed so as to give it a glossy sheen and there were tinges of red within which I saw elements of her father. The hair hung softly in ringed curls across her shoulder and her back, and I thought then about how striking a form she was, almost ethereal and ghostly.

As I approached the window seat, she did not stir, and I slowly sat down. I saw her face and I understood the truth in what her father, Tom, had told me about the love which she had inspired in all who met her. Her green eyes remained fixed upon some indefinable place within the trees which surrounded the hospital. She was indeed a most beautiful creature, her eyes soft and large, framed by gently curved cheekbones which lifted her face and caused her mouth to appear pursed. Her lips, although without the benefit of rouge, were red, cushioned and tender as if awaiting the kiss of her long-dead beau.

I was so struck by her countenance that when she spoke it caused me to start somewhat.

'Have you brought news of Sibelius to me?' Her voice was low and smooth.

'I have not,' I responded, 'just news from your father.'

'Father, I know Father's message already,' she said. 'He loves me and that is why he keeps me here. It is… for the best, I am told.' There was a sharpness to her voice.

'Why did you ask about Sibelius? Was it not Nikolas Darke that you loved and were betrothed to?'

'I did, and I was, but I said goodbye to Niko. We had our time for farewells; Sibelius gave that to us.'

'Then you do not believe that Sibelius murdered his brother?'

'Sibelius Darke was the bravest, kindest and most gentle man I ever knew. He did not kill Niko! Nor any of those children either, he did not have it within him!'

'But the evidence would say differently. I have read the newspapers; I've even spoken to those that were there.'

'Then you are a fool,' she laughed. 'Do you really believe everything you read in the press? Even I know that they lie and exaggerate in order to sell the latest edition – and I am supposedly a lunatic.'

'But what about the Dolorian Club, Bethany? He was seen by more than two dozen witnesses leaving the blazing building in his wake. He walked through that club armed to the teeth and killing all who stood in his way, including Dr Earnshaw, the man who arranged his membership of the club. You cannot deny that he was guilty of that.'

'Were you sent by Dr Jepson?'

'No, why?'

'Because Jepson has sent dolts like you before – I do not know why, perhaps it is for his own amusement. He is sicker than most held within these walls.' Her eyes fixed on me for an uncomfortable period of time and I found myself looking away from her to avoid her scrutiny. 'The Dolorian Club was a place of evil; it was the place where the demon Surma was reborn. Do not tell me that Sibelius was a guilty man for killing everyone in that building.'

'I am sorry but I cannot see it,' I said. The poor girl was obviously damaged.

'They watch me here still, you know,' she said, a small upturn of her lips showing some amusement.

'Who?'

'The club and its members, those who worked their evil with Earnshaw.' She spat the name as if the word burned her mouth.

'You do mean Dr Charles Earnshaw? He was known to be a good man, well known for his charitable work; he was Darke's most famous victim.'

'He was never a victim,' she murmured.

'He died in the fire, Bethany; the few that survived said Darke shot him. I think that makes Earnshaw a victim.'

'Then you are madder than I,' she said. 'He dragged Sibelius into it all, even tried to get Sib to join them but he wouldn't. No, Sib killed them instead.' She laughed aloud, a noise that seemed more of a wail, more of pain than humour. A tear formed in her eye and she threw her head sideways into the wall sharply, striking it with a crack. I reached forward to stop her, but she turned on me. 'Do not touch me. I belong to my love. The one who still visits and talks to me, the one who died so that I could live. Oh how I wish I was dead with him now!'

'A ghost, Bethany? Are you saying that a ghost comes to you?' I suddenly thought of the figure at Frith Corner, the image of Sibelius Darke hovering above the ground, trying to speak to me. An apparition caused by my own drunkenness, nothing more.

'Of course, he speaks to me in the night, when no one else is here;

he speaks soft words into my ears and sometimes even stands at the foot of my bed.'

'I do not believe in ghosts, miss. They are a sign of an unsure and desperate mind as far as I am concerned.'

Bethany smiled at me and did not say another word. I stayed by her side for another twenty minutes, but despite my questioning she would say no more. She sat staring out of the window, a gentle smile upon her face, her eyes glazed and thick with unspent tears.

I knocked upon the inside of the door and heard it unlocking. I had hoped to discover more detail about Darke the man but had only found a confused and maddened young woman, lost and wasting away in her tower. The only new part of the puzzle that I had found was the involvement of Dr Earnshaw. I had heard the name in passing in my earlier investigations but decided that I should attempt some further enquiry into him.

I paused for a short while in the grounds of the asylum to add to my notes while they were fresh in my mind and draw some sketches of Bethany Finnan, waiting to be rescued by a ghost who lived within her broken mind.

***

That evening, after midnight, I sat in my rooms, piecing the details of my conversation with Bethany into my larger piece of work. Despite being angered by the lack of detail that she had given me regarding Darke, I found that I could not shift the image of her face from my mind. There had been something about her presentation which I had found morbidly engaging. The girl had been taken past the edge of sanity through her experiences with Darke and was living testament to the dark power which he must have used on all around him. Bethany had obviously been taken in by him, as had her father, and this only made me wish to learn more about the man and to find out when and why he had turned into such a monster.

I was disturbed by the sharp knock of a messenger boy on my door. This was a normal; I had promised Purkess that I would be willing to attend a murder scene no matter how late or early the hour. I was a man who usually slept very little and enjoyed the excitement of being at the scene as soon as possible. This was considerably more prefer-able than having to search for dry scraps from the police, long after the bodies had been removed.

The note was sent by Inspector Thomas and, written in his usual brusque manner, it stated: *'Dead girl, Cuthbert Street, you are expected – AT.'*

Within twenty minutes I had arrived at my destination, where I found a small crowd gathered at the end of the road. I pushed my way through and when seen by the officers, who recognised me, I was let through to walk the twenty or so yards to where the body had been placed.

Like the three other recent killings, the freshly murdered girl had been ruthlessly butchered and carefully positioned to create the max-imum impact upon those who saw her. Although sitting upon the floor, the victim, little more than a child from what I could ascertain, was tied to the iron railings outside one of the street's properties. She was fastened by her wrists, her arms outstretched, crucified and reach-ing to the world for comfort and mercy, of which she had obvi-ously been given none. Her neck had been dramatically broken and her head lolled to one side resting upon her shoulder. Her legs were splayed wide in front of her, and the lower part of her body was cov-ered in her internal organs, which spilled out of a wide cut from the top of one hip to the other, almost bisecting her. Although sickening to see, I found that I could not draw my eyes from her.

'They're getting worse, Sam.' Abe Thomas's voice came from behind me and I turned to see him looking disconsolately down at her.

'Do we know who she is yet?' I asked, pulling my sketchbook out from my bag.

'Local girl, Catherine Davies. She was found an hour ago by one of my men; he must have only just missed whoever did it. She's wearing work clothes so she must have been in service somewhere in the area. Someone will know where.'

'Just like the others then?'

'Mm, we discovered the name of the jointed girl, Eloise Davison, known to work kitchens in Marylebone by all accounts, another girl in service. There is a wider pattern, it is not just victim type. They all suffered singular cuts from a large and keen blade, all of the bodies were positioned. There is even a witness account of a 'golden woman' seen in the area shortly before the body was found.'

'Golden woman? Are you sure? That sounds very odd.'

'Yes, but it ties together with the 'jaundiced woman' seen at the last murder. The description was similar this time: a "tall, dark-cloaked lady with golden skin, running from the scene at speed". You should get drawing quickly if you want to capture this one. I've been told not to let you near any murdered girls, if any more happen.'

'What have I done so wrong, Abe? I didn't think I'd insulted anyone in the police lately.'

'I know,' he said, lowering his voice. 'But someone up top's not happy with the access I've been giving to you.'

'But I'm just doing my job. Isn't it best that I see it so the truth is published?'

'It is Samuel, it is – but it's not about you personally, I think it is the press at large. My superiors want to keep this quiet for as long as possible, and they don't trust your kind.' There was the edge of a smile on his lips and he let out a short laugh as he slapped me on the back. 'Get on with it quick, boy. Before we both get put out of a job.'

I needed no further encouragement and set about making sketches of the scene. I already had in mind the front page, an amalgamation of all the recent murders with each pictured surrounding the central image of their starting point – the twelve dead bodies at Boston Place.

'Can I step a little closer, Abe?' I asked, glancing over my shoulder. He nodded.

The girl had an honest, gentle face; her eyes were open and stared down at the ground, but I could see no hint of terror or pain in them. Her hair was pulled tightly back into a bun, held in place by a number of small pins and a delicately crocheted net that held it together. Her skin, although pallid and grey, was soft and smooth and it was plain to see that she cared for herself well and obviously worked somewhere where cleanliness and appearance were important. Her lips, once red and full, were now blue and waxy, parted slightly as if about to speak. In that moment I felt something that was alien to my mind and did not sit right; it was a mixture of pity and sadness. I was normally immune to such barriers to objectiveness.

I felt an uncomfortable twinge in the corner of my eyes and coughed slightly, checking to see if Thomas had noticed.

It was as I stared at her lips that I saw something that did not belong there: a triangle of white stuck to the inside of her bottom lip.

'Abe,' I called. 'Has anyone looked inside her mouth?'

He bent down beside me, studying her face.

'No, not to my knowledge,' he said, prising open her jaw. A square fold of paper lay upon her tongue and he reached a finger into her mouth to retrieve it. After pulling out the piece of paper, he returned his fingers to her mouth and, to my horror and sad expectation, he withdrew a cut spike which had been forced down her throat. He wrapped the spike in a handkerchief before carefully unwrapping the paper. It was a handwritten note. The words were in Latin: *Profectus venit per dolorem.*

Through pain comes progress.

7

Sent Before the Beak

I could hold the story back no longer and the Inspector finally agreed with me to make it public. We retired to the Bay Horse, a regular haunt of Abe's and somewhere where I held a good enough relationship with the landlord to ensure that the Inspector's drinks flowed freely enough to keep his mouth working.

'Tell Mr Purkess to go with it,' he said, draining another whisky at my expense. 'Tell him to make sure that it doesn't say my name anywhere, but he can tell the world the whole bloody lot – the bit about the golden woman, the names of the girls that were killed, all of it.'

I itched to leave and to let Mr Purkess know. There had been reporters from other newspapers sniffing around at the last two scenes but, with no official word from the Inspector or his seniors, and all witnesses in fear of a beating from Thomas's men if they spoke out, any story was but a rumour. I sat at the table scribbling notes, which I would later write up and present to Henry Cope with my pictures, telling him to send them to the engravers with our Inspector friend's blessing. Abe, becoming looser of tongue by the minute, added words to my scribbles and, through whisky-clouded eyes, took in all I wrote. He retained some vague level of sobriety, however, as he bade me keep some of the more particular details from the newsstands to afford him the power of knowledge over the general public.

I settled back in my seat and stared hard at the drunken bear before me; his large frame had begun to sink down into itself and I knew that it would not be long before he would leave to take in the air and undergo a sobering walk back to the station. I had known the man drink to a degree that would have laid me flat upon my back for days on end; Abe Thomas, however, knew precisely when to call a halt to proceedings and how to pause for enough time to be able to stand and talk straight enough to return to work.

I had wondered, in the past, if he had always been this way. Was his habitual inebriation the result of his experiences in Whitechapel six years previously? I had come to the conclusion, based on our discussions regarding Darke, that perhaps guilt played a major part.

I decided that I should try to press this matter.

'I have a question for you, Abe,' I said, taking a gentle sip of ale. 'One that has been annoyingly prominent in my mind for a couple of weeks now.'

His eyes were closing a little. Time was short before he left.

'Go on,' he murmured, reaching for his glass.

'It has to do with Sibelius Darke... now please do not anger, I know that it is a matter which has caused you some discomfort to talk about to me in the past.' He bristled somewhat, but did not speak. 'You told me that you were prevented from holding him; that you had him in your hands and were powerless to stop him,' I continued. 'Why is that? He was an obvious suspect; Inspector Draper interviewed him on more than one occasion. You said yourself that you knew he had done it. Why would anyone want to stop you?'

There was no flash of anger in his eyes, no sudden torment to him; in fact he did not flinch at all at my question. His face broke into a rueful smile and he drained the glass of whisky in his hand.

'Samuel, I am not so much of a drunk that I will tell all I know for a few shots of whisky and the appearance of friendship. You are a journalist at heart and you work for a paper that has been proven to love a good scandal. I will not give it to you.'

'You are right, Abe, but if ever there was a line of truth come from my lips it is this: George Purkess is not interested in the past. He cares not one jot for the story of Sibelius Darke and those terrible murders which you were witness to. If I went to him with your version of the events of six years ago, he would laugh me out of his office. This is just my interest, Abe. My query into everything I've ever heard about Darke. It is obviously something which has annoyed you, which continues to annoy you. Tell me, as a friend, and I promise it will go no further than these walls. Why was he allowed to continue to kill?'

Thomas had a sullen look upon his face. He shuffled to the end of his bench and made to stand. The world rose up to meet his heavy frame and for a moment I thought that he might just rush down to meet it halfway, but he did not and his legs held his weight.

I thought that I had lost him but he leant forwards and I felt his hot and sour breath upon my skin as he spoke softly into my cheek.

'There are higher powers at work in this world, Sam. Powers that make the rules, pull the strings and that will kill, yes kill, to maintain what they have. Sibelius Darke was a terrible murderer, a killer and eater of children, of that I have no doubt; but he was a pawn. A pawn who turned on his masters, but it was the masters who directed him. Look to the club that he burned to the ground; look to those who did not die, that is where you will find your scandal. But I did not tell you this.'

And with that he righted himself and stumbled towards the door and out into the busy afternoon street.

***

I submitted my writings and sketches of the servant girl murders to George Purkess personally the next day, including the full list of the names given to me by Inspector Thomas of the victims from Boston Place: Florence White, Patricia West and Annie Flanders, among others. George was apprehensive at first, but eventually decided that the opportunity to beat the other papers to the full story was too good to miss – and my scoop hit the front page the following Saturday to great success. Circulation for the 'Boston Place' edition surpassed anything *The Illustrated Police News* had achieved in the past. The public lapped up the horror and potential danger of 'A merciless killer with a razor-sharp blade' stalking the streets of West London and the 'mysterious golden woman' sighted at the murder scenes. George's happiness was matched by the ire of Henry Cope who, if anything, despised me even more. Over the next two months I found myself somewhat out in the cold in terms of work. There were no further murders related to the Boston Place killings although, as expected, sightings of large men armed with devilish knives sprang up all over London and beyond, even as far north as Edinburgh. The only work that seemed to come my way were long days spent in the courts, sketching defendants and recording notable incidents of the trials of the day. These assignments generated within me the firm belief that I was being punished in some way. Possibly by Purkess for my continual badgering about Darke, but more probably from Cope.

Some artists and writers in the employ of old Mr Purkess were content to spend their days comfortably sitting within the law courts and away from grisly scenes of crime. There must have been a dozen others who were bitterly jealous of Cope's desire to cage me within the court buildings, and I would have gladly passed on the work to them if I could have.

I could not, however. If I were seen to be turning down assignments given to me by Cope, it would only give him further excuses to downplay my importance to the newspaper and the light of my necessity would fade before George Purkess. I prayed for another murder to save me from the boredom of it all.

This is not to say that suddenly all murder and mayhem ceased within London. Knives were drawn, throats were cut and the stain of blood continued to soak into pavements and floorboards. All whilst I was stuck for endless hours listening to lawyers pontificate, judges snore, and petty criminals beg for forgiveness.

It was as I entered the second week of my entombment in the courts that my life saw a change which was both unexpected and unexplainable.

It had been a slow morning in the court of Judge William Edwards. My day had been filled with almost nothing of note: petty burglars and con men, late payers and pox-ridden harridans who passed themselves off as 'ladies'.

The prosecuting counsel for the day had spent as much time in these chambers as I over the past week. He was a short, round man by the name of Richard Warriner. Although relatively new to the bar, Warriner was ambitious and attempted to use the courtroom as his own private theatre. He fought hard for every case that he brought before the judge, which set him apart from his peers, many of whom appeared to see their time in chambers as time wasted when it could be spent drinking and socialising. Warriner had a piercing nasal tone to his voice, which only made my hours spent in this cold limbo more difficult to bear.

I had written little in my notebook and had amused myself, in a brave attempt to stave off the ennui of the day, by drawing pictures of those who sat willingly in the public stalls in pursuit of entertainment. The pictures that I drew of them placed their caricatures in terrible situations, both of a deviant and violent nature; heads were lost, limbs taken viciously from them, as they starred in their very own newspaper covers which would never be published.

I was just starting a new 'faux edition' with the thrilling headline 'Eaten alive by mice!' when the next defendant was brought before the bench and I found myself pausing to give her my full attention.

She was a slight and pretty girl, but proud, perhaps five or six years younger than I; she held herself well in the dock and gave eye contact to those in court. Her flaxen hair was tightly drawn into a bun and I wondered whether she was normally this well kempt or had tidied herself up for the benefit of her situation. She had bright eyes, full of life and fire, and her face was well scrubbed. At her side stood a small dark-haired boy no older than ten who, unlike her, stood shivering and tearful. He was painfully thin and I wondered when he had last been afforded a good meal. He remained pinned to the girl's side, his mouth a taut line.

As the clerk of court began to speak, the girl pulled the boy's cap from his head and straightened his unruly hair somewhat.

'The defendant will give her name!'

'Alice Griffiths,' she answered.

'Your Honour.'

'Alice Griffiths, Your Honour, begging your pardon.' She attempted what I can only imagine was supposed to be a curtsey to the judge.

The clerk walked slowly to the bench, where he handed over the details of the case to Judge Edwards, who was in his natural position: slumped at the bench, giving little sign that he was interested in anything more than the impending call for lunch. He glared over his spectacles at the papers, murmuring to himself under his breath as he read. After what seemed like an age, he finally spoke.

'Miss Griffiths,' the judge began, 'I see that you are accused of petty theft. The theft of a loaf of bread from the stall of one Harold Gardener. How do you plead?'

'Not guilty, Your Honour.' She rose as she spoke. Although addressing the judge, her voice held within it an element of disgust at the proceedings. I sensed defiance and found myself putting down my notebook.

Richard Warriner lugged his large frame to its feet and strode slowly over to the stand, beginning his performance. 'You plead not guilty and yet there are several witnesses who saw you steal the bread. How can you *not* be guilty?'

'It was not theft!' she snapped. 'I took the bread because it was mine to take.'

Judge Edwards, who had been staring idly around the courtroom until this point, suddenly jumped to life and, placing his spectacles upon his nose, glared down at the young girl.

'Young lady,' Edwards's voice was reedy and thin, 'do I understand it correctly that you admit to taking the bread from the stall but still see yourself as the innocent party in this matter?'

'I do, Your Honour.' She held her head high. 'Mister Gardener owed me money. My brother and I had been helping him on his stall and, at the end of the day, he refused to pay me. I took my payment; that is all.'

'And where is Mr Gardener?' the judge asked. A response came in the form of a tall, bearded man, who rose up from his seat at the side of the court.

'I am Harold Gardener, Your Honour,' he said, pulling his hat purposefully from his head.

'And is this true, Mr Gardener? Did you have this child and her brother under your employment and then refused them payment?'

'She worked for me, Your Honour. She was a good grafter, did more than most. That's what made it even harder for me when she ended the day stealing. I would have employed her again but a day's wage is not a loaf of bread in my eyes.'

The judge snorted in disbelief. He had obviously never needed to wonder about the worth of a day's work before.

'If a day's work is not a loaf, Mr Gardener, then what is it worth?'

'Half a loaf.'

'Half a loaf of bread?' His eyebrows raised above his spectacles. 'Then why did you not pay her?'

'I meant to, after she had worked another day for me,' Gardener replied in a matter-of-fact voice. 'I saw no reason in tearing a loaf in half and leaving the rest to ruin. Best to give her one loaf when next she worked.'

'And when would that have been?'

'It could have been the next day, it could have been a week later. I have others working for me like this, they never complain… or steal.'

'Liar!' shouted the girl. 'You're well known for cheating people. I only worked for you because we hadn't eaten anything like a meal in a couple of days.' She was silenced by the judge, who spoke over her to direct his own anger at the stallholder.

'Mr Gardener, I would think that if a person was asked to do a day's work, only to be told that they might be paid in the future – and only if and when they were needed – then they would be as defiant and forceful as this young lady; and they might even be of a mind to ensure that payment was received even if they had to take it without warrant.'

There was a murmur throughout the assembled public and I saw that the two other members of the press had started to furiously scribble in their notepads: 'Judge admits that stealing might be just' would be the headline in the following days.

'No, Mr Gardener,' he continued. 'In light of the facts presented before me, which include your very own words, I do not believe that young lady has stolen from you. In fact, I think that I would have preferred a very different case to be held in my court this morning; for I believe that you yourself are the thief in this matter.'

Gardener made to speak but was held silent by the forbidding hand of Judge Edwards as he turned to the counsel for the prosecution.

'Mr Warriner, I know that you have little control over the cases which you are asked to bring into my court, but I find that you have wasted my valuable time this morning. It is my judgment that this coster should pay monies to the court of no less than three shillings and I ask that he not be brought before me again, lest I feel of a mind to give him a custodial sentence.'

The judge shuffled in his seat, raised himself up and peered down at the young woman and the boy beside her. 'Now then, young lady, I wish to address the matter of your living circumstances. I see from your arrest papers that you are at present living on the streets. Is this correct?'

Before Miss Griffiths had a chance to reply, Warriner immediately saw his chance at redemption and jumped to his feet.

'M'Lord, if you do not wish to see a young woman and her child of a brother wandering the streets, might I suggest that the young lady and her brother be released from the court and taken to a place of safety? I am a trustee at a suitable house where unfortunates such as these are put to good use and given good Christian guidance and protection.'

'No!' cried Alice. 'We have been in places like that before. I do not wish to return. I would rather we starve on the streets. I promise to find somewhere to live, Your Honour, I just need time to do so.'

The judge nodded in agreement before continuing. 'I am sure that you speak very well, young lady, but the facts of the matter are that you and your brother are, at present, homeless. The basis of your innocence is now of no consequence. I agree that you were within your rights to take what was owed to you, but I cannot release you onto the streets if you cannot give an address. You give me little choice but to ask the court to arrange for you and your brother to be taken to the workhouse, where you will be given a bed and a roof and whatever gainful employment is seen fit for you.'

'We can't go back to the workhouse, Your Honour,' Miss Griffiths pleaded, pulling her tearful brother into her embrace. 'I know what them places are like; I don't want to go to our deaths.'

I watched the girl and her brother intently; she was an attractive thing, too good to be wasted on the workhouse. Perhaps I could stand for her, and even offer her temporary shelter? She came with baggage, but he looked half fed to start with and it wouldn't cost much to feed them. It was an unnatural thought that I had, not normal for me in the slightest. Providing charity was not something that I had ever done before but, looking at the girl before me, I decided that it could reap its benefits.

Judge Edwards had now clearly become bored and pulled out his watch; lunch was imminent. 'I'm afraid you give me little choice, young lady. No one else will give you an address, will they? It is the only option in this matter. Now, I see that it is time for a short break in proceedings. We will return in one hour when I shall see the next case.' He stood to leave, causing a bustle among the court as all made to rise.

'I will stand for her, Your Honour!' I cried, jumping up; the eyes of the court all fell suddenly upon me.

The words that came from my mouth surprised even myself.

What a fool I was.

***

I have always been a solitary type. Even as a child, I never craved or needed the company of others. Whether it be sitting in my rooms drawing, or walking the streets of York, my most comfortable and enjoyable times were those that I spent alone.

It was because of this natural inclination for solitude that I found myself quite shocked by my offer of shelter to the girl and her brother.

'You may stay for as long as it takes for you to find yourself some regular work and afford lodgings of your own. I am sure it will be soon,' I said, as we entered my rooms. Despite my father's best hopes for me as a gentleman of London, my place of residence was a humble one. Barely furnished, it consisted of four rooms: a bedroom, a small kitchen, a bathroom and a living area, which held a set of chairs and my writing desk, upon which I would spend the majority of my hours at home either drawing or writing. 'Use the cushions from the chairs,' I said as we entered the living area. 'I have spare blankets that you may use to make some kind of bed for you both. Will that suffice?'

The girl looked wholly dumbfounded by my offer, although I think it was in a good way. I was glad that she had not read the thought that had passed through my mind in court.

'Yes, of course,' she replied. 'We will be no bother, I promise. I have some friends who can help me; it'll be for no more than a couple of days. We are both so grateful.' She held the boy close to her; his eyes had not left me for one second since leaving the court.

Benjamin was his name. He was unnaturally quiet and I wondered if he were a mute. Even when I asked him a direct question, he would not answer and instead pushed himself tighter into his sister's arms. After a few attempts at pleasant conversation, I decided that I was wasting my time with him and continued talking to the girl. I did not refer to him, for I did not want to draw attention to his presence at all; if the child wished to be rude and non-communicative then I would leave him to his misery. If the girl met my needs, I felt sure of my ability to persuade her to drop him in return for a place of safety and security.

Alice, despite my earlier worries that she would be a foul-mouthed and opinionated brute, turned out to be quite pleasant when engaged in conversation. She was well read, aware of the affairs of the world and enthusiastically interested in my work. She told me how much she enjoyed the illustrations she had seen on the covers of *The Illustrated Police News*, and had often wondered about the sort of man who was employed in this task. She asked to see examples of my work, which I showed her without question; normally I would have refused such requests, unless they were from potential publishers or buyers, but I found her nature somewhat disarming and before long I found myself enjoying the pleasant surprise of her company. In some ways she reminded me of Victoria and, as our day went on, the image of Mrs Coleman's daughter began to appear within my mind, much to my shame.

My estimations of Alice's age were correct as she told me that she was nineteen, ten years older than her brother. Alice and her brother, like myself, had a father in the clergy. Their mother had died giving birth to her third child, a baby girl who survived her. Their father coped with the death of his wife through drink and gambling, leaving the care of Benjamin and the newborn child to their older sister. Very soon he had established large and insurmountable debts, losing both his parish and, as a result, their home into the bargain. He had ended up in debtor's prison, the baby was given up for adoption and Alice and her brother found themselves placed in the Paddington workhouse. Their father lost to them, and their baby sister never to be found, Alice and Benjamin spent just over two years in the work-house before deciding that a life on the streets was a better option.

Late in the afternoon, Alice and I (accompanied by her dumb shadow) journeyed out from my rooms and visited the last of the stalls at the nearby market to buy some food that she promised to cook. To be quite honest, I had not had a home-cooked meal since Mrs Cole-man's fare back in York and the thought of such secretly filled me with some excitement.

Alice's skill in the kitchen was basic but adequate and, for that first evening that she and her brother stayed with me, I found myself almost forgetting about Sibelius Darke and the murders of those poor servant girls.

'You live a strange life, Mr Weaver,' Alice said as we stood in the kitchen late on that first evening. She had settled her silent brother down to sleep after dinner and we had adjourned to the kitchen, where we sat at my small table.

'Strange? My life is not strange, it is the way I have designed it and it pleases me very much. I answer to no one; I have the time and space to complete both my work and my interests, and am very much the master of my own destiny. What is so strange about that, other than it is probably the deepest wish of any sane man?'

She smiled and looked down at the glass of port wine that I had poured for her, having retrieved the bottle from the back of one of my sparse cupboards.

'I think I said it wrong,' she said. 'I meant that *you* are strange, you are quite unexpected in many ways.'

'Why thank you, Miss Griffiths!' I laughed. 'Firstly you criticise my lifestyle, then you further insult me by telling me that I am odd as well. Is there any other aspect of my persona that you wish to mock?'

She looked at me, thoughtful for a moment. 'I am sure that I could find plenty. Where would you like me to start?'

My laughing stopped and I looked at her shocked, but relieved when her face broke into a smile of its own.

'Mr Weaver, I say that you are strange and unexpected, because despite your cries to the contrary, you can be quite friendly and kind.

I know that you say how much you prefer your own company to that of others but, when your barriers come down, you can be most charming. And what other man in London would have offered to take in two strangers to save them from the workhouse? None I would say, none other than those who would do it for purposes other than plain good nature.' She paused suddenly and reached out her hands across the table to touch my own. 'Unless of course you had other purposes in mind.'

A vision of Victoria suddenly flashed before my eyes at her touch and I withdrew my hands quickly. Pulling my chair away from the table, I stood.

'I would say that you were correct in your first assumption, Alice. You and your brother are guests in my home until you are able to find more permanent accommodation. I am not that kind of man; I was in the past but no more. Now, if you will excuse me, I have a long day ahead tomorrow and will bid you good night.' I walked towards the door, turning as I did so and catching her expression, which was a mixture of shock and guilt. 'Do not be upset by my reaction, Alice. Be thankful. I have a cruel nature and a tendency to hurt those who become close to me. Sleep well.' And with that I left her and took to my bed, thinking of Victoria, of terrible shame and of guilt-sodden regret.

***

In the later years of my youth I became a sullen and rude individual. I spent long hours out of the house, working as an apprentice artist and writer at the *York Herald*. Out of working hours, I would tour the pubs of the city, observing the harder side of life around me. Often I would not return home until late in the evening, sometimes worse the wear for drink, and Mrs Coleman would fuss around me, attempting to get me to eat something wholesome before I retired to my room.

My father was rarely at home either. Since Mother's incarceration, it would seem that he had been freed to spread his ministry further, spending long hours, like me, around York aiding the 'welfare' of the fallen and broken. I knew this to be a lie, of course. I did not know what he did on those evenings away from home, but I doubted it was to help anyone but himself.

My anger towards him was immense. He was immoral and disgusting to me, having failed in his duties as a husband and a father. He had had his own wife locked away to pursue these addictions and had left me to my own devices and the care of his house staff.

Mrs Coleman, although I know she was disappointed by my lack of presence in the home, felt maternal love and worry for me. She would urge me to eat well, always having a breakfast ready for me each morning, no matter how unwell I felt, and would ensure that my clothes were kept clean and my appearance presentable before I left the house for work. I complained loudly and bitterly at this suffocating behaviour, but knew deep down that she meant the best for me and was only trying to replace the care that Mother would have provided if she had not been imprisoned. What she thought of my father's actions I can only begin to imagine, as I am sure she knew the true nature of his ministries.

However, my relationship with Mrs Coleman's daughter, Victoria, was somewhat different. I took advantage of my position as the son of her employer in a terrible way. I abused her good nature; I lied to her, giving her hope; and then I cast her away when my actions caused a problem. For it was when I had not long passed the age of eighteen that she fell pregnant and my world began to fall apart.

She came to me with the news in secret; she was excited and took it as a sign that we should be together. I had put these thoughts into her head for years, with the grievous intent to get what I wanted from her, and now she discovered how untrue my words were.

'Are you sure it's mine?' I asked her coldly.

Her eyes were suddenly red rimmed as she realised that there would be no happy future for her in all of this. There would be no fairy tale of the young servant girl saved from a life of servitude by the dashing son of her employer; a fairy tale, I regret to say, that I had fed at every given opportunity since first drawing her into the dark folds of my affections.

'We will go to see my father about this; he has been helping poor unfortunates like yourself for years. He will know how to fix the problem.' Her face was like melting ice, slowly drooping in the real-isation of her circumstance. 'But there will be no mention that it is mine, none at all. As far as my father and your mother are concerned, I am merely helping you in this terrible situation. There is a way out of this for both of us, but if you talk of what has gone between us I will make sure that both you and your mother are put out onto the streets. Do you understand me?'

Still she did not speak, but nodded her head. There, it was done.

She told a good tale to my father when we went to see him. A tale of a delivery boy whom she had met but once and whom she had never seen again. I am not sure that he believed her, yet he played along and spoke to Mrs Coleman amid her tears and anger at her fool-ish daughter. All the while, Victoria did not speak of what had gone between us and I, for my part, did not involve myself in any of the discussions or actions hereafter.

It was decided that the child must go before being born. Father knew of a 'discreet friend with medical experience', whose services he had called on in the past for circumstances similar to these. Mrs Cole-man took my father's assurances of the man's abilities in good faith and, less than a week after Victoria's admission to me, she was taken in Father's carriage to a property on the south-western fringes of the city for the procedure.

The maid did not survive.

***

I left my rooms for court duty the following day before either Alice or Benjamin awoke. They had both benefited from a bath the pre-vious evening and at that moment, curled up on their cushions and bedding, they did not at all resemble the homeless waifs that they had appeared just twenty-four hours previously. I had told them to dispose of their old clothing and given them some of my old shirts to wear, as well as trousers, which they had rolled up to fit, much to our hilar-ity the previous evening. I had promised to take them out later in the afternoon to purchase suitable new clothes and shoes.

I wondered how long it had been since they had both slept safely under a roof – probably not since before their father was taken from them.

Throughout the next week I remained stuck on court duty and the days were dull, full of petty burglary and deceit, with only a smattering of violence and bloodshed. Alice and Benjamin spent their days either searching for work or making my rooms more homely. On the first couple of nights I found myself a little uncomfortable upon coming home to a cooked meal and something close to family life, but I admit that I came to be thankful for the snap decision to take in lodgers. Although remaining unnaturally quiet, Benjamin began to speak a little in my presence. This 'conversation' was limited to one or two words but it was progress in my eyes and, although I still harboured intentions in the depths of my mind to discharge myself of the boy, it was better than having a noisy child running around, disrupting everything. Alice, on the other hand, was fine company, well educated up until her father's downfall, and equally well read. We would spend our evenings sitting quietly talking and telling each other about our past lives. The act of sharing felt strange, and of course I did not mention all of the details of my childhood and the dalliances and deaths, but she was interested and seemed to enjoy my company. She continued to promise that their stay with me would be short but I did not press her on this matter; I was content with the situation.

I decided that it was time to continue with my hunt for information regarding the activities of Sibelius Darke's club, which Abe Thomas was so insistent had played a larger part in his killings. I intercepted Mr Purkess as he left the offices and told him that I felt my services were not being best used in the law courts and that I would only be available for murder cases. He looked shocked but agreed in principle and told me he would speak to Cope upon his return tomorrow.

When I next saw Cope I could tell that he did not know whether to be pleased or dismayed for, although he had plenty of other artists and writers at his disposal, it also meant that I had escaped the shackles of the prison he had created for me.

'You will not get the court job back, you know!' he said, to which I merely nodded and smiled.

I had a small lead on the club; I had been given a name by a hansom driver associate of mine, a trusted source of information. The name he had given to me was Gerald Hopple, a former superintendent of the Dolorian Club. Hopple had disappeared from public life for three years after the fire, but had now returned to London to work as a valet to Lord Bracken in Kensington. I had written to Hopple stating that I was a nephew of a club member who had perished in the fire; I said that I was planning on writing a book in memoriam on the medical and charity works of my dear uncle and wished to discover more about his last hours. With the offer of a reward for this information, Hopple, of course, agreed and wrote that he would be pleased to meet me at the Rainbow on Fleet Street. Hopple told me that he would take a seat at one of the booths at the rear of the establishment and that I should ask for him on arrival, under the name Arthur Banks.

Upon arriving I ordered a drink and was directed towards a dark and secluded spot away from the general hubbub of the tavern. From my view at the bar, Hopple kept his face very much in shadow, and it was only when I came close that I realised why he had wished to remain out of sight.

'Mr Banks, I presume?' I said as I approached the table, holding out my hand to him.

He turned slowly towards me, bringing the whole of his face into the light of the gas lamp above the booth. The right side of his face was deeply etched and eroded; rough lumped and red, it wept in places, looking sore to the touch. Pink, shiny skin hung down over the place where his right eye had once been, giving the impression of a man whose face had been made of wax held too close to a great and oppressive heat. He had lost the majority of the hair on the side of his head also. He wore small, round glasses for the vision out of his one remaining eye, and there was nothing resembling an ear on the right side of his head. Where his ear had been there now remained nothing but a red, glossy lump scorched by the flames of the Dolorian Club. I found myself staring uncomfortably at him.

He reached out a white-gloved hand to me which I shook gently as I sat down.

'I apologise for the shock of my appearance, sir.' His voice was thick-edged and raspy. 'I never was the most handsome man in London and seem to be even less so now.' There was a slow wheeze in his breath and I wondered just how much damage had been done to him in that terrible blaze.

'There is no need to apologise, Mr Banks, or is it safe to call you Hopple now we are here?'

'Mr Hopple will do,' he breathed. 'But let us keep our conversation low. There are those who watch still. You say you are here on club matters, regarding your uncle Dr Earnshaw. Speak quickly, for I do not wish to dwell on those times.'

'Of course, sir,' I said. 'We are obviously both busy men.'

I found myself watching the sinews on his neck, which stuck out like tightened strings on a cello; it seemed as if they would break through his paper-thin skin at any moment. 'I understand you were the superintendent at the club for many years before Darke and the fire. Did you know my uncle?'

'I knew all the members,' he said. He paused momentarily, his eyes searching my face. 'Dr Earnshaw was indeed a long-standing member, one gracious enough to sit in the inner circle.'

'What can you tell me about him? I last saw him when I was but five. I knew he was a medical man but my mother would never speak of his character.'

'He was a great and learned man, in my experience; never short of a kind word or deed, hard working and dedicated to his poor family.'

'Poor family?'

'Yes, both of his children died very young. That is how he came to meet Sibelius Darke in the first place. Darke photographed his children – post mortem. A strange and morbid business, if you ask me, but then you only have to look at how Darke turned out to see that.'

'Did you know Darke well?'

'Not really. He was a member of the club, of course, recommended by your uncle, in fact, but he never seemed to fit in. It was all a bit above him. He was a career-minded individual, desperate to drag himself out of his immigrant squalor but, in the end, his nature got the better of him.' His breathing became more ragged, and he stopped talking to regain his wind. 'I apologise, sir. My lungs are not what

they were; the damage from the fire goes much deeper than these out-
ward scars.'

'Did the club know what Darke was up to?' I asked. 'Were they
complicit with his crimes?'

'The gentlemen of the Dolorian Club were fine, upstanding members of society; they still are fine and upstanding. They have nothing
but the success of society at their heart; I am sure that they were not
involved in the sins of that monster.' He paused, realising that he was
becoming angered once more by the memory. 'Enough of Darke,
though; too much time has been given to that beast. You wished to
find out more about your uncle, did you not?'

'Yes, of course. Do carry on,' I replied. 'When was the last day you
saw him?'

'Well, it was on the day of the fire, of course. He had arrived early
in the morning and took his seat in the second-floor study to read
the papers. He told me that he was not to be disturbed unless on
club business. He was pleasant; Dr Earnshaw was always polite and
friendly towards everyone in the club. It was a day much like any
other, until Mr Darke arrived requesting to see your uncle. Dr Earnshaw took great pleasure in this news, asking that Darke be brought
to him immediately. He seemed to have been expecting him, which
was odd, as your uncle only tended to meet with other members of
the inner circle.'

'This inner circle, can you tell me who they were? I should like to
try to contact them to invite them to the memorial.'

'They were private men – they still are. I am sure that they would
not be pleased if I should begin to bandy their names around to all
who would listen.' He fell silent and looked down at the table.

'You are obviously a very loyal man, Mr Hopple. I take it you are
not in the employ of the Dolorian Club now?'

'I am not, but they were good to me following the fire.' His voice
cracked as he spoke. 'I hid, you see. When Sibelius Darke started the
blaze, and began shooting and killing anyone he saw, I hid in a store
cupboard and prayed for my life. I crouched on the floor, listening to
the screams of the dying and the roar of the flames and I entreated
the Lord to save me, but the fire came to me, it took the door of the

cupboard – and that is when I ran. I ran through the flames, my skin crackling in the heat. I fell through the door of the club, tumbling down the steps onto the street below. I was thought to be dead at first and, had it not been for one of the club members, I would have been left. He saved my life, he revived me and he made sure that I was given the medical attention I needed.

'I was taken to the Sussex County Hospital in Brighton, where I stayed for two years at my saviour's expense. When I finally left the hospital he offered me employment back at the club, which I took for a few short months before moving on to work as a valet for Lord Bracken. The original Dolorian Club had burned to the ground, but many of the members were not there on the day of the fire and so, thanks to the good graces and finances of my saviour, it simply moved location. I understand the club still operates from his London home.'

'And your... saviour, was he a confidant of my uncle?'

'Why yes, he was also a member of the inner circle. I understand they were great friends.'

I shuffled slightly in my seat.

'I understand, of course, that these gentlemen wish their privacy to be respected and maintained at all times, but I would like to contact this friend of my uncle's. Could you perhaps give me his name?'

The ragged breathing of the man filled the short silence as we stared into each other's eyes.

'You mentioned the possibility of a financial reward in your first communication,' Hopple said. His eyes did not move from me. I pulled out my wallet, and he continued. 'The man who saved the club and who indeed saved me on the day that Darke brought about his evil is Lord William Falconer. I doubt that he will see you; he is a proud man, protective of his company and suspicious of those seeking his attentions.' He took the money from my hand, a look of shame crossing his face. 'I will take my leave of you now,' he said. 'I hope all goes well for your... memorial.'

Without another word he shuffled from his seat and left me. As he walked out of the door I allowed a broad smile to plant itself on my face.

***

After leaving the Rainbow, my mind fizzing with this new piece of information, I made my way to the police station in the hope of catching Abe Thomas to run the name of Falconer past him. He was not there, however; the desk sergeant told me that he had been called away on a matter of some urgency.

'Has there been another murder?' I asked, wondering if this day could get any better.

'I cannot say, not least to you, Mr Weaver,' said the sergeant. 'I read your piece in the paper, we all did, and we are all under strict orders from above to not speak to you or any of your lot.'

'Of course,' I smiled. 'If the good Inspector returns, please pass on my best regards and ask him to contact me, if you would.'

I spent the afternoon wandering the streets of Paddington and Marylebone, checking the drinking houses that he normally frequented, in the hope of seeing some sign of the Inspector. There was none and so I returned to my rooms, hoping that Alice had prepared a good meal.

As I walked down the corridor, I heard the sound of voices coming from the other side of the door. I paused for a moment. I recognised Alice's voice but the other was unknown to me. It was not Benjamin, it was far too deep; this was the voice of a man. How dare she? How dare she invite a man back to my rooms; had she no sense of dignity or gratitude?

I flung the door open and strode in, but rather than finding some kind of illicit liaison, Alice was in the kitchen making tea when I entered, and an older gentleman sat in the chair at my desk, looking out of the window. Alice rushed to the kitchen doorway, holding my teapot.

'Sam,' she said, smiling. 'Your friend Fred Draper has just arrived to see you.'

At the mention of his name, the man turned to face me. Of course, I knew this man well, very well indeed. Ever since my arrival in London, I had ceaselessly attempted to hunt Inspector Frederick Draper down.

And now, it would seem, he had found me.

8

An Inspector's Fall

Inspector Frederick Draper had disappeared soon after the news of the slaughter at the Dolorian Club and the death of Sibelius Darke had hit the front pages. Unidentified sources inside the police had made it common knowledge that Darke had been under the watch of Draper during his investigations and had been interviewed at least twice. How Darke had managed to slip through the net and continue to carry out such wilful bloodshed was a matter of some embarrassment to both Draper and to the police as a whole.

Draper's office had been cleared and, despite the best efforts of some of London's top newspaper correspondents, there seemed to be no sign of the man whom everyone held to be as guilty as Sibelius Darke himself for the terrible crimes that had been committed.

Rumours abounded that Draper's father, himself a high-ranking member of the police force, had arranged for Frederick's disappearance. There was talk that he had been relocated to Southern Africa, working under an assumed name for the High Commissioner there, Sir Henry Bartle Frere, in a minor accounting and administrative role. *The Times* even sent one of their correspondents out to find Draper, a search that proved fruitless when they came up against some good old-fashioned British secrecy and stubbornness.

I had conducted my own investigations, of course, interviewing many who had known Inspector Draper during the Darke murders, including Abe Thomas. Details were few and far between, however; I had descriptions of him, and amassed recollections of fleeting encounters with him, but nothing that would give me any clues as to the nature of his disappearance or his final destination.

And now, six years after the public outcry at Inspector Draper's failure to prevent the murders, here he was – sitting bold as brass at my desk and accepting a cup of tea from Alice.

I remained as calm as possible and took a seat opposite him. He was a tall man, lean of face; his pale skin stretched across angular cheekbones. There was a patch of hair atop his head which seemed to have been carefully arranged with the design of fooling those around him as to the number of strands still growing there. His small beard, which was of a similar but slightly darker colour, was well trimmed and neat. He was stylishly dressed, wearing a dark brown suit of good tailoring, set off by a pair of well-crafted, finely polished shoes. He did not give me the impression of a man in hiding at all; in fact, there was nothing about Frederick Draper that suggested he was in any way in fear of discovery.

'You are a difficult man to find,' I said, unable to take my eyes from him.

'I have good friends,' he replied, his voice sharp. 'When you look after your friends, they will always reciprocate when the need arises. Of course, there really should not be any need to find me. I am not an interesting man and people have lost interest in old news; only the most dogged individuals remember my name and try to hunt me out.' His eyes flashed at me as he spoke.

'Of course,' I said, as Alice brought me a cup of tea. 'I find that, when something or someone piques my interest, my dogged nature will come to the fore.'

Alice had returned to the kitchen and I heard light whispering coming through the doorway. Benjamin was probably in there with her.

'Alice!' I called, 'Harridge's on the high street will be closing shortly. Would you mind taking Benjamin and fetching something for dinner tonight?'

She quickly realised that I required some privacy and led Benjamin from the kitchen. The boy dawdled and smiled at Draper as he passed.

'I shall see you shortly, young master Griffiths,' I said.

'Bye,' Benjamin muttered, before hurrying after his sister.

'The boy has not stopped talking about you, Mr Weaver,' Draper said, smiling. 'He tells me that you saved him and his sister.'

'Benjamin can talk? He has said no more than five words to me in a fortnight, and yet he freely converses with you. I must be doing something wrong.'

'You are doing nothing wrong; that is often the way with children and their heroes. Give him time; perhaps even try speaking to him. You will be amazed at how much he has to say.' He paused for a second before continuing, 'Why did you take them in? What kind of play is it?'

'Play?' I replied. 'You think the worst of me. There is no play here. Call it a whim, a sudden lapse in concentration; I do not have them often.'

'That is what I hear. It was a great surprise to find them both here when I arrived. Much of what is said about you must be wrong if it was just out of the goodness of your heart.'

'I suppose it depends on who you have been speaking to – who was that by the way?'

Draper grinned and took a sip of his tea.

'Like I said, Mr Weaver, I have good friends and colleagues that look out for me. Much like yours.'

'Mine? What friends do *I* have?'

'I am referring to our mutual friend, Abe Thomas. He is one of the reasons for my visit to you this evening.'

'But Abe told me that he did not know your whereabouts.'

'And that is why he is a good friend. He tells me that you have been asking a lot of questions about the Darke case and I think he is becoming worried that you may cause yourself more trouble than you expect. I share his concerns. Despite your apparent obsession with the case, there is much that you do not know, much that could place you and yours in danger if you persist.'

'There is no need for concern. I can look after myself,' I said, settling back in my chair. 'I have an interest in the murders, that is all. Sibelius Darke was a vicious murderer and cannibal who killed members of his own family, slaughtered and ate children and burnt down a gentleman's club. All of this is public knowledge; I am just trying to piece the story together – for my own ambitions.' I glanced at his expression, which, despite his best efforts to contain it, betrayed a slight twitch. 'I am not seeking some great conspiracy here, Inspector.

It doesn't hold much weight with me, I'm afraid, although it would sell more papers if it were true. You see, I have listened to the fearful ramblings of those who feel that there were greater powers at work. I have even heard that Sibelius Darke was innocent. How do you like that?'

'I like it a lot, of course,' he said, allowing himself the smallest of smiles. 'He committed crimes; he was seen coming out of the Dolorian Club as it burnt to the ground; he did not hide his face from the many witnesses. However, I still do not believe that he killed his father or brother, nor that he murdered and ate children. How is Miss Bethany Finnan, by the bye?'

I froze. 'You know that I have visited her?'

'I do. In fact, I know a lot of those whom you have seen regarding your little investigation. I understand that you enjoyed a little visit to Kent. Lovely part of the world, such beautiful countryside, and fine pubs too by all accounts.' His words, although soft and friendly, came from a hardened face. 'You see, Mr Weaver, you are ruffling feathers with your blundering, feathers that should remain untouched. I did not lie when I told you that I was concerned for your welfare. I cannot impress on you heavily enough how dangerous this path is. Leave it now and no harm will come to you – or your house guests for that matter.'

I sat forwards.

'Are you threatening me, Inspector?'

'Please, not Inspector any more, I am afraid; I have left that life behind now. Just plain Mr Draper will do.'

'Are you threatening me, *Mister* Draper?'

'Why no, Mr Weaver, I would not do such a thing. I would like you to think of me as a messenger and friend; a kind face delivering a warning. Understand what I am saying to you: this will not end well if you continue.' He lifted his cup to his lips a final time and drained the contents before standing. 'I'm afraid I must leave. Think on what I have said. There are those that care for you, Mr Weaver. You have Alice and that sweet young boy to look after. I will see myself out.'

He walked towards the door. As he turned the handle, I called over to him.

'Inspector? Mr Draper? One last thing before you leave – something Bethany said to me that I did not understand. What is Surma?'

He paused for a second before replying.

'Surma? Yes, it was spoken to me by Sibelius Darke himself. He told me that, in Finnish folklore, there is an underworld – a place where all souls go when they pass from this life. They call it Tuonela, I think. Anyway, at the gateway to Tuonela stands a beast called Surma, a vile creation tasked with preventing anyone from returning from the underworld. Nobody knows fully what this beast is supposed to look like as it devours anyone attempting to pass back to our world. Darke believed that this beast had been summoned to stalk the streets, committing the very murders of which he stood accused. Now, I am a practical man. I believe in the truth of science and fact and only in what I see before me; but there were things at work back then which, even now, I am wary of… and you should be too. We will not meet again. Goodbye, Mr Weaver.'

He closed the door gently behind him as he left.

***

In the short time between Draper leaving and Alice and Benjamin returning with supplies for that evening's dinner, I managed to scribble down as much as I could regarding my conversation with the elusive ex-inspector. As I worked I thought about his visit; was it a friendly call from a companion of Abe Thomas's, genuinely worried about my welfare and that of those I held dear, or was this man in some way connected with the mysterious and shadowed gentry behind the Dolorian Club? Whatever the answer, I had finally come face to face with the last of those who had played a key part in the latter days of the killer who occupied so much of my mind and time.

My smile was broad as I poured myself a large glass of brandy to celebrate. Details of a meeting with Inspector Frederick Draper, a man who had eluded the public and press for over six years, would surely be the final twist of the arm that I needed to persuade George Purkess to let me write my article. I could even envisage being given the power to take full control over the piece, even expanding my work into a book on the Darke murders.

When Alice and Benjamin came through the door, I could not contain myself from rushing towards them and sweeping Alice off her feet in joy, even chancing a peck upon her cheek, while little Benjamin stood in open-mouthed bewilderment at my happy actions. My good humour was infectious enough, as we set about laughing together and dancing around my small rooms. Benjamin, of course, did not dare to ask me the reason for my joyful nature, but Alice pressed for answers. I would not tell her the full details of the story, though, and managed to restrict my answer to just a few words.

'My fortune has come to me – it has found me out!' I cried. 'Just you see, the pair of you, just you see how my name will soon be known and my pedigree savoured.'

We sat down for a happy meal at the table in my kitchen, the three of us, and I can honestly say that I had known no happier repast in all of my days, humble and plain though our dinner was. I found myself talking merrily with Benjamin, who suddenly, as if by some stroke of magic, had found his tongue. It gave me such happiness to see this child, who I had only witnessed being solemn and shy of face, turn into such a larkish youth in the blink of an eye. Alice too shared my relief at Benjamin's transformation and I am sure that there was a tear in her eye at the sight of her young brother seemingly returned to her at last from the torpor of misery and worry.

Draper had been correct about the boy; he was obsessively interested in my work and my involvement with murder cases and the like. I lost count of the questions that he asked of me. Indeed it was a glowing and happy lad that was put to bed by his sister that night and the memory of his face, smiling as he slept, is one that has always stayed with me.

'I cannot remember the last time I saw him so content,' Alice said as she returned to the kitchen and began to wash the dishes from dinner. 'You have lit a spark in him that has not been there for a very long time; I am grateful for that.'

There was a comfortable silence in the room and I settled back in my chair with my glass. I looked on Alice at the sink and the warmth I felt was like a long-forgotten associate, returned by chance and a stranger to the senses, but gratefully welcomed.

'Oh, I forgot to tell you in all of the excitement of the evening,' Alice said, drawing a plate from the sink and placing it on the side to drain. 'I was offered some regular work today. There's a new agency opened up in offices on the Marylebone Road; a friend of mine, Ellen, got taken on two weeks ago and does well out of them. They arrange temporary service work in some of the big houses in town. Nothing major of course, just some scullery work, laundry and the like. The man at the office, Mr Tandry, says that someone from my background and upbringing will most certainly get offered a proper job sooner or later; he said I had great potential. I start in two days' time.' She turned to look at me and gave a nervous smile.

'That is wonderful news, Alice. I knew that it would not be long until you found your feet.'

'Yes, well. Of course it means that Benjamin and I should be moving on once I get my money. That will make you happy, I'm sure.' Her eyes searched mine for a reaction; I placed my drink on the table, stood and stepped over to her.

'Alice,' I said, my voice low. 'I am happy that you have found this work, but really, there is no need for you to be leaving here in a hurry – in fact, there is no need for you to be leaving here at all.' I reached forwards and took her hands in my own. They were soft and her fingers moved in response, taking mine.

'Are you sure? I mean, I thought we were a burden to you.'

'My rooms would feel too large without the pair of you,' I said, looking down into her eyes. 'I think I would feel a little lost, in fact.'

Her lower lip trembled a touch and she smiled at me then, throwing her arms around me as I drew her close. It felt good to be close to her at last – it felt right, in fact, and I moved to kiss her.

At that moment there was a loud knocking at the door.

'It seems you are a man wanted by others as well,' Alice said, giving me the briefest of kisses before pulling away to answer the door. 'Maybe it is another long-lost friend come to give you good news?'

Behind the door stood a young lad holding a note in his hand, and I knew immediately what the message would be. There had been another murder and Abe Thomas was indeed being a loyal friend.

'I will not be long, Alice!' I called, grabbing my coat and satchel.

'We have lots to talk about!' And leaving her smiling softly at me in the kitchen doorway, I left.

***

I hailed a cab from the end of Amberley Road and told the driver to take me to the address given by Abe. The messenger boy had provided no other instruction and the note was written in Abe's usual sparse and curt tone; simply an address and his initials. I felt gladdened to have received it, as I had wondered whether I would hear from the man again following my article in *The Illustrated Police News* about the Boston Place deaths and the more recent murders of the young girls. I stepped out of the cab at Hanover Gate and saw that there were policemen stationed at the entrance to Regent's Park, the inside of which was consumed by fog. Two constables stood on watch at the gate, preventing any members of the growing crowd from entering. As I approached, they stood a little taller, one of them holding out his hand to bar my entrance.

'No one but police past this gate,' he said.

I was about to start my argument with the man, an argument that would start with the name Inspector Thomas, when I felt a sharp tug at my elbow. I turned to see Sergeant Eastwood, a policeman who worked at Abe's station; he leant in close and whispered in my ear, 'This is not the entrance for you, Sam. Follow me up the road a little. The Inspector is waiting for you.'

Without speaking, I followed his instruction and walked at a quickened pace behind him towards Portland Place, where another entrance to the park lay.

There were two constables in attendance. However, just behind them stood the large figure of Abe Thomas, who beckoned me in as I approached.

'You haven't been here, Sam, right?' he hissed, throwing his arm around my shoulders and leading me in. 'My head would be on a spike outside Scotland Yard if it became known that I had told you of this.'

We hurried into the dark. The dank chill of the late September evening hung in the air and the fog gave Regent's Park a hazy and sinister appeal, the trees and bushes of the park lit only by the lantern that Abe carried. In the distance, I could see other torches dancing in the blackness; there was obviously a lot of activity here this evening, which hinted to me that it would be a scene well worth attending.

'Is it another murder, Abe?' I asked as he rushed me along the path. He nodded.

'The call came in not one hour ago. A gentleman travelling home from his club by carriage spotted an altercation between a tall cloaked figure and a young girl on Park Road, near Clarence Gate. The gentleman called out of his carriage and the figure took flight, dragging the girl away. By the time he got the carriage to stop, they had disappeared from sight. He made off after them, telling his driver to alert the police. By the time we arrived, it appeared he must have caught up with them at Hanover Gate. His body was shredded, almost unrecognisable. I cannot take you to him; it would be too obvious. He is a well-known figure apparently, a friend of the Chief Inspector.'

'Why have you called me, Abe? Why risk yourself for this?' I said.

'There's something not right about this whole mucky business,' he snarled. 'Someone up top has got the wind up their jacksie. My men have all been put on the gates of the park; they've been barred from entering. It's the city police that are inside, so don't worry, they won't recognise you. If this continues though, then soon it will be just like it was before...'

'Before?'

'Back in Whitechapel, back when Darke was on his rampage. It was the same then; the powers-that-be tightening up everything and overriding the officers on the scene. I would never be able to live with myself if I let it happen again.' He pulled us to a stop and dragged me in front of him so that he could stare into my eyes. 'I want you to record it, Sam. I want you to record it and make sure that it doesn't disappear, that it doesn't get forgotten as just a few unimportant deaths of girls that no one cares about! I care about them, Sam. I care and others should too!'

His eyes were bloodshot, his normally ruddy face a pale grey colour as it glowered down on me, lit by his lantern. It was clear that he had been caught unawares by this incident and had not had the benefit of his sobering walk before being called.

'I will take it to Mr Purkess, I promise you, Abe,' I said.

'Yes, right. Well, you should know that the cordons of the park were sealed pretty quickly. I am sure that our man is long gone but there is a chance that he still lurks in the shadows.' He paused for a second to watch my face blanch. 'The first we found was just up here,' he said, charging off ahead of me.

'Are they linked to the others? I asked. 'Have you found a spike?'

He snorted at me then. 'Spikes, Sam? If it's spikes you want then you won't be disappointed.' A lone constable stood at a tree ahead of us. At our approach, he raised his lantern and shouted over. The Inspector called out his name and introduced me as a police artist; the constable looked a little suspicious but said nothing, stepping out of the way so that we could see the tree.

There was indeed a spike; just the one, though. It had been driven into the tree with great force, pinning a single left hand to it. The hand was small – a woman's – and had been severed at the wrist; the large spike was nailed through its soft, white palm.

I sketched it quickly; all the while Abe Thomas stood at my shoulder hurrying me on, telling me to move on to the next tree. The next scene was not twenty yards ahead and manned also. Abe went through the introductory rigmarole once more and another hand – the right – was revealed to me.

'I don't need to sketch this, Abe,' I said. 'It is in my memory and I will do it later. Is there another?'

A sad smile crossed his face as he ushered me onwards. 'Another?' he said. 'We haven't got started yet.'

A large lump surged upwards from my stomach as I began to realise the enormity of what I was witnessing. The next two trees wore the forearms of the poor victim and then we moved onwards to the upper arms. Each body part, each piece of now useless dead meat, had been perfectly and precisely cut. Although my mood became low as we trudged onwards through the dark and misty park, I still had – at the back of my mind and developing by the second – a vision of how the final drawing would look on the cover of George's newspaper in the coming week. I imagined a clock face, each number represented by a picture of a body part nailed to a tree, and in the centre a picture of the victim's face, whenever we finally came across it.

From the hands and arms we moved onto the feet and legs, and I wondered at the mind of the murderer. What strength and willpower would drive a person to behave in this way? What purpose was there in the slicing apart of such innocence, merely to display them thus?

My mind was sick and my heart weak with sorrow by the time we came to the torso; for here the killer had dedicated the most time and effort in their work.

They had chosen a large tree, and it was needed: the torso had been secured by a large spike through the top of the spine, the chest opened and emptied. Each of the poor girl's internal organs had been nailed to the branches around it, with the exception of the intestines, which had been draped over them, garlands on some satanic Christmas tree. I retched and vomited immediately.

Abe patted me on the back and bade me to recover myself so that I could draw it. I had the feeling then that this was some bizarre form of cleansing for me; that someone somewhere had devised this murder scene so that I would be forced to draw it, eyes held open to witness the horror, in order to purge me. I did as he asked; I slumped to the ground in front of the tree and drew it, although my eyes smarted with tears at what had been placed before me.

'Can I have a moment, Abe?' I asked. 'There is... much to draw here and I would work better if not observed.'

He agreed and led away the sickly looking constable who had been given the task of guarding the tree. I shone Abe's lantern up into the tree and began to sketch this abomination. I worked quickly, but with great detail; I thought it best to record more than was required and tone it down for the audience at Mr Purkess's behest for publication. It took me about ten minutes, no more, and, as I lifted the lantern from the ground and was about to call for Abe to return, I spotted something up high in the branches – a movement.

I pushed myself to my feet, raising the lantern's light higher into the air. The movement had been quick and fleeting, probably a squirrel or roosting bird. As the light hit the branches they shook, more violently this time as if something up there in the blackness was trying to avoid the lantern's glare. The leaves rustled and there was a loud creak as it moved once more. Surely no squirrel could cause this much noise?

'Abe!' I called, as loudly as I dared, wondering if my voice would be heard over the hammering of my beating heart, whose pounding now filled my ears. 'Abe! I have finished, would you come back? I think it is time that we moved on.'

The Inspector and the young constable made slow progress in returning to me and all the while I did not take my wide eyes from the branches above me.

'Move on?' said Abe. 'There is nowhere to move on to now, lad, apart from home to our beds, for we have not yet discovered the head. Although I know a place where we can get a late drink to wash this all awa…'

He saw the look in my eyes as he approached. 'Sam?' he said. 'What is it?'

'Above,' I breathed, with all of the effort that I could muster from my strangulated throat. 'There is something abo…'

It dropped then; a large, cloaked mass which fell with force onto the young constable, knocking him to his knees. In a flash, before either Abe or I could react, a large golden blade, flat and thin, appeared from within the folds of the cloak and swung like a scythe, slicing the young man's head clear from his shoulders. All this before the poor boy's body had even realised what had happened and crumpled into a heap upon the grass.

Despite his size, Abe's reactions were quicker than mine and he pushed me to the ground, away from him, as he attempted to draw his pistol from inside his overcoat. He was not quick enough; the golden blade loosed his hand from his wrist as he pulled the gun clear and attempted to take aim. For a short moment, time seemed to stand very still; Abe stared in disbelief at his arm before him, his hand falling to the ground still gripping the pistol, his index finger remaining poised on the trigger.

The figure in the cloak was tall, a good head taller than I, and remained fully shrouded, showing little of what lay beneath. The hand that bore the blade seemed hidden inside the sleeve and its other hand appeared gloved in some kind of tight gauntlet, also gold in colour. Of the face there was no sign – the hood was drawn well down, hiding any sight of the man.

I shuffled backwards quickly, trying to regain my feet.

'Abe!' I called. 'Abe, we must run. We must leave this place!'

The figures of Abe and his assailant stood frozen.

Suddenly Abe screamed and threw himself at the hooded man, attempting to wrestle him to the floor. He did not make it further than one yard. I saw the blade shoot from the base of his back, only to be pulled upwards, dividing the man and leaving at his left shoulder.

I cried in horror, scrabbling backwards, trying to get away from the hooded figure, and came upon something soft. I looked down to see Abe's severed fist in my own, the gun still in its fingers. I pulled the pistol free and pointed it at the figure, pulling on the trigger and firing. I knew that my aim was true and my target easily within my sight, but the bullets did not bring it down. With each shot a respond-ing noise rang out, as if the bullets were striking metal, as if the figure wore armour under its cloak.

The figure turned, leaving the body of Abe Thomas split before it, and strode towards me. As I threw my empty gun towards it, I looked up at the golden blade raised in the air; my end, it seemed, was close.

What happened then was the most remarkable thing. The blade appeared to shimmer and change shape, as if it had become heated enough to melt. It shrank and thickened, withdrawing into the sleeve of the figure's cloak and, as it was just about to disappear altogether, I saw that it had moulded itself into the form of a golden hand.

My expression must have been one of horrifying disbelief, which did not improve when the hand lifted to pull down the hood of the figure and I saw its face for the first time. The face of a beautiful woman.

I am an educated man. I have visited the museums of London and seen pieces of art on display that have been created by man, but I have never seen anything as shockingly stunning as the face which I saw before me in that moment. I compare it to art because it is that which it was most like. It was like a carved bronze, only moulded from pure gold, statue-like and impassive, expressionless and devoid of all sign of life. She leant in, bringing that solemn mask close to my face. Apart from my own childlike whimpering, there was no sound; not a whisper of noise came from the golden woman, no breath. Time seemed to stop and, unmoving and cold though her eyes were, I could feel that I was being closely observed, like some oddity or strange antiquity in a circus. Stinging sweat ran down my forehead and into my eyes.

The moment was broken by the sound of approaching voices in the distance. The gunfire had obviously been heard, and the police were on their way.

The golden woman stood up suddenly, raising her right arm, which immediately melted into the form of a sword once more. As the voices grew nearer she lowered the sword until it hovered unmoving above my head. I closed my eyes and waited.

My death did not come.

I heard the flutter of her cloak and when I opened my eyes the golden woman had gone, disappeared into the darkness. I crawled over to where the divided body of Abe Thomas lay. To my surprise he was gasping for breath.

'Abe,' I breathed. 'Do not worry, help is on its way.'

He tried to speak but his voice was a gargle of blood, which he coughed weakly from his mouth.

'Dolor...' he spat, his words rimmed red. 'That is the key... find the Dolorian Club.' He choked again and spat out another mouthful of blood. 'Go!' he spluttered. 'Don't let them see you here. Don't let them hide it again.'

There were men's voices now and I knew that at any moment I would be seen. Abe was gone and I touched his bloody face briefly before hauling myself to my feet and, after pulling free the iron spike which held the torso to the tree and stuffing it into my pocket, I ran in the opposite direction to the approaching men. I heard the screams and the cries as they discovered the bodies of Inspector Thomas and the young policeman.

Finding a gap in the railings at the edge of the park, I did not stop running until I reached home.

As I burst through the door, I saw Alice standing in the doorway of my bedroom, waiting for me. She saw the blood on my clothes, the expression on my face and the tears in my eyes; she ran to me and held me close.

I did not tell her then what I had witnessed that evening; in fact, I hardly spoke at all, merely to say that I had been with the police, working. After pouring myself a large brandy, which I downed in one swig, I undressed and took to my bed, where I held Alice to me. Eventually, sobbing like a child and cursed with dreams of the deadly Golden Woman, I slept.

9

Those Who Watch

When I awoke the next morning both Alice and Benjamin were out. I had slept fitfully during the night; I felt tired and broken. My legs, unused to the exercise and effort expended during my escape from Regent's Park, burned with lethargy and I near shuffled into the kitchen to prepare some coffee to wake me fully.

I sat for a while at my desk, looking out of the window while I drank. The horror of what I had seen had not left me, and I doubted that it ever would. Abe's final coughed words resounded around my mind, repeating themselves each time with emphasis and force.

It is strange, but the sadness which I felt that morning was as much for myself as for the good Inspector. I thought about my past revelry in matters murderous, when I had regarded them not as terrible incidents of great violence and repulsion, but as opportunities for the furtherance of my career. What had made me this way? And were my current circumstances some kind of penance for my sins?

If I did not have Alice and Benjamin then I am sure that I would have shut myself away that morning and sunk into a deep despair, the like of which I have known just once in my life before, following my mother's committal to the asylum.

In the days after her sudden absence I refused to attend school and spent long hours in my room, lying in my bed staring out of the window. Mrs Coleman would bring me food regularly and try to mother me into eating but I rarely did and, after a few weeks of this stubborn behaviour, my health began to suffer. I lost a great deal of weight – my constitution was not strong enough to fight off sickness. I became weak and pale and prone to long coughing fits, during which I would bark and wheeze.

Father came to me daily, imploring me to eat and to venture outside, offering me treats and rewards if I would obey, but from him I wanted nothing. He had taken away the one bright constant in my life and he would not be forgiven. Thinking back on this time now, I recognised that it was childish and pathetic in the extreme to punish my father for taking Mother away. It was not him suffering to be sure; he had not changed his daily routine at all and continued to spend as much time away from home as before her incarceration, probably more.

It was Victoria who brought me out of the mire that I wallowed in. She came to me each day, sitting on the edge of my bed and talking to me. Just talking. She did not get any response but then, in truth, I do not think that she expected any. She did not implore and beg me to eat, like her mother; nor did she make promises like Father. No, she just talked. She told me about her day and the chores she had completed and she told me of the gossip from town that she had heard from her mother and her friends. She told me of the gardens and the work that Mr Morgan was doing, digging new beds in the lower lawns or planting daffodil bulbs around the apple and pear trees in the orchard ready for the coming spring.

I lay and listened to her each day. The sound of her voice became a soothing balm to my troubled mind; a soft and constant reminder that life in the world continued without my attendance. One day, perhaps four weeks into my self-induced confinement, she did not come. I watched the clock for nearly three hours, wondering where she was and what she was doing. Finally, when my curiosity could bear it no more, I pulled back my covers and, with effort, swung my legs over the side of the bed, so that my bare feet touched the cold floor. I pushed myself up on unsteady legs and stood for a moment, balancing myself before walking towards the window. In the garden Mr Morgan was planting bulbs, just as Victoria had said, and Mrs Coleman was hanging out washing. It was a bright but cold day with a soft breeze and, for a while, I simply stood watching the white sheets swaying in the gentle wind. I looked to the clock once more; still she did not come. I shuffled towards the door of my bedroom and opened it, holding it ajar and peering out of a crack in the small world that I had created; all was silent in the house.

I stepped outside onto the landing, my feet enjoying the feel of the runner carpet which lay along the length of the hallway leading to the stairs. I made my way down the stairs; still there was no sound from the house other than the occasional creak in the risers as I descended.

I walked into the kitchen. It was warm and my head was filled with the comforting smell of freshly baked bread, which made my stomach complain at the lack of attention I'd paid it. Victoria stood with her back to me at the stove. She held a frying pan in her hand and was cooking eggs; she did not turn or acknowledge my presence. On the broad wooden table was a plate with thick-sliced buttered bread and I sat down and reached for it.

'Can you not wait for your eggs?' Victoria said suddenly, and I jumped with a start. She smiled at me before bringing the pan over and depositing two fried eggs upon my plate beside the bread. I said nothing and picked up my knife and fork, wolfing down the late breakfast.

'I will draw a bath for you shortly,' she said. 'But do not worry – I shall not be attending or helping you with that.'

I looked up at her and smiled weakly.

'Thank you, Victoria,' I said, preparing to stand.

'Do not rush. We have all day to bring you back to the land of the living. Perhaps after your bath we can walk in the gardens together?'

'Yes,' I said. 'Yes, I would like that very much.'

As I sat drinking my coffee and waiting for Alice and Benjamin's return, I thought of the day that my father's plain but loving house-maid brought me out of my misery and, despite it being a warm memory, tears ran down my face when I thought of the pain, misery and humiliating end with which I had rewarded poor Victoria.

***

The road was busy outside. Carriages, cutting through for the Harrow Road on their way to the Edgware Road, and central London beyond, ambled past. Barges, some drawn by heavy horses, made their slow way on the Paddington Canal. It was a grey day, one which fitted my mood on waking, but the sun was attempting to break through the clouds, occasionally escaping their cover to dance on the water of the canal, which dominated the view from my window.

When it cleared, it brought a warm yellow glow to the street and waterway, and I found myself temporarily in awe of this scene which I had taken for granted for so long.

Thinking back on my discussion with Frederick Draper, I wrote a short letter to Edward Higgins. I asked after his well-being and whether he had given any more thought to contacting George Purkess regarding his ghost stories. According to Mr Purkess, he had not received any such letter as yet, but he told me that he would be glad to meet Higgins and offer him the opportunity to appear in the newspaper. I then asked whether Edward had noticed any suspicious visitors in Pluckley. If it was known that I had visited Kent, Draper and his associates would know that I went to learn of Sibelius Darke through Tom Finnan. I thought of the veiled threats given to me by Draper and, through my liking of Tom Finnan, would not have wished these threats to extend to the landlord of the Black Horse or his sister. I smiled upon thinking of Higgins and his charming manner; how I would be glad to have the opportunity to enjoy a drink with him again.

It was as the sun's autumn light shone golden upon the finished letter on my desk that the door to my rooms opened and Alice and her brother came in. Benjamin looked a little nervous at first but, after a tap on the shoulder from his sister, he ran over to where I sat and threw his arms around me.

'Alice says you had a late night with the police,' he said. 'Was it a murder? Did they catch the killer?'

I smiled a little, driving the memory of Abe's murder from my mind. 'It was not so bad, an accident involving a carriage,' I remarked. 'Nothing for you to worry about. Now tell me where you and your sister have been this morning. I hope not to buy sweet things from the baker again.'

'We have not been doing anything of the sort,' Alice said, coming over and laying a hand on each of our shoulders. 'We have been down to the agency I told you about, to see if there was any work today. Mr Tandry asked me to return later this afternoon as there may be some evening work at an event in town; kitchen work, nothing more, but it's a start.'

'It is indeed,' I said, putting my arm around her waist and drawing her close so that I held both her and her brother tightly. I felt a sudden surge of emotion, which I fought hard to repress, before jumping to my feet and announcing that we would be going out for breakfast.

We broke our fast in a small coffee shop on the Harrow Road and there Alice and I told Benjamin of how their stay with me would not be so temporary, and of how we thought to enrol him in a school nearby. He seemed overjoyed at this; he had never had the benefit of any formal schooling like his sister and had relied on her teaching.

I left Alice and Benjamin after breakfast. They had friends to see and I had given Alice some money to buy herself and Benjamin some clothes fitting for a young lady entering the employment market and her soon to be school-bound brother.

I had shaken the horror of the previous evening's events from my mind and now thought of them as terrible actions which it was my duty to report and visualise. I had learnt a valuable lesson from my experience in Regent's Park: a call to wake up from my revelry in all things murderous and terrible. It was as though I had been given the opportunity to make a new start for myself. Therefore, with the decision made to unburden myself, I returned briefly to my rooms to collect my satchel of works and headed into town to see the proprietor of *The Illustrated Police News.*

***

Mr Purkess had never worn such a dark expression.

I walked in slowly, placing my satchel on the chair in front of his desk.

'I understand that you wish to see me,' I said, looking towards the floor. 'Mr Cope said something about a visit from the city police earlier.'

He said nothing but motioned towards the chair. I seated myself in silence. I thought of reaching into my satchel and bringing out my sketchbook to show him the fruits of my terrible evening with poor Abe Thomas, but I could tell from his expression that he would hear no word of it. He leaned forwards, his arms resting on the desk.

'Mr Cope is right; I did have a visitation from the law today.'

His voice was ire and fury tightly contained. 'They asked after you, Weaver; they were very persistent. It would seem that there was another 'incident' last night, something in Regent's Park, where two policemen and a member of the House of Lords were butchered.'

'And another servant girl!' I cut in, with anger of my own that he did not deem her worthy of mentioning.

'...and another servant girl,' he replied. 'One of the policemen murdered was Inspector Abe Thomas, a good friend of mine, a good friend of our newspaper and, of course, a good friend of yours also.'

I made to speak but he raised his hand and continued.

'Witnesses at the park say that our good friend Inspector Thomas was accompanied by a young man fitting your description, who was introduced as being a police artist. Were you aware of this?'

'I was aware of this, sir; in fact it was the reason...'

He held up his hand once more. 'Were you with Inspector Abraham Thomas last night in Regent's Park and were you witness to his death?'

'I was.'

'And did you run away from the scene before the police arrived?'

'I did, but...'

'The police are very interested to speak to you, Mr Weaver. They came to me this morning, asking for your address.'

'You didn't give it to them, did you?' I said, thinking of Alice and Benjamin.

'No, I did not, although I doubt that it would have taken them long to track you down... if I hadn't told them that you were with me all night.'

'You did?'

'Yes, I thought to protect you – and the reputation of this very newspaper – although, sitting here now, I cannot for the life of me think why. They are very angry men, Weaver, very angry indeed. Two of their own killed, and a lord – Lord Blakenbury – who was a personal friend of the Commissioner himself. They are taking this matter very seriously indeed.'

'I saw the lad die,' I said. 'He did not have a chance; he died very quickly. The lord was already dead when I got there. I didn't get to see his body.'

Mr Purkess turned puce with rage and leapt to his feet, slamming his hands upon his desk.

'But what were you doing there in the first place, you stupid boy! You knew how angered the police were by our coverage of the servant girl murders and the deaths at Boston Place! They said we made them look incompetent and they barred us from any further involvement. Why were you there?'

I nervously straightened myself in my seat.

'I went because Abe asked me to go,' I answered.

'But he was most probably drunk! What were you thinking?'

'I was thinking that Abe Thomas was one of our most trusted associates and that if he saw fit for me to attend a scene, then go there I would. I wish that I had never been, if it makes you feel any better. I had no wish to see my friend – our friend – die in such a horrible manner. It is something that will always be with me.'

Purkess could see my upset at Abe's death and his face softened a touch. He took his seat again, shaking his head, and opened his cigar box, snipping the end of a cigar before lighting it.

'Well, I think I put them off your scent,' he said quietly. 'I swore blind that you were with me. Even Mr Cope, someone whom I would have thought would have relished your downfall, backed up my story. I think that they believed us. However, I have agreed that we will hand over all sketches and drawings done by you relating to the servant girl murders, and that is not negotiable – it is the price for your head being off the block.'

I nodded my newly saved head and agreed; the thought of giving over any of my works to the police abhorred me, as I knew that they would be lost forever, but I had enough that I could keep back.

'What about the sketches I made last night?'

'I will keep them. In my safe. Let us call it a bargaining tool to keep you straight in the future.'

I pulled them out of the satchel and handed them over. Mr Purkess placed his glasses on his nose and looked through them; the horror was clear upon his face.

'Such a terrible thing to do to someone, especially a girl so young,' he said, shaking his head. 'I hope never to see such murder upon our good streets again.'

'But what about the next time?' I asked. 'There will be more deaths, more girls murdered before this is all played out, you know. It will not stop.'

Purkess looked up in surprise and removed his glasses.

'Oh, but it has,' he said, the hint of a smile on his lips. 'Have you not heard? They caught the killer last night, shortly after finding the bodies of Inspector Thomas and the young constable. Chased the killer across London they did, until they finally caught up with them. The murderer was brought in, although I hear he suffered grievous injuries in the arrest.'

'He?' I exclaimed. 'Did you say he?'

Mr Purkess looked a little shocked at my outburst but continued all the same. 'Yes, "he" – as if it would be anyone other than a man who committed these crimes. He was a tinker from a camp just outside Belsize Road. They caught him by the railway line up at St John's Wood. He had a set of tools, including a large knife, a hammer and a bag with railway spikes in it, like those used in the murders. Feathers his name was, Jack Feathers; the police say they knew him as a thief who specialised in scrap metal and the like, but they are sure it was him.'

I thought of Abe's final words, how he had said that it would be brushed away, made to be forgotten by those who wanted to make it disappear. Anger boiled inside of me and I thought of telling Mr Purkess about the Golden Woman, of how I had seen the true killer up close, but I did not. Mr Purkess had obviously been given the hard word by his visitors that morning and it would be useless to try to persuade him otherwise. I thought of my good humour after Frederick Draper's visit the previous evening, and of how I had envisaged striding into the office today and amazing Mr Purkess with my story of Draper's reappearance and of the Dolorian Club's involvement in the Darke murders; but again this was only suspicion and accusation. In truth I had no real proof that the club was anything more than a group of respectable gentlemen terrorised by a child-killing cannibal. There would be no way forward with either the Golden Woman or the Darke cases without further investigation into the club and its apparent benefactor, Lord William Falconer. I decided to stay quiet.

I left the offices with promises of good behaviour and a solemn oath to my employer that I would lay low for the foreseeable, in terms of my involvement with the police.

Henry Cope, his face as smug as I had ever seen it (I am quite sure that he eavesdropped on conversations between Mr Purkess and myself, from the other side of the door), told me as I left that he would be sure to contact me if there were any stories abroad regarding lost dogs or broken windows. I thought of parting from him with a cutting remark, but bit my tongue and stepped out onto the street without a word.

***

That afternoon I accompanied Alice to the employment agency; I wished to meet this Mr Tandry for myself to ensure that the agency was as above board and reliable as Alice had described it. Benjamin came with us also and, as we walked along the Marylebone Road to the agency's offices, he continued to pester me about my work, wanting to know if he could attend scenes of crime with me. I knew that murder cases would be off the menu for a while – a fact that I was quite grateful for, following my brush with death. And so I agreed that, should I receive the call, and should the work be appropriate for a young lad to attend, then I would of course allow him to shadow me. I just hoped that I was not assigned court duty again, as it would be interminably dull, as well as sullying the heroic ideal that Benjamin had of me.

The offices of the Marylebone Service Agency appeared nothing more than a sparse-looking shop front and it was obvious that they were a new enterprise. Alice led us inside to what appeared to be a simple office arrangement. There were two desks, both unmanned as we entered, and a tall lockable wooden cabinet. There was little decoration other than a number of certificates framed upon the wall, a tall shelf upon which sat a solitary large ledger and a very sickly plant, which stood behind one of the desks. While Alice called out into a room at the back for Mr Tandry, I decided that the agency had obviously not had the benefit of a woman's hand in its layout and presentation.

When Tandry appeared I found him to be a very odd fellow indeed; small and weaselly, he gave the impression of someone who had been dressed by a blind man with access to a theatre's costume box. His trousers were a pale yellow, bright and gaudy and were a good four inches shorter than they should have been. His jacket, made from velvet which had never seen a brush in its life, was a colour that could only be described as a 'dirty orange' and bore on its lapel a cloth flower, which may have intended to represent a carnation, although this would have been many years ago. Tandry's face was round and shiny, as if coated in a thin layer of wax, and his lips were thin to the point of invisibility, dancing around his mouth in a nervous manner as if by their own accord. His hair was red and curled, although not natural in either respect, and seemed to be rigidly held, as if by some sort of lacquer.

He came bustling out of the back room all of an angered dither, a presentation which immediately changed when he noted that Alice had company with her.

'Miss Griffiths, Miss Griffiths, thank you for returning today, ha ha!' he said, taking her hand. 'Very prompt, very reliable and I see that you have brought someone with you, Mr...?'

'Weaver,' I said, shaking his outstretched hand, which was limp and cold to the touch. 'Mr Samuel Weaver. I am a close friend of Miss Griffiths.'

'Of course!' he said, waving his arms in the air in a most extravagant manner. I stepped backwards a little and bumped into one of the desks, making Benjamin snort and dissolve into giggles. I glanced at Alice, who gave a tight smile, which I returned. 'We are new of course,' Mr Tandry continued. 'Only set up in the last month, but business is glorious and we are always happy to take on such quality as Miss Griffiths here.' He turned quickly to Benjamin and gripped him by the shoulders. 'And I see that you have returned to me once again, young man. Are you ready to take up my offer of work? Ha ha! I am sure we can find a little something for you.'

'That will not be necessary,' I cut in, and pulled Benjamin towards me. 'Young Benjamin here will not be entering the employment market for a few years yet; he has school to attend.'

Tandry did well to hide his obvious annoyance. 'School, yes, a man needs an education, of course he does. Oh well, if school should not work out for you, then you know where we are. And you, sir!' he exclaimed. 'I take it you are a working man. What industry is yours?'

'Journalism,' I replied. 'I am a writer and artist for the newspapers. You will probably have seen some of my work; it is widely read.'

'Oh I am sure,' he said, turning back to Alice. His expression had dropped at the mention of my work; he had obviously lost interest. 'Now then young lady, I told you that work would arrive for you and arrive it has; good work, in a respectable house, yes, yes. Ha ha!' His eyes flickered wildly and his voice became quite excited. 'I have need of serving staff for a ball this evening, Knightsbridge. Does that take your fancy? I take it you feel confident in serving, of course you do, of course you do, ha!'

Alice made to answer but he walked away from her and into the back room, returning seconds later with a large brown paper package, which he said contained two sets of uniform in her size, one standard linen dress for kitchen work and one smarter black uniform which she was to wear that evening. He gave her the time and the address scribbled on a piece of paper; she was to go to the rear entrance of the house and introduce herself, giving Mr Tandry's name.

Without allowing us scarcely another word, he ushered us towards the doorway and out into the street. We took his cue and left, barely containing our mirth at this strange little man, who lingered in the doorway, waving to us until we were fully out of sight.

***

Over the next two weeks Alice gained a flurry of work from Tandry's agency, which left me spending a great deal of time alone with her younger brother. I found myself enjoying the opportunity to get to know Benjamin. There were no further reported murders of servant girls; however, this was not proof that the killer had indeed been caught, and in fact I knew full well that this had not been the case.

Surprisingly enough, after my meeting with Mr Purkess, work did not completely dry up for me and I was able to allow Benjamin to accompany me on a couple of assignments. As promised by Mr Cope, they were of low quality. For the most part, I mainly worked from home on 'second-hand stories': these were the dire pittance of artwork for the newspaper, where the complete written account would be purloined directly from a rival publication or one of the dailies, and I would be expected to conjure up suitably evocative images to match. Unlike me, Benjamin seemed to enjoy this work, as it gave him the opportunity to sit at my desk with me, and draw his own interpretations of the stories. His imagination was a wonder to see and I even found myself including some of his ideas in my own drawings, which pleased him greatly.

I had been in touch with St Stephen's School on Westbourne Park Road, and had even visited the premises with both Alice and Benjamin. They had both found the school to be agreeable and it was decided that Benjamin would start his classes in the new year. For Benjamin it was an exciting time: a new school, the opportunity of making friends and, to cap it all, time spent with me. To any outsider, life appeared to be heading in the right direction for all of us.

Constant in my mind, however, and taking up all of the hours that I did not spend either working or with Alice and Benjamin, were my investigations into the Dolorian Club and Lord William Falconer.

Falconer was not a difficult personage to track down, being well known throughout London society. A relatively young man, he had inherited his estate from his parents, who had died under most unfortunate circumstances whilst visiting lands purchased by them in the Cape Colony. Falconer's father, Lord Arthur Sedgewick Falconer, was an avid game hunter who had become entranced with the Cape during a trip to Southern Africa in his youth. As soon as young William was old enough to be shipped off to preparatory school, his father had acquired ten thousand acres and taken his wife, Lady Edith, with him to view their lands, shoot some big game and generally lord it up over the local population, a state of affairs which came naturally to them both. Indeed, their maltreatment of those in their employ was often decried by the more liberal-thinking commentators, one of whom famously stated: 'The Falconers seem to be most careless in the number of staff who pass through their houses, and it is a lucky whelp who survives the process.'

Like her husband, Lady Edith was said to be very fond of shooting and killing wild animals. Some even dared to announce her the better marksman of the two, a claim which she neither denied nor hid from. She positively revelled in all types of blood sport and even employed a photographer to accompany them on each of their trips to record her victories over Mother Nature and her fauna.

The couple's unfortunate demise occurred during one such trip into the veldt, when their shooting party was set about by elephants, who for some reason had taken exception to being fired upon. How they had ended up being led into such dangerous paths remained a mystery. In fact, the only survivors of the incident were their native porters, who claimed that the Falconers had refused their warnings regarding the minimum safe distance to be maintained between a large group of gun-happy aristocrats and a herd of protective and angry pachyderms.

Young William then found himself, at the age of eight, an orphan and the proud owner of unimaginable wealth and lands both in Britain and elsewhere in the Empire. It appears that he coped with his parents' death well and took to the job of ownership and dominion over all he surveyed with great aplomb, removing himself from school immediately and employing private tutorage, which was conducted at his estate in Hampshire. As he grew into a young man, he was surrounded by his father's most trusted confidants, who helped him to manage his inheritance. He was a confident young man, one who learnt early how money brought power – and how power in turn brought in more money. This is not to say that Falconer was a man who greedily amassed wealth only to sit atop his piles of money; far from it, he was well known for his lavish spending on parties and social occasions, as well as his generous outpourings to charities of his choice. In fact, he was well known about town and the entertainment establishments of London fought for his approval and attendance, whether they be restaurant, drinking club or theatre. Theatre, in particular music hall with its singers, comic acts and magicians, was his one great passion. He had been known to involve himself financially in such establishments as The Canterbury and The Old Mo, paying for repairs and refurbishments and even sponsoring acts that he enjoyed and in which he saw potential. He kept an open-ended reservation for a private box in each of the main music halls in London, and would often be seen at more than one in an evening.

Although in his thirties and London's most eligible bachelor, he had never married. There were, of course, rumours of lady friends and illicit liaisons, of beautiful women kept in lodgings of various degrees of grandiosity throughout the city, but that is all they were – kept women, playthings and ever-hopeful dreamers, who waited for the door to knock and hoped that, when it did, it was not a messenger telling them that their time was up and a new edition was waiting to move in.

Often Falconer would disappear, sometimes for weeks at a time. There was talk of travel abroad in Africa and across Scandinavia; but, of course, as with everything else about the man, while facets of his life were known, the whole picture was never revealed.

Of his associations with the Dolorian Club, even less was known. I sought out each of my 'people in the know' – cab drivers, barmen and society watchers – and none of them knew anything further of his involvement other than that he had joined the club at a young age, was a regular visitor and that he often spent the night there; although of course, now that the club was run from what had been his main London residence, this was hardly surprising. The club was situated in Marylebone, Cavendish Square to be precise, and I visited the area often following the death of Abe Thomas and in light of my new-found interest in Falconer. I took up a regular spot in the square, where I watched the daily comings and goings whilst posing as a pavement portrait artist.

I had been given a description of Lord Falconer by a hansom driver who had carried him in his cab on more than one occasion. He was said to be a tall man with pale, well-groomed hair and piercing ice-blue eyes. He would generally, according to my source, be impeccably dressed and carried a cane topped with an ivory carving of an elephant, presumably in memory of his lost parents.

I counted myself as most unfortunate, in those first few visits to scope the club, as I did not see him either arrive or leave. However, I saw plenty of other men enter and exit the doors, a great many of whom I hastily sketched. I planned to take these sketches to my contacts once my surveillance was completed, which I told myself would be upon my first sighting of Falconer. I could then attempt to create a list of Dolorian Club members.

During the second week as a surveiller I even began to expand my search for Falconer, attending the music halls in the evening. For these excursions I took both Alice and Benjamin with me, as it gave me an additional layer of disguise to be seen as a member of a family on a night out. Of course, the other effect of these night-time entertainments was that my 'family' also got to benefit from an evening out, and the entertainment provided by all manner of singers, comedians and magicians. It was the magicians who provided Benjamin in particular with the most joy. He stared open mouthed at their illusions and apparent enchantments. (I had a passing interest in magic myself and had attended the Egyptian Hall, a theatre in Piccadilly, on many occasions upon first coming to London.)

Despite our trips to the theatre and my attendance in Cavendish Square in between work assignments, no sighting of Lord Falconer was evident; it would seem that he himself had conducted his very own disappearing act.

My frustration continued to grow to almost unbearable levels until one evening, when I finally took my wards to the Egyptian Hall. Upon leaving the show with Alice and Benjamin, I saw, across the atrium, the figure of a man dressed in hat and tails, identical in appearance to the description I had been given of Lord Falconer. He was tall, slim built, in his early thirties and carried himself with that natural haughtiness to which only the upper classes can lay claim. He had sharp, bright eyes which sat above an aquiline nose, under which he sported a thin yellow moustache which appeared to be groomed to the point of obsession. He was dressed smartly for the evening and most importantly carried a slim black cane, the top of which was ivory in the shape of an elephant. I had my man at last and, in a sudden and spontaneous move, I crossed the hall to confront him.

As I approached, he looked up from his conversation and saw me. The slightest hint of a smile crossed his thin lips; was he expecting me? How did he know me? I was not to find out as I suddenly felt a hearty slap on the shoulder and was grabbed from behind.

'Well, here is a surprise!' came a booming voice. 'What the devil are you doing here, man? Why did you not tell me that you came to shows at the Egyptian?' Higgins gave me a wide smile and shook me by the hand. 'Weaver, old boy! Fancy seeing you, I would have thought that you would deem a magic show to be all poppycock and claptrap.'

'Well it is, it is!' I replied, somewhat taken aback. Over his shoulder, I could see Falconer leaving through the main doors and glancing over his shoulder to wave at me. Good God, the man was taunting me!

'Are you all right, Weaver, you look a little lost? You haven't been spooked by the performance have you?' The face of Higgins loomed before me again, blocking the view of my lost quarry. I shook myself back into the moment.

'Of course, I am fine, Edward. It takes more than the sight of a disappearing woman and a lucky choice of card to make me believe in that tripe. However, my young friend here is entranced by it all, and so I put up with it.' I gestured to Benjamin and Alice, who had come over to where we stood. 'Edward, this is Benjamin Griffiths and his sister Alice; they are good friends of mine. This here is Mr Edward Higgins. I am sure that I have mentioned him to you – he shares your love for all things magical.'

Higgins took Alice's hand gently in greeting before clapping her young brother on the back.

'A pleasure to meet you both, I am sure,' he said. 'Don't let Samuel convince you of anything but that magic is real and the supernatural is there to be discovered. He is a dreadful bore and will try to tell you otherwise.' He turned to me. 'I'm sorry, Weaver, I should have told you that I was in town, but it is only a short visit. I return to Pluckley first thing in the morning. I promise you that we will meet up next time I am in London. Now if you will excuse me, my carriage is waiting outside, so I must dash.' He fixed me with a steely smile and shook my hand again, with promises of future meetings and incomparable drinking sessions.

I saw no more of Falconer in the days that followed the Egyptian Hall, not even at his house in Cavendish Square, and my annoyance at his lack of appearance began to gnaw at me once more.

It was at the start of the third week of my watching the club that I finally decided to take matters into my own hands. I had assembled a good collection of drawings of the club members to work on in the future, as well as sketches of a number of other visitors, workmen, servants and the like – enough for a comprehensive study of the club and its patrons. It was late in the day, and the square was beginning to quiet, as I strode across to the front door. There was no bell but a large knocker in the shape of a stag, a small detail which did not escape me. I knocked confidently on the door and stood back a little, brushing down my jacket in an attempt to appear more formal. It was opened quickly and I found myself face to face with a short man with unnaturally white hair and dark, forbidding eyes. I had observed him answering the door on countless occasions and had sketched him more than once, but those views from across the street did not prepare me for him. He was shorter than I but exuded an aura of power and threat like none I had met before. He wore simple black attire; however, his posture gave the unnerving feeling of one that would have been more at home in the garb of a soldier. His arms were taut at his sides and there was a tension in his upper body; here was a man who would snap my neck as soon as look at me.

'I am here to see Lord Falconer,' I said.

'There is no one here of that name,' he replied. His voice, heavy like oak, was a rumble which seemed to resonate in the air; he carried an accent but not one which I immediately recognised.

'Is this not his house? I understand that Lord William Falconer is the owner of this property. If he is not here then when will he be?'

He laughed a little then and appeared to relax somewhat. 'The master of the house lives here no more, but then you already knew this, Mr Weaver. Tell me, did you expect us to open the doors to you and invite you in for a drink, or maybe some supper?'

'Well I...'

'Perhaps I could introduce you to the members of the club, help you to put some names to your sketches?'

I turned to look across the street. Two men stood there, my bag and easel in hand; they smiled to me and tipped their hats before walking away with my belongings.

'That is my property!' I proclaimed. 'Have them bring it back this instant!'

'When you set yourself against my master's friends, then everything of yours is ours to take at will. Everything and... anyone.'

I was never a gambling man. I had tried it, of course; what young man hadn't dreamt of outwitting their opponents in a game of chance or cards? I had had some small interest in games of chance, but not enough to forge any willing endeavour. When it came to cards, however, I'd thought I would be a natural, due to my facility to lie and read the behaviour of others, and I was – to a degree. For although I could easily read the minds of the other men around the table, I lacked the one vital asset of a good sharper: to be able to hide my own feelings with anything but ineptitude.

Upon those last words spoken to me, my face must have dropped a full ten inches and the realisation of his threat struck me as hard as any closed fist. My stomach lurched in sickness.

'My name is Mávnos,' the man said, a broad smile stamped upon his face. 'Go home now, Mr Samuel Weaver. It is there that you will find the man you seek, although he will be more than occupied with a special task saved just for your loved ones. Tell my Lord that you have seen me. He and my other friends should have finished their work by now and will not harm you. Hurry home now, you may just get there in time.'

I did not give him the satisfaction of seeing the torment in my face and ran from the doorway, desperately searching the square for a cab to take me back to my rooms and whatever hell awaited me there.

***

As I burst through the door a scene from a nightmare met me. The main entrance room, and I was quite sure the other rooms of the house, had been completely ransacked. Furniture was overturned, cupboards had been emptied out and my many drawings – and not just those relating to case work – lay ripped and torn upon the floor, much of them lost forever. I prayed that the hiding place of my most secret and treasured items remained untouched. This damage to property and place was, however, insubstantial when compared to the sight that met me on the far side of the room. There were two intruders of completely mismatched sizes.

The larger of the two was a hulking brute nearly twice the size of any normal man. He wore a well-tailored but aged suit, and atop his head sat a tweed flat cap. His face was round and lumpy, bearing many scars, especially around his eyes, and I immediately identified him as being a boxer of some sort, although I doubted he would have been matched in size by any other. He had a scar upon the left side of his neck, large and star shaped, and so near the windpipe that it is a wonder the man had survived the wound.

At his side stood the shorter of the two men, although he still stood at least a head higher than myself, and would have looked down upon most men. He too wore a brown suit; however, his looked as if it had been better maintained and was cleaned regularly. He had a thin, mean face which drew to a point at the end of his nose and gave the impression that it had been twisted and pulled out of shape.

They stood and grinned broadly at me as I entered; it seemed not to bother them a jot that they had been disturbed in their actions – in fact it was more likely that they had been awaiting my return.

And then there were Alice and Benjamin. Both were roughly tied to chairs and both had suffered at the hands of the intruders.

Alice's cheeks were swollen and bruised, glowing red and sore; it was clear she had been struck repeatedly. Blood came slowly from the side of her mouth, staining the dress that she wore, a present from me not one week earlier. She was conscious but only just so, her head lolling from side to side. Upon seeing me she tried to speak but was silenced by the large brute, who held one large paw over her mouth whilst the other grabbed her hair.

Benjamin had suffered a similar fate to his older sister, although he was gagged with a dirty cloth from the kitchen. He was frighteningly aware of his condition, his eyes wide and tense as if attempting to scream with his blocked mouth. The reason for his fear was clear: the smaller of the two men held a long, thin knife poised over one of the boy's thighs, ready to cut him.

The man spoke in a reedy voice. 'Good afternoon, Mr Weaver. We had been expecting you, of course, but not so soon. You seem to have caught us in the act a little, isn't that right, Mr Soames?' He turned briefly to the large man, who said nothing but nodded.

'Leave them alone,' I stammered. 'This has nothing to do with them, they know nothing of my business. Where is Lord Falconer?'

At that moment another figure appeared, stepping out of my kitchen with cup and saucer in hand; it was the tall, thin man from the Egyptian Hall.

'We were just wondering how long it would take you to race here from the club,' he said. His voice was rich and musical, but he was oddly accented, as if English were not his first tongue. This was not what I had expected of him at all.

'Lord William Falconer?' I asked, although I already knew the answer.

He bowed slightly before taking a sip of his tea. 'I am indeed he and I am afraid that this is not a social call, Mr Weaver. I am simply here to deliver a message to you. It is a message that I am sure you will fully understand.' He motioned to the large man, who immediately took hold of Alice's throat. She made a small whimpering sound; her eyes were wide in terror.

'Please,' I cried. 'Please let them go. Do not involve them in this.'

'Oh we intend to, Mr Weaver, just as soon as we have delivered this message to you. But, now that you are here, we can do our job and leave you alone. It seems you have a bit of tidying up to do.' He waved a long arm around at the mess upon the floor. 'I suppose this is what happens when you have little ones running around the house. They get everywhere, don't they? Like rats.'

'Tell me your message and go, please,' I begged.

'Well, it's a funny thing that, isn't it?' He turned once again to the dumb brute holding Alice. 'You see the message, although being very clear in its intentions, contains no words.' He turned to the smaller of the two men. 'Mr Dawes, I have not the stomach for any further violence today. I shall wait downstairs in the carriage. It was lovely to meet you at last, Mr Weaver, if only for the briefest of moments. We shall not meet again and, if we do, be in no doubt I will have you gutted like a pig.' He dropped the full cup to the floor, where it smashed. Stepping over the broken pieces, he retrieved his elephant-topped cane which was leaning by the doorway. 'Goodbye.'

He did not shut the door behind him and my eyes immediately returned to the two men holding Alice and Benjamin.

'Alone at last,' said the smaller man, Dawes. 'I don't know what you've done to upset my boss so much, but you've got him terribly angry. Maybe it was that you stole some money from him, is that it?'

'No... it's–'

'Not money,' interrupted Dawes. 'Well then, maybe you took something of value. Did you steal from him, took something you shouldn't? We've all done that sort of thing, haven't we, but it's another matter to get caught.'

'You don't understand... I haven't...'

'You can deny it all you like but we've got a message to deliver, which brings me back to this boy.'

'Please don't...'

'You see, we came in here, my friend Soames and I, and we see what a terrible mess this place is in, terrible mess. And so I turn to Mr Soames and I say, "This is what you get when people don't have consequences for their actions," I say. It's a terrible thing when people don't think of their responsibilities. They need to be shown the way, and they need to know what is right and what is wrong. Now, I see this boy and I think that this boy needs a lesson, before he starts following your example and not showing respect to those that deserve it. So let's give him that lesson, shall we!'

He plunged the knife downwards into Benjamin's thigh with great force.

I went to jump forwards but saw that a man of Soames's size could snap Alice's neck in an instant.

Through his gagged mouth Benjamin screamed, a dull howl of pain. Yet the man did not draw out the knife; he held it in place, gripping the handle firmly.

'Now, you have to tell me, Mr Weaver. Does this seem like a

message that you understand? Does it?' At his last word he turned the handle of the knife, twisting the blade with unnatural relish and enjoyment.

'I understand!' I shouted. 'I understand the message!' Tears ran down my face. What had I done?

'That's good, Mr Weaver. That's good that you understand, because if we get sent another time to see you then who knows what might happen?' Slowly, and with a final agonising twist which made Benjamin's body shudder, he withdrew the knife. Blood began to pour from the wound, running like a tap onto the floor under the chair. Benjamin lost consciousness then, a small mercy perhaps. 'You see, next time it might be the lady that we give our attentions to. There's terrible things you can do to a young girl to send a message. Terrible, nasty things, eh Soames?'

The grin on Soames's face grew broader. He stroked Alice's head softly for a moment, and I could see that he was thinking back upon an awful memory that was dear to him.

Alice sobbed quietly, the sound muffled by the paw of Soames. She looked directly at me but I could see that there was no anger there, just grief and terror at our current situation. I mouthed the words, 'I'm sorry.' The torturer spotted this and howled with laughter.

'Oh, Mr Weaver! It would seem that our time here is at an end. Our master awaits us downstairs, and you and your good lady obviously have a lot to talk about. Perhaps you can tell her how you have seen the error of your ways and how you will be a better man in the future. Let us hope so; for if Mr Soames and I have cause to return then I am afraid that I will have to steal her heart away from you. I will take it and even take her pretty lips as well, and that's before my dear boss sticks you like swine. Come on, Soames, let's leave these lovebirds and hope that Sam here gives us good reason to come back here. Good-bye, Mr Weaver. I hope to see you again very soon.'

The men departed, and I, lost in tears and agony of my own, desperately tried to staunch the blood which pumped from the hole in Benjamin's leg, before untying Alice.

10

Deep and Grievous Wounds

The wound in Benjamin's leg was deep and wide; it would not stop bleeding no matter how much we bound it with torn sheets. He was pale, dangerously so, and slipped in and out of consciousness, seemingly unaware of his wound and complaining of how terribly cold he was.

'We need to get him to a doctor quickly!' I said to Alice, as she held him tightly to her. 'We should take him to Lock Hospital at the end of the road – there will be a doctor there who will know better than me how to stop this bleeding.'

I looked at her briefly; her eyes were locked on me. She had not spoken a word since our unwelcome visitors had left. She had not asked who the men were, or what my connection to them was.

'Let us help Benjamin, get him to a doctor and out of danger. Then I will explain everything to you, I promise,' I said. She began to cry small sobs of worry. I leaned over to kiss her on her forehead. 'They will not hurt you again, Alice. They will not hurt any of us again, I will not let them.' I took Benjamin from her. 'Come, before he loses any more blood.' I helped her to stand and we left my ruined rooms, all broken furniture, torn paper and bloody chaos.

Within minutes we burst through the doors at The Female Hospital, screaming for help. A trail of red had been left in our wake along the pavement of Amberley Road amid a sea of concerned faces, as people appeared at their doorways, watching Alice and I run sobbing towards the hospital, carrying Benjamin between us.

A small, bespectacled man stepped from behind his desk as we entered. 'This is a women's hospital,' he said. 'You will have to take him to St Mary's; they will help him.'

'He is dying!' I shouted. 'He will not make it to St Mary's; surely there is a doctor in the building who can help?'

At that moment a lean, sharply dressed man walked out from behind a set of doors to the side of the desk.

'What is the meaning of this commotion?' he asked.

'Please!' I cried. 'The boy needs immediate attention – he has a leg wound and is losing blood. There must be somebody here who can help us, or he will die.'

The gentleman looked me up and down before glancing at Alice, who was herself the worse for wear as a result of the treatment meted out to her.

'Bring him this way,' he said, opening the doors behind him. He turned to the old man at the desk as I carried Benjamin past. 'Mr Umbridge, please send to St Mary's, inform them of our situation and ask for the assistance of Herbert Holmes; he owes me a favour.'

The man wore a smartly brushed, black woollen suit, and looked as if he had never worked a day in his life; however, the leather bag which he now held at his side showed him to be a doctor – Doctor J. P. Lubbock to be precise.

'Put him on there. And keep pressure in the wound; press as hard as you can!' ordered the doctor, as we entered a large examination room with a cushioned bed in the middle. Thankfully it seemed that, in the case of Dr Lubbock, we had found a medical man confident of treating emergencies.

'I do not suppose you will tell me exactly how the boy came upon this injury?' the doctor said, examining the wound, which began to bleed anew as I removed my hands.

'They were accosted on the Harrow Road, not half a mile from here,' I answered, the lie slipping effortlessly from my tongue. 'The man ran away when he saw me approaching. I did not give chase as I knew that the boy was in danger.'

'You were right, of course.' The doctor stuck his finger into the hole, which brought a muffled groan from the semi-conscious boy. 'The wound is dangerously close to the femoral, although I think it has been merely nicked.'

'Will he die?' Alice asked, her eyes imploring the doctor for an answer.

'No, he will not die,' he returned sharply. 'Although he will need hospital treatment for his wound and he will be weak from his loss of blood. The man who did this to you, do you know him?'

'I do not, sir; I didn't catch a good look at him. He just came out of nowhere, and attacked my brother and myself. He scarpered when this kind man came to our assistance.' Alice forced a smile at me then.

'Well, your brother does indeed have a lot to thank this gentleman for. He will have lasting injuries but his life can be saved. When my man from St Mary's arrives we will dress the wound as best we can, and get him sent to a more suitably equipped hospital.'

'Any costs, sir. Whatever it takes, I will gladly pay it to secure the boy's health,' I said, taking Benjamin's hand in my own.

'You are a rare man,' the doctor said, eyeing me. 'I am sure that the child will thank you for your aid in the future.'

At that moment the door opened and another man breezed in. He briefly surveyed the scene and nodded in a friendly manner at both Alice and myself, before removing his jacket and addressing the doctor.

'Good lord, John,' he exclaimed, a smile upon his face. 'I thought you left all this behind to look after your French-gout-ridden fire-ships!' He waved Alice and me away. 'Come on then, let a real doctor through – let's see if we can't help this boy and get him back to my ward before he contracts a bout of some female malady from this place.'

The grin upon his face was infectious to a degree, and his confident manner sent a cool breath to my heart as I realised that Benjamin would come through this with his life. Within twenty minutes a carriage from the hospital arrived for the boy and, after thanking Dr Lubbock for his aid, we left for St Mary's with the eternally jovial Dr Holmes.

***

The last time that I saw my mother I was nineteen years old. I admit that I had rarely visited her; I hated hospitals, the smell, the cloying sickness that surrounded me as I entered and the sense of decay and death which seemed to be inherent in the very brickwork. The experience of forcing myself to make the journey to see her drew the life from me, leaving me sullen. The ward in which Mother was held, although lightly painted and high ceilinged, felt oppressive to anyone entering. For the residents, those who had no choice but to remain within the walls of the building, it would seem that there were some benefits to being unsound of mind. Lucidity and clarity of thought, for these poor unfortunates, were rare, not just owing to their partic-ular brand of madness and hysteria, but because of the very fact that they were held within such walls, surrounded by other fragile minds. Indeed, in the case of my own mother, I always felt that had she not been committed to such an institution she would have recovered from whatever ill had caused Father to imprison her.

When last I saw her she was greatly changed from the days when she had been taken from our home some five years earlier; she had aged in those few years and had become pale and drawn, as if she were little more than a ghost of the person she once had been. Her eyes, once so full of blue sparkle and delight at my presence, were now dull and grey with large shadows hanging beneath them. She had always been a lady who had taken so much pride and care in her appearance, but this was gone now; any self-respect had crumbled with her heart and sanity when these were broken by the man she loved.

Father never visited her to my knowledge. He told me that he did, often stating that he would be going to The Retreat to see her and always coming back a few hours later with news of her well-being; but I knew that this was not the case. There were no entries by him in the visitor's book in the main atrium and I took the time to speak to the attendants, whose care Mother was under, to ask them of other visitors; there were none. I had long since known that my father had given up on my mother in the pursuit of his other interests.

Whenever I pushed myself into a visitation, my time with her was often short, for my stomach churned and a bitter taste sat in my mouth just to look at her. We did not speak any more than a few words to each other. I would offer her vague and paltry news of home and the gardens, and she would answer in a brief dull manner. When I left, it would always be a hurried affair; I would take her hand briefly before kissing her gently on the forehead and bustling past the atten-dants into the fresh air outside. Each time, following my exit, I would walk the five minutes to the centre of York to drown my sorrows, sitting sullenly and lost in dark thoughts, daring myself never to visit her again.

Father never asked me about my visits and, in truth, I do not know what I would have said to him if he had. We hardly spoke at all in the months prior to my leaving for London. I had nothing to say to the man and, when the time came that we did at last speak frankly to one another, it was the last time that any word was uttered between us.

***

Dr Holmes had been a saint to us, and especially towards Benjamin. He had taken us personally to St Mary's and accompanied the boy on his stretcher, talking gaily to him all the way, until we reached the ward. There Benjamin had been tended to by the kindly nurses and given a draught to ease the pain. Holmes left us for a short while, returning to swiftly stitch and dress the wound whilst the boy was mercifully unconscious.

'He will sleep through the night,' Holmes told me after taking me aside. 'I have given instructions that you and the young lady may stay with him if you wish. And I will return in the morning to see how the little man is doing. I do not doubt that he will be able to go home after a short stay with us.' He placed a hand upon my shoulder. 'He will be in considerable pain for some time I would imagine, and he will probably require a stick of some kind; I doubt if he will ever run anywhere again.'

The good doctor shook my hand warmly and departed with a wave to Alice, who was still in shock from the whole ordeal. The happy nature and gentle attentions of Holmes, combined with the traumatic circumstances, had caused me to forget that I was standing within a hospital, something which would have normally filled me with revulsion.

I returned to Benjamin's bedside, where Alice sat holding the sleeping boy's hand.

'Alice, I need to explain,' I said, sitting beside her and placing my arm around her shoulder. She did not resist my affections, but instead turned to sink into my embrace, sobbing quietly. We sat there for a while in silence until finally she removed her head from my chest and spoke.

'Tell me now, Sam. I am ready to listen.'

And so I told her. I told her of my obsession with the killer Sibelius Darke and of how my investigations had led me to Lord Falconer. I told her of the Dolorian Club and of how I suspected that they were also behind the current spate of murders in the area. I told her of Abe Thomas and his death at the hands of the hooded killer and finally, with regret, I told her of the true nature of Frederick Draper's visit and of how I had ignored his veiled threats towards her and Benjamin.

All the while she listened intently and, when I had finished, she did not react with anger, as I had feared, but instead was quiet and kind, telling me that I had been doing the right thing in trying to expose the men behind the murders. For a while we sat in gentle conversation and I vowed to her that this would be the end of it, that I would not push either Alice or her brother further into danger.

'I have decided that you and Benjamin should go to stay at my family home in York for a while, until all of this settles down,' I said as I held both of her hands within my own. 'You will be safe there and the housekeeper, Mrs Coleman, will look after the two of you like you were her own. It will not be for long and I will come up to York to collect you myself when all of this has gone away. Please, Alice. Do this for me, do this for all of us.'

'But what about you, Sam? How can you expect me to leave you to the mercy of those terrible men?'

'I will be fine,' I replied. 'And I would be more content if I knew that you and Benjamin were out of harm's way. No one will touch you in York, I promise you, and I can protect myself better if I do not have to worry about your safety.'

Reluctantly she agreed and in the early hours of the morning she climbed onto the bed with Benjamin and slept. I bothered one of the nurses for some writing paper and a pen so that I could write to my family home in York.

I will not divulge the full details of my letter, other than to say that it started with an apology for my hasty departure and the dearth of communication from me since. The rest of the letter was lies, to a point. I said that I was successful in my job, that my editor and the owner of the newspaper found me irreplaceable. I said that I had met a delightful young woman, Alice, who had moved into my home with her brother and they were both as close as family to me now. Unfortunately, however, due to incidents related to Alice and her brother's background it was not safe for them to remain in London at the moment. The lies flowed easily. I was of course a writer and as such my aptitude for fiction was inbuilt. Finally, I asked that they be looked after for a short while and that I would, despite what I had said in the past, travel up at the soonest opportunity.

The letter finished, I settled back in my chair and, with a last lingering look at my new family asleep before me, I closed my eyes and rested until morning came.

***

Surprisingly, I received a reply to my letter promptly. One week later Mrs Coleman met us at King's Cross station and, after overprotective fussing, long embraces and promises to be reunited shortly, I watched the little party wave from the carriage window as the train pulled away.

I stood on the platform until the train disappeared fully from view before leaving the station and hailing a hansom to take me to the Strand and the offices of *The Illustrated Police News*. My employers had, most surprisingly, been very understanding of my recent absence. As far as George Purkess and Henry Cope were aware, I had been forced to travel to York to attend the funeral of my mother and to assist dear Father in the ordering of her affairs. As I strode through the doors of the offices I even saw a hint of sympathy in the eyes of Cope (his own elderly mother having passed away not three months earlier, a fact of which I was aware and which formed the basis for my lie).

'Hello, Mr Cope,' I said, my voice suitably subdued and tears welling in my eyes to complete the picture. 'I am sorry for my absence. It has been a very trying time and I am grateful for your understanding.'

Cope looked as awkward as I had ever seen the man.

'Do not mention it, Mr Weaver,' he said. 'A death in the family is a terrible thing for all concerned. Of course you were aware of my own mother's demise. I understand what you have had to deal with. Mr Purkess also passes on his condolences.'

'Thank you again, Mr Cope. Tell me, is he in at present? I very much hoped to see him in person to thank him for his patience.'

'No, I am afraid not. He has not been in all week in fact – family matters of his own. He has sent messengers every day, of course, requesting news of this week's edition and making decisions on stories as always. I will let him know that you have returned.'

'I would be most grateful. Shall I return to my rooms and await your call?'

'Yes, there is always work and I shall no doubt be in contact presently. We have a new contact in the police who has asked after you personally, an Inspector George Langton. He has taken on poor Inspector Thomas's position.'

'He asked for me?'

'Yes, nice man he seemed. He said he had followed and enjoyed your work immensely in the past and wondered when you would be sent to attend an incident with him. I shall of course let him know that you are back, if you wish?'

My back stiffened somewhat. 'Of course, I would be glad to meet him when the opportunity arises,' I said. 'Send a boy around when I'm required. And once again thank you. It is good to know who your friends are in such difficult times.' I shook his hand and left, wondering if this Langton was indeed a follower of my work or, more likely, attached to the Dolorian Club and Falconer.

Over the next week some work did trickle through from Mr Cope, some of which was of the dull court variety, while other pieces included post-incident interviews and accompanying sketches of robberies, beatings and fires. I was thankful for the work when it arrived, but also enjoyed the spare time that I had, during which I worked at home on my written manuscript of the Sibelius Darke affair. I had decided to cut my losses and halt the investigations into Lord Falconer and the Dolorian Club. I had lost enough from my blundering and was glad that I had come out of the ordeal with both Alice and Benjamin still alive. I would send my completed work to Mr Purkess, but I would leave it up to him as to if and when it was published. My time with Alice and her brother had shown me that there were greater things in life.

I received letters from Alice and Benjamin on an almost daily basis, telling me of how well they had settled into my old family home and of how warm and loving both Mrs Coleman and Mr Morgan were towards the pair of them. Benjamin had been enrolled in a local school and was very much looking forward to starting his lessons, while Alice had begun the search for work in York.

I missed them both. It was strange to me that, although they had been a part of my life for such a short time, they had left a void and I often returned to my rooms expecting to find them there waiting for me; Benjamin desperate to know where I had been and Alice smiling and warm, happy to see me. In those two weeks, following their move up to York, I struggled at times and wondered how I had ever been so content on my own.

***

I had begun to sink into a funk. At times I even thought of packing up and heading back up north myself to be reunited with Benjamin and Alice, even if it meant facing up to my past indiscretions. This changed, however, after I arrived home one evening from a particularly nasty stabbing outside the Crown and Anchor in the Strand. The incident itself came as quite a shock to me as I had actually witnessed the crime in question.

I had stopped in for a drink on my way home after dropping off some sketches at the office, when an argument started between two men at the bar. I recognised one of the men, Neil Bates, a man well known locally as someone who dealt in stolen and smuggled goods. I do not know the true cause of the argument but I could guess that it would be one of two reasons: money or women. The voices of the men rose to a point where all other conversation in the bar stopped.

'You cheated me, Batesy!' the smaller man snarled. 'I bought them fish off you in good faith – you said they was fresh! They was rotten within a day!'

'And they was,' replied Bates. 'They was fresh when I got 'em and I sold 'em to you the same day. What you do with them after you hand over yer money is up to you. Don't you go blaming me.'

The men suddenly noticed the silence around them and Bates got up to leave, finishing the argument with a particularly coarse reference to the family history of the other. The door had just closed on the departee, when the smaller man charged out of the pub, bottle in hand.

Like most others in the bar, I raced after him, not necessarily to stop the inevitable assault but more to witness it. I reached the open doorway just in time to see the bottle broken over the head of Bates, and the remaining broken glass jammed hard into his throat and pulled outwards, causing the skin on his neck to turn to ribbon. In that moment all time seemed to freeze and, as I later drew to horrifying effect, a huge spurt of blood shot outwards covering all within its reach, including me. The attacker threw his weapon to the ground, where it smashed into pieces on the paving slabs, and immediately ran off down the road, closely chased by a number of men. I, however, found myself catching the falling victim, and attempted with great futility to stop the blood from flowing from his neck wound. By the time the police arrived on the scene there was no more blood left to flow and I was sat on the sodden ground cradling a bled-out corpse. Neil Bates had suffered the consequences of his final dodgy deal.

And so it was that, not one hour later, I traipsed slowly back to my rooms covered from head to foot in drying blood, and wondering how on earth I was to get my best suit cleaned to a degree where I would ever feel comfortable wearing it again. As I opened the door I was shocked to discover a figure waiting for me in the doorway of my kitchen.

'Oh good God, Sam!' she cried. 'Please tell me that that is not your blood!'

'Alice, what are you doing here? Where is Benjamin?' I thought for a fleeting moment to run into her arms, such was my joy at the sight of her, but my present state prevented such an action.

'Benjamin is fine,' she said. 'He is under the care of Dr Furnbridge, whom I understand you know, and is looking forward to starting at his new school. He is in good spirits, although he misses you dearly. Mrs Coleman fusses over him, although she continuously calls him Arthur and then stops and curses herself. Who is Arthur, is he a boy you knew?'

I bit my lip for a moment before speaking. 'Arthur? No, I have never heard of him before. Perhaps she had a son of her own once, although I'm sure I would have known of him. Anyway, tell me about Benjamin, is he truly happy?'

'He is, in part.'

'In part – what do you mean, in part?'

'He has seen how unhappy I am without you, Sam. It was his idea that I return, although he wants me to persuade you to go back to York so that we can all be together. But enough of that – this blood, where is it from? Please do not tell me that you are still in danger?'

'No, I think that the danger is past for now. Life has been… well, a little dull without the pair of you around.'

I bathed and changed. Alice cooked us both a meal prepared with whatever meagre provisions she could find in the cupboard, a place which had quickly reverted to its bachelor state.

'I thought of going to see Mr Tandry tomorrow, to find out whether there's any work for me still. It would help to see us through until you get work back in York.'

'York?' I said coughing slightly.

'Yes, York, like I said. Well, now Benjamin is settled, I thought that it would be good for us to move to York and start a new life there.'

'New life?'

'Oh come now, Samuel. Do not tell me that you have forgotten your promises from not two weeks ago? You told us both that we would be able to start a new life once things had settled down. Why not in York? You have a home there, Benjamin is happy. I'm sure that you would easily get a good job with one of the newspapers there. Maybe you could even find someone to publish your Sibelius Darke story.'

'I want *The Illustrated Police News* to publish it. That has been the plan for years – that has always been the plan. London will be safe for us all soon, I am sure. Benjamin can come back; you can get more work through Tandry. Our future is here, Alice. I cannot go back to York.'

'But why?'

'Because... because I do not believe in going back,' I snapped. 'I have left that place behind – and all it represents!'

'But what of Benjamin?'

'Benjamin will not stay in York a moment longer than he has to. Please stop now, Alice. I cannot talk about this any more.' I stood from the table and carried our plates to the kitchen.

'But, Sam, I do not understand,' she called after me. 'I know that you left York under some kind of cloud, but that doesn't have to be a problem for us.'

I paused. The anger I felt was not towards her and in that moment I wanted to tell her everything about the reasons that I fled York – but I couldn't.

'It is more than that, Alice. Much more, but I will not talk about it. I will not talk about anything to do with moving back there. This discussion is over.'

Although she followed me to the kitchen, she did not press me any further on the subject. Our conversation was polite and cordial and I wished that I could have opened my heart to her, but I did not. For now, I was glad that she had returned to me and the wound created when she and Benjamin left was partially healed.

***

The following day, Alice did indeed visit Mr Tandry, who was most pleased to see her. According to Alice, he nearly tripped over his own feet in his excitement when she walked through the doors of his office on Marylebone Road. There would 'of course, ha ha!' be work for someone of Alice's quality; in fact, she could head straight up the road to a nearby address in her uniform and say that Mr Tandry had sent her. The work, he said, would be regular and long standing if she proved her worth. She returned to me shortly afterwards to change into the grey dress that Mr Tandry had provided.

I was sitting at my desk putting the finishing touches to a truly terrifying picture related to a scene that I had attended earlier in the week. Builders renovating a nearby convent on Earl's Street had uncovered what they first thought was an ancient priest hole. In fact, it transpired that the dark and musty space that they had found beyond a bricked and plastered wall at the back of the chapel was no more than one hundred years old and contained the skeletons of no less than three nuns, still dressed in their habits. This situation was a pure blessing for me and I threw myself into creating something which would stun Purkess and his readers. I needed something to push myself back into the limelight and make myself indispensable once more. In my mind, the threat from Falconer and the Dolorian Club had now passed and it was time to return to my rightful place at the top of Old George's list.

Alice was almost hysterical with excitement, happy to be back with me and filled with eagerness to impress her new employer.

'This is a great chance for me to help build something for us,' came her voice from the bedroom as she changed. 'I have thought about our discussion last night, Sam. If this works out for me then I think we could arrange for Benjamin to come back to us, in time for him to start at St Stephen's as we originally planned.'

'Mm,' I replied. The words had gone in; however, I was deeply engrossed in my work.

She spoke again but, I confess, I did not hear her words. In fact, I heard very little more of what she said. It concerned 'new beginnings' and 'putting our troubles behind us', yet my mind was elsewhere.

I was shaken from my concentration when she danced through from the bedroom and landed in my lap, throwing her arms around my neck.

'When will you be back tonight?' I asked.

'I think it will be sometime after midnight. Apparently there is a special function this evening. It is the perfect opportunity to make a good impression, Mr Tandry says.'

'Then go and do your impressing,' I said with a smile, kissing her lightly on the cheek. 'I shall be here when you return, probably still working on this damned picture.'

With a final embrace she breezed out of our home and I spent a short moment looking towards the closed door with a warm feeling inside. Perhaps she was right, I thought; perhaps this was where everything changed for us.

And I was correct; for she did not return.

11

A Bringer of Death

My only job, before coming down to London, was as a junior correspondent at the *York Herald*. Most of my days were spent running their errands, a job which I hated and abused as often as possible, taking myself off to wander the streets, observing and sketching as I had done when a child.

After one year of service I was finally given the opportunity to show my skills when, from nowhere and quite to my surprise, I was asked to help on a story for one of the senior writers, Jack Bartlett. Mr Bartlett had always been a man whom I had held in greater esteem than his colleagues due to his morbid interests in the darker side of city life. Although I possessed a higher degree of awe and respect for the man, I craved his job and saw myself as usurping Jack Bartlett at my soonest opportunity. I was superior in terms of the vivid realities of my writing and the added bonus of the picture portrayals which I could also offer. He knew this; I had made it clear to him. I had shown him my work and my art, and I had told him that I wished to be in his position as soon as my work was recognised. At that time I did not think it bothered him. He was a confident man with years of experience – what fear could he have of me, a mere upstart boy?

One particular day Jack took me aside and told me how he wished to nurture my talents and help me on my way. He had been investigating a number of brothels in the area which, rumour had it, were controlled and owned not by the criminal classes but by a small group of seemingly respectable gentlemen about town. This fellowship kept these houses running in town both for their own uses and for the revenue and profits which they could bring in. Jack was well known in the city, and would undoubtedly be turned away should he attempt to gain entry to one of these establishments. I, however, was an unknown, the perfect person to avail myself of their services whilst collecting clues as to the true ownership of these establishments. I could also use my artistic skills to portray their degradation and sordidness in all of their nasty glory, capturing the faces of those within and of the girls who earned their shilling. I would, of course, he told me, be given the recognition due to me for assisting him in this project. I was simply to attend one of the brothels over the course of a few nights and, after making my excuses, leave and accurately draw and make notes on what I had seen. This would be the making of my career; it was all but assured.

I had decided upon a story that I would tell if asked regarding my background; I was to be a solicitor visiting York.

I was nervous of my task, although kept this well hidden, as I had promised myself that I would not throw away this golden opportunity. Mr Bartlett had given me a list of the brothels and suggested that I visit one on Fossgate first, which was renowned in the area as the place for well-known gentlemen about town to visit.

I approached the tall, smooth painted door with not a little tension; although confident of my ability to lie and give the appearance of someone I was not, I was still a young man who had had very little experience of dealing with womenfolk, not least those womenfolk who plied their trade through sin and iniquity.

There was no bell or knocker in sight, and at first I wondered whether the address that Bartlett had given me had been false, for there was no sound coming from within. With less force or confidence than I would have liked or intended, I rapped upon the wood with my knuckles. There was no answer at first and still no noise from within, and I began to wonder if there was some type of coded knock required, upon which the riches and joys of the brothel were unlocked to the visiting gentleman. I knocked again, this time with slightly greater force, and, at last, I heard the rough sliding of deadbolts from inside and the rattling of a key in the large lock. The door began to open and I was immediately struck by noise as loud music and laughter rang out of the slowly opening crack. As it opened wider the door frame was immediately filled by a smartly dressed man of impressive size and threatening face. His head was high domed and looked almost polished in the light of the gas lamps.

'Are you expected?' he boomed down at me.

I did not answer immediately; I found myself staring up at the man with an open mouth that would normally mark me as slow witted.

'I... er... no,' I stuttered; my lips, it seemed, were not fully under my control. 'I do not think that I am expected. I was given this address by a work colleague who told me to pay a visit if I were ever in the area. Perhaps I have made a mistake.' Suddenly the thought of entering such a place twisted my stomach and I cursed my own overconfidence at putting myself in this situation.

'Well that all depends, boy,' the man said, his face relaxing with a warmth that I only supposed was sarcasm. 'This colleague of yours, did he tell you what to expect once you had entered? Did he give vivid detail to his recommendation?'

'Why no, sir!' I proclaimed. 'He is a gentleman and would not openly discuss such matters. He merely told me that if I wished to see a different side of York and I had money to spend on... company, then this was the place to visit. Was he wrong? If he was then I can only apologise and take my leave.' I began to turn but felt a large paw upon my shoulder.

'Money to spend, eh?' His eyebrows raised a touch. 'If it's money you have, then this may be the place for you. Why don't you step inside for a while and see if we have anything that takes your fancy.' With the grip of his hand still firmly in place he drew me inside.

In truth I had not been fully prepared for the attack on the senses that the interior of this house brought upon me. I stepped immediately into a large lounge area, busy with both young girls and men old enough to be their fathers. They drank and cavorted, danced and lay upon the long, soft seats which littered the room. The noise was varied and loud and I wondered why I had not heard it from the street outside; there was laughter filling the room, from light, tinkling giggles to raucous, hearty guffaws, which seemed to burst from every corner. The music being played was that of the music halls, bawdy and coarse, hammered out on an upright piano by a wide older woman, who encouraged those about her to sing along. The lighting of the house was varied too; lamps hung from the walls, casting a soft glow down upon those in their range, yet these areas of warmth were offset by corners of darkness where it was difficult to make out exactly what went on, the only signs being shifting limbs and shadowed faces.

The atmosphere was smoky both from the cigars shared by amorous couples and also from hookah pipes, of which there were a few placed around the room. The scent that they gave off was decidedly not from tobacco; it was more heady and perfumed, full of sharp spice and soft flowers. The air made my eyes water, a powerful and overpowering change from the fresh night of the street.

I am sure that my expression of wide-eyed innocence did no harm to the character which I wished to portray to those inside, but it is true to say that I had never experienced a place such as this in my young life. To see such obvious debauchery and flagrant immorality set out in all of its terrible glory both shocked and, I am ashamed to say, stirred private feelings within me that I would not normally reveal in such a public place. My open-mouthed wonder was, of course, noted by my guide, who shook me from my stupor by slapping me suddenly between my shoulder blades.

'Was this perhaps not what you were expecting, young sir?' he laughed, leering. 'Let me get you introduced and see if we cannot turn that look of yours into a smile. Isabelle!' he called to a woman on the other side of the room, who was facing away from me and talking to a pair of older gentlemen. 'Isabelle, we have a new visitor. Won't you come over and give him the benefit of your welcome!'

As she turned I saw that she was, without doubt, the most attractive woman whom I had ever laid my young eyes upon. Her hair was a dark red in colour and, although pinned up in tight curls, I could tell that it was unnaturally long. Her green eyes were wide and inviting, almost innocent in their aspect – almost. She floated across the room to where I stood and smiled warmly at me, a look which I attempted to return. I must have looked every bit the young and callow fool, out of my depth and grinning like a simpleton.

'Good evening,' she said, holding out a long-gloved hand for me to receive. 'I do not think I have seen you within our sugared walls before. I am Isabelle; I am here to make your visit memorable. Would you like a drink? We have most kinds.'

'A drink would be most welcome, miss,' I stammered, feeling the flush of my face lighting up the room. 'Brandy would be good at this time.'

She laughed gently, and walked to the trolley at the side of the room where she filled a glass, which I am glad to say was large in its volume.

'Tell me,' she said as she passed it to my grateful fingers. 'How is it that such a charming young man has not graced my eyes before? Are you new to York?'

I took a large gulp of the drink.

'I am from Leeds,' I said. 'Here on business for the evening. I travel back tomorrow. A colleague told me that I could not stay a night in York without paying your house a visit and may I now say that I can see why.' I wore my most charming smile, although later I imagined it to be weak and boyish.

Our conversation continued, if a little stilted in places. However, despite my best attempts at social pleasantries, together with her obvious skills at making gentlemen feel comfortable, I cringed inside at my feeble abilities to talk to the opposite sex. I was also very distracted by my need to observe the men in the room, some of whom I recognised as well known in York. Others that were not known to me I studied as closely as I dared; I planned to make carefully drawn studies of these men after leaving this place.

I took two more large drinks before I came across the large obstacle that I had expected to encounter.

'So tell me,' my hostess said, as bold as you like. 'What takes your fancy? Anything in the room?' She placed her hand on my arm and gently motioned around the room to the various young ladies who appeared to be unattended at the time.

A bead of sweat broke on my brow.

'Well it's, er... I do not know quite what to say,' I stumbled. 'I mean, they all look most delightful. Perhaps I could just step outside again and get a breath of fresh air? It seems awfully hot in here all of a sudden.'

I started to turn, looking towards the door, but my arm was suddenly held tightly by Isabelle. She nodded to the large bald man at the door who quickly rushed over to where I stood and, laughing, threw his arm around my shoulder.

To all around it would have looked like he was an old friend embracing and guiding me but, I can assure you, this was no friendly gesture and he used his obvious strength to lead me away from the door and up the stairs.

'Don't you worry,' Isabelle whispered into my ear, as we followed her up. 'You aren't the first young man to get hit by a case of the collywobbles on his first visit, and I have no doubt that you won't be the last. I have someone upstairs who we keep for such occasions and who would just love to spend time with you.'

The drink had suddenly hit me quite hard and the staircase began to spin. If it had not been for the large man, half carrying me up the stairs, then I am sure that I would have fallen.

'No, really,' I slurred. 'I think if you would just let me get some air...'

We reached the top of the stairs, where the large man pushed me up against the wall next to a closed door. He reached into my coat pocket, pulling out my wallet.

Isabelle knocked gently on the door and entered.

'Charlotte, I have a young man who is keen to make your acquaintance.' She turned her head to the man, who had now emptied my wallet. 'How long does he get, Harold?'

'I'd say a good hour, Isabelle,' he replied, taking me by the shoulders and pushing me into the room. 'There you go, fella.'

I stumbled into the dimly lit room to see an older woman sitting on the bed with a drink in her hand. She was large, impressively so, and wore little clothing. I stood for a moment staring at her. Both Isabelle and the man, Harold, stood behind me.

'Well then, boy,' said she on the bed. 'Are you coming over here or do I have to get up and come to you?'

The couple behind me laughed and turned to leave, Harold giving me one last slap on the back. I felt drugged and hazy, as if caught in a dream. I did not move from where I stood. The woman got up from the bed and came towards me just as the door slammed behind me. It was a jolt which seemed to wake me from my stupor.

As the large woman came close to me I threw my hands up, pushing her away, so that she tripped backwards, landing heavily on the floor. I turned and threw open the door, running out of the room towards the staircase.

Isabelle and Harold were halfway down the stairs when I neared them. I tried to shove my way in between them and found Harold to be an impervious brick wall of a man. Isabelle, however, was small and light – and my push sent her tumbling down the stairs. Harold threw his arms around me, pinning mine to my sides, and we both watched as Isabelle landed at the bottom of the stairs with a sickening thud, her head bent sideways at an impossible angle.

In that small moment all time stood quite still and I looked at her beautiful face, her pale green eyes and her wide, red-painted lips which were parted, and from which now began to leak the smallest tear of blood.

Harold released me from his hold, ran down the stairs to her and crouched over her body, holding her head as if to put it straight again. I found myself following him, my feet slowly tripping down each step in shock. As I reached the bottom and looked down at the dead girl, Harold suddenly lurched upwards at me, his large boulder of a fist connecting with the side of my face.

The world span violently before sinking into darkness.

***

I awoke with a start. I had been dreaming of chasing a young woman whose face I was unable to clearly define. It was as if I was looking at her through thick fog, her features fading in and out of sight but never truly in focus. We were running through a large house and I could not tell if she was scared and in fear of me, or if this was some sort of game of tig like children play. Each time that she came within reach I stumbled and she slipped through my grasp. I was becoming frustrated – angry even. Why could I not catch her?

We ran along a wide landing, lit by candles, at the top of a large staircase and suddenly I felt true cold fear. The chase was out of my control; she would slip and fall down the stairs, I had to stop her, to save her. I sped up and neared her once more, the staircase beckoning, almost sucking her towards it. As she reached the top step I threw myself forwards in an attempt to stop her from falling, but she was merely a shadow and I found myself tumbling through her form. As I hit the floor I began to roll down the stairs, feeling the sharp stab of each riser as it struck my body. I could see the bottom of the staircase approaching and I knew my death awaited me there. I closed my eyes, braced for the impact and woke.

It was dark in my sitting room; the last embers of the fire were dwindling into barely noticeable orange flecks. I was sitting in my armchair, my drawing pad on my lap and on it a completed picture of two men pulling away crumbling bricks to reveal the skeletons of dead nuns. I could not remember completing it. I looked up and saw that the clock on my mantelpiece showed three o'clock in the morning and wondered whether Alice had returned whilst I had slept. There was no light on in the bedroom; perhaps she had found me asleep and decided that the armchair was the best place for me.

I pushed myself to my feet and stepped lightly towards the bedroom door. My eyes tried to focus as I peered into the darkness beyond and to my bed. It was empty and untouched. The party was going to be a big one, Alice had said; perhaps it was a particularly late one. I began to worry about her travelling home alone; the streets of Marylebone, although a great deal safer than their East End counterparts, were still no place for a young girl, and I cursed myself for not arranging to meet her. I could go out now and try to find her, but it would be hopeless; I did not know the house where she was working and might spend the rest of the night wandering the streets of Marylebone in vain. I placed some kindling on the ashes of my fire, blew it gently to life and settled back in my chair, my tired eyes on the clock upon my mantle.

I dreamt again, this time of a baby, no more than a few weeks old. The babe was laid in a cot which I had discovered at the foot of my bed. Unaided, the crib rocked gently, the small child sleeping deeply within. The child was pale, though, deathly so, and I found myself wondering if it was due to the terrible cold that I felt. As I approached I saw that upon the child's pale skin were cracks, as if it were made from porcelain like a doll, and I found myself reaching out to touch its skin to see if it were real.

As my fingers neared the child, the crib's rocking stopped suddenly and the tiny figure began to stir. The cold in the room sent chills through me, starting at my feet and quickly rising throughout my whole body, causing me to shiver. I withdrew my hand from the crib and folded my arms, rubbing my shoulders in an attempt to warm myself. The child's eyes opened and it stared up at me. It began to cry. A terrible sound which sent shots of pain to my ears. I was dreaming! This was a dream! Why was I standing here listening to this horrible sound? I shook myself violently. I had to wake! I had be free from this terrible noise!

I awoke laid on the floor in front of the dead fire. Sunlight streamed through my window, blinding me, sending a pain into my head. My clothes were damp and cold with sweat and I forced myself to my feet. Looking up at the mantle, I saw that it was nearly nine o'clock. Alice had still not returned and immediately all thoughts of my own pain and shock disappeared. This was not right; she should be back with me by now. Without thinking, I made straight for the door.

***

When I arrived at the Marylebone Service Agency the doors were locked and there was no sign of life. Noting a small coffee shop across the road, I went in and took a window seat where I could watch the agency's doors from a place of warmth and comfort.

I am usually a patient man; it does not bother me one jot when others are late for appointments. I am most happy in my own company and others' tardiness only reflects badly on them, not me. On this day, however, as I wondered about Alice's whereabouts, I could not have been more agitated at having to bide my time. I constantly glanced at my pocket watch, cursing as the minutes crawled by at a lacklustre rate. This would not do, I told myself. Ten more minutes and I would head off to the police station to report her missing.

It was as I paid my bill and stood to leave that I saw the outlandish figure of Tandry strolling down the road as leisurely as you like. He was dressed in a suit of bright green velvet, a colour which was only drowned out by the glare of his curled red hair. I could see why he had taken so long to reach the agency as he seemed to stop and talk to everyone he passed, laughing and cajoling them, slapping shoulders and shaking hands, a broad smile fixed upon his face.

As he neared the doors of the agency I ran over the road to meet him.

'Mr Tandry!' I called, waving to get his attention. 'Mr Tandry, might I have a word with you?'

As he looked up and saw me approaching I could see some confusion in his eyes; he obviously could not instantly remember our last meeting. Without taking his gaze from me he withdrew a large set of keys from his pocket and began to pick out the one he required.

'Good morning, sir. Ha ha! And it is a fine morning, is it not? Full of sunshine and hope. Ha!' He thrust the correct key into the lock and pushed his way inside the door.

I followed him in.

'Work is it, young man? Work that you are looking for? I have plenty for a bright young gentleman like yourself. Plenty to do.'

'No,' I said, trailing him around the office as he took off his coat and hat. 'You do not remember me, do you, Mr Tandry? I came in here a few weeks since with a young lady and you kindly arranged some work for her. Alice Griffiths, I am quite sure you remember her.'

His eyes flicked downwards quickly and the smile on his face took on a fixed and mask-like countenance.

'My dear man, a great many people pass through these doors, yes they do, a great many. And unfortunately I am not the young gentleman I once was, I can be dreadfully forgetful. A few weeks ago was it? Alice? I'm not sure I do recall her exactly.' He turned towards the large, dark-stained bookcase set on the wall and pulled down a ledger.

'Yes, a few weeks ago, I came in with her; her young brother was with us also. Surely if you do not remember that meeting you will remember seeing her yesterday? She came to you a little after two o'clock and you arranged some work for her, a party in Marylebone.

He had begun to open the ledger on his desk but stopped as I spoke, quickly closing it again.

'Yesterday, you say? Quite impossible. Yes, quite impossible. You see, I was not here yesterday, the agency was closed. Are you sure that it was here that she came? There are other agencies in the area, perhaps you are mistaken.' He placed the ledger back on the shelf and turned back, the smile now quite faded from his face.

'No, Mr Tandry, I am quite sure that it was you whom she saw. She returned home to me immediately and said as much.'

'I think I know the girl you speak of, but I can assure you she was not here yesterday.' He grasped my shoulder as if to lead me back to the door and out onto the street again. 'Now, if you will excuse me, I am a busy man, very busy. I have people to see today, yes, lots of people to see.'

'But she did not come home last night, Mr Tandry,' I implored, standing my ground. 'I am worried for her safety.'

He moved away from me then and sat down behind his desk. He let out a small laugh as he reached for the drawer at his right side.

'Young man, if I had to deal with all of the problems of gentlemen in London whose ladies received a better offer and did not return to them, then I should be a far sight busier than I already am, a far sight.'

I watched his hand as it slid into the drawer; I saw the grip of a pistol.

I threw myself across the desk, sending both of us crashing to the floor. My fist struck him twice on the side of the head but I am no pugilist and my punches did little more than cause him to fight even harder. I sat on his chest as he struggled violently, attempting to throw me off. I continued to hit him, each time with greater force. The blood sprayed upon the floor and walls around us.

Time and again I struck him, and he reached up with short arms trying to deflect my blows, trying to reach for my throat. I had lost all control now and brushed his arms aside, pinning them to the floor. With him finally under my power, I spoke.

'Where is she?' I demanded. 'Where is Alice Griffiths?'

With blood-stained teeth he smiled at me then. After all that I had done to him – he smiled.

'Speak!' I yelled. 'Speak! Tell me where you sent her. Tell me where she is!'

But speak he did not. Instead he laughed at me, a terrible gargled laugh which spat blood up at my face, red, wet flecks which covered me.

This man did not fear me and he would not tell me what I needed to know. I trembled in anger, and looked towards the pistol which had been knocked from his hand to the floor by the doorway – too far. I reached onto the desk, grabbing a large glass ashtray.

Slowly I brought it into his view. His expression did not change and he continued to chuckle, an act which only increased my anger. I struck him with the ashtray. He died instantly, but I did not stop. Again and again I brought the heavy glass down onto his face.

I sat for a short while on his corpse. The room was almost silent, the only sound my own ragged breath, as I sought to compose myself whilst looking down at my handiwork. Tears ran down my face, mixing with the flecks of Tandry's blood that decorated me. What had I done? What was it within me that made me a bringer of death?

My tears turned to wracking sobs and I fell sideways from the man I had killed, laying on the floor beside him. For a while I stayed there, staring blankly up at the walls, which had not escaped Tandry's dotted decoration.

As my eyes scanned the room, they fell upon the clock on the wall; I could not lie here all day, it would not be long before someone tried the door of the agency and peered through the window to see the pair of us, killer and victim laid down together in stillness.

Rolling to my feet, I dragged Tandry's body into the back room. There was a small kitchen and a door which led into the back alley of the shop fronts. Returning to the main office, I locked the entrance door and hastily scribbled a note saying that the agency would be closed until further notice. With luck the body would not be discovered for a few days. I made to leave through the back door, pausing momentarily to return to the office. There I retrieved both pistol and ledger before making my escape.

12

They Come in the Night

I awoke in darkness and pain. My head swam as if immersed in brandy, and I could feel the left side of my face swelling and throbbing intensely. What little light there was filtered through the roughly woven hessian sack over my head. I went to remove it but my hands were immobile, tied behind my back as I lay upon the floor. The room stank of stale alcohol, of beer long since flat and soaked into the boards on which I lay.

I could hear distant mumbled voices, as if on the other side of a door; words spoken in anger.

I shook my head slightly, trying to wake myself from the stupor that had been forced on me by the thundering fist of the man named Harold. I do not believe I would have been less stunned and damaged by his hand had it been made of brick itself.

I thought of Isabelle, lying prone at the foot of the stairs, her neck twisted, the bones at the top of her spine attempting to force themselves free from within the pale smooth skin of her throat. It was an accident; surely they would see that? It was not intentional in the least; why would I ever want to kill the girl?

The voices outside the door grew louder and then stopped suddenly, falling into an edged silence, only broken by the sound of a key rattling in the door. Heavy footfalls followed and large rough hands picked me up and sat me on a chair, causing me to let out a feeble groan. My hands, still bound behind me, were pressed against the back of the chair, the wooden spindles pushing hard into my wrists.

As the sacking was pulled from my head, and my eyes adjusted to the light, I could see Harold standing in front of me. He did not look a happy man.

I made to speak but the raised palm of his right paw was enough to quiet me.

'It seems you have provided me with a problem, boy,' he said quietly, with the expression of one looking upon an errant nephew. Pulling up a chair to sit opposite me, he continued, 'You see, when young lads like you come through the door, not knowing their arse from their elbow and generally making a mess of the place, then I am of a mind to take you straight out the back and beat you into a bloody pulp. But unfortunately I am not the person to make these kinds of decisions. I am just a simple doorman, hired to keep the peace and to beat, break and evict any whom I am told to.' He reached into his pocket and withdrew a carved ivory cigarette case, opening it and pulling out one of the white sticks within. He closed the case swiftly, then tapped the cigarette on the ivory before raising it to his lips.

The silence pulled knives through me as I waited for him to continue.

'I love my job,' he said, blowing a large gust of smoke into the air above my head. 'I get to be in the gracious company of the ladies of the house; I will usually have a small drink or two as the night goes on and sometimes I get to use my fists to crush the face of someone who won't pay their bills when they're asked nicely.'

He took another large drag on his cigarette, the end of which glowed menacingly red in my direction, and continued. 'But this is why tonight's turn of events has brought me so much sorrow, for it is not I who gets to choose the men that get a beating. No, that job, on most nights, fell to our hostess. For Isabelle – you remember Isabelle? Tall girl? Red hair? Broken neck? Well, she was a woman without equal, a beautiful hostess, kind and warm – she was a real lady.

'Now, when your sorry face appeared at our door tonight, I had half a mind to kick your arse and chase you off, but Isabelle told me to let you in. It was her decision to bring you into our little house and that, you might say, was her downfall, in more ways than one. And where is she now, I hear you ask? Well she is in the very next room, cold on the floor and awaiting the undertaker.'

I began to shake at this point, gently, in the legs at first, but, as the full realisation of my actions dawned on me, it quickly spread throughout my body.

'It was an accident,' I said, the words falling from my mouth with difficulty as my tremor grew.

'Of course it was, of course it was,' he said with a short smile. 'But accidents have consequences and consequences must be met, and this is where the problem that you have given me lies.'

He pulled hard on the cigarette between his thin lips, the red tip glowing ferociously as he took it from his mouth and brought it to my chest, pushing it gently through my shirt until the burning ember touched my skin. I howled in pain, an action which did not dissuade him from his task as he brought the burning tip to my chest a further four times. When he had stopped, and my cries subsided, he spoke again.

'You see, if it was up to me I would have you in pain in a great many ways before finishing you off and dumping you in the Ouse to float away with the rest of the shite. But it is up to my dear boss, who is a pleasant man, but one who I've seen do terrible things to people like you in the past. Isabelle was a particular favourite of his, and I've taken to thinking that maybe my way might be a little more merciful. Because I have seen my boss take the eyes from a man with nothing more than an old spoon…' He leant in close; his face was just inches from my own and I smelt whisky on his warm breath. 'Do we understand each other?'

I nodded shakily.

He stood before removing his jacket and rolling up the sleeves of his shirt. His roughly tattooed forearms were broad, probably even wider than my legs, and I thought about the punishment to come, a punishment that I would undoubtedly not survive. 'Now then, son. What will it be? Me or him?'

I could not speak for fear of what was to come and braced myself for his onslaught.

He raised his eyebrows. 'So, no answer is it? Then I think it will be me.' The leering smile left his face, to be replaced by the stern look of a man intent on murder. 'Could I ask a last favour of you, before you go? Could you not flake on my first strike? Let me have a little fun first.'

His fist hit me like thunder, hard on the left-hand side of my face, bursting the skin. I was knocked from the chair and landed in a heap on the floor. He knelt down beside me, gripped my hair and lifted my head in one hand, before punching me a further five times with the other. I felt the cracking of bone and knew that my cheekbone had been broken. I groaned as he lifted me up again and placed me back on the seat.

'Good lad,' he said. 'Still with me for a while yet.'

He struck me again, this time in my stomach, forcing all of the wind in me to wheeze from my broken lips in a fine mist of red over his clean, white shirt.

I was not strong. To most eyes I was little more than a child, and I knew that I would not last much longer at the hands of old Harold. Tears ran from my closing eyes as I felt my fate rushing towards me.

Before the next strike came my attacker was brought to a pause by the sound of voices from beyond the door. It would be his master, and I prayed then that I would die quickly rather than suffer more at the hands of this supposed torturer of men, Harold's employer.

'It would seem that my dear boss will have his fun with you yet, boy,' said Harold as he withdrew from me and awaited our grim visitor.

The door opened and the silhouette of a tall man stood framed in the doorway.

'Harold!' he snapped. 'Is this the wretch that murdered my Isabelle?'

Although my head swam with pain, the voice of the man made me lift my head towards him, as he entered the room and stepped into my sight.

I allowed myself the most ironic of smiles that my broken face could afford and let out a croaked reply.

'Yes it is, Father,' I said. 'It was me who killed her.'

***

The journey back to my room was hurried. Head down and holding the ledger tightly underneath my coat, I bustled my way through the busy streets, fearful of the slightest noise around me. At any moment I expected to hear a police whistle and turn to see uniformed officers running towards me shouting, 'Murderer!'

I shook uncontrollably. I had taken lives before; I knew this, of course. But never in this manner. I had finally turned into a monster. After stripping off my bloodstained clothes and washing myself, I picked up the ledger and opened it for the first time. What if Alice's name was not written in it? Had I killed an innocent man? The answer was resolved quickly, however, as I found her name within.

She was listed on the previous day's date, Thursday 1 November 1883, as Miss Alice Griffiths, Service Maid required for large dinner party at a gentleman's club in Cavendish Square. In that moment I knew Alice's fate. The club in question was the very same one that I had watched for days: the Dolorian Club, home of Lord William Falconer. I slammed the ledger shut and, after hiding it underneath my mattress, I put on my coat and left for the police station.

I was fully aware of the difficult position that I might be about to put myself in. To report Alice as missing would only lead the police to the Marylebone Service Agency, and of course to the mutilated body of Tandry, but I had to know if she still lived. I could have taken another route to discovery and gone to see George Purkess; surely he would have heard if there had been another servant girl murder, but if my theories regarding the Dolorian Club's influence were correct, then any such murder would have been hushed.

No, what better way to put myself in the clear for the death of Tandry than to lead the police straight to his body? I would report Alice missing with the police and hope that my hard-earned relationships with the lower-ranking officers on the streets might bring about news of her.

I reported to the desk at Marylebone station and saw the familiar face of Josiah Grant, a desk sergeant of long association. As I approached him he scoured me with dark eyes.

'Josiah,' I said. 'I have something to report.'

His eyes continued to bore into me and I could tell that something was amiss. He looked back down at the large book in front of him and continued to write.

'It is a missing person,' I continued. 'I have a missing person to report... Josiah... Sergeant Grant. I am here on police business.'

'Name of missing person?'

'Alice Griffiths. She went out to work yesterday evening and has not returned.'

Grant had begun to write her name but stopped himself as I spoke.

'Come back in two days,' he intoned drily. 'She is not a missing person unless she has been gone for three days.'

'But, Sergeant, I fear that she has come to harm. Girls are being killed in the area; you know this.'

A wry smile broke onto his face.

'Oh yes, of course girls have been killed, Mr Weaver. We all knew that – and you made sure that the whole world knew about your supposed 'golden woman'. In fact, I think you'll find it was not a golden woman who's responsible for the crimes as you claimed, for we caught the real culprit. Your musings have been very well read in these parts and make us look fools. Then of course came the deaths of Abe Thomas and young Jim Worthing in the park. There are many around here who blame you personally for that.'

'But the man you caught was not the killer,' I implored.

He brushed away my pleading with a stroke of his hand.

'The killer was captured, Weaver, and he sits now in Newgate awaiting the noose. If this girl of yours has gone astray then it will be purely to rid herself of your stain, nothing more. And if she is dead then it's another on your conscience. Now leave here, before your attendance is noted by my colleagues and you find yourself in a cell with harsh company.'

I needed no further encouragement. There was nothing for me there, no hope of comfort nor concern from the law. If Alice were indeed dead then I could not expect any help from the police. They would raise their heads soon enough when the body of Tandry was discovered.

Of Tandry's murder I felt no remorse. He was an agent of evil and was responsible for his own fate. If he indeed was under the employ of Falconer and the Dolorian Club then I was sure that, given their contacts in the police, no stone would be left unturned in the search for his killer, but without his ledger there was nothing to lead them to me.

I returned home, stopping off only to buy a bottle of brandy. I needed time to think, time to work out my next move. I was sure now that Alice was indeed dead and my only hope at retribution was to bring the whole fetid organisation, from Falconer downwards, to its knees.

Uncorking the bottle, I poured myself a large glass and began to look through Tandry's ledger. It was unremarkable at first glance, merely a list of names and jobs spread throughout Marylebone and the surrounding area. I sought out the entries regarding Alice and found detailed notes of her work, the role she was required to perform by the employer and the address where she was needed. Each of these entries was correct, in terms of what Alice had told me herself about where she had been and what she had done. It was upon finding and noting her first job and moving to close the book that my eye was caught, however.

'Felicity Moore.'

There in bold letters, recorded for work on the night before her death, was the name Felicity Moore, the girl nailed to the tree in St Peter's Park whilst I was in Pluckley. Stunned now, I studied the book more earnestly, finding that nearly every page revealed a new victim: Eloise Davison, the dark-haired girl jointed and left in a heap in the middle of the road; Catherine Davies, left crucified on the railings on Cuthbert Street. As I turned each page, more names were revealed to me, names of the women whom I had seen laid out on the floor of that terrible house in Boston Place: Florence White, Patricia West, Annie Flanders... until finally I saw her – Mary Pershaw, the girl whom Abe Thomas himself had sent to the Marylebone Service Agency; the girl who had, for some reason, murdered her only child before being sacrificed in Boston Place's ungodly ceremony. Binding all of these names together was the final truth: each of these girls had at one time or other worked at Falconer's home in Cavendish Square. I was sickened by what I had discovered, but I knew that, in the right hands, this ledger would be enough to bring the culprits down. I resolved to visit Mr Purkess the next day, ledger in hand. He would know what to do with this evidence; he surely could not deny me now. I would tell him everything – of the Dolorian Club, of the Golden Woman, Bethany and Tom Finnan; he would know it all.

I drained my glass and poured another. Tomorrow I would free myself of this knowledge and I would watch Falconer be brought to justice, but tonight? Tonight I would drown my misery at Alice's demise.

It was as I collected together all of my drawings of Boston Place and the subsequent servant girl murders that I came across the battered tin box given to me by the owner of the Princess Alice, meant to be passed on to Tom Finnan. For some reason I had almost forgotten about it, caught up as I was with events after returning from Pluckley. It was large in size, quite deep and it rattled when shaken. Suddenly I felt a maddening urge to get inside it, to find out its secrets. After searching my rooms for a suitable implement, I took at it with a hammer and the iron spike that I had taken from the tree in Regent's Park. The lid bent back, until finally the lock snapped and the contents of the box were revealed.

I had acquired a number of mementos from Sibelius Darke's reign of terror: the odd photograph taken by him in his role as a post-mortem portrait photographer, letters written in his own hand, even a fire-damaged Frodsham's pocket watch, bought from a very shady gentleman who swore that it belonged to the beast himself. I had no reason to doubt the seller; the watch seemed genuine enough, and it even had a foreign inscription which I later discovered was in Suomi, the native tongue of Finland, where Darke's family originated before settling in Whitechapel.

Of course the words were all nonsense to me, but the meaning of the inscription did not get any clearer once I had it translated. The only translation I could find was: 'Don't paint the image of a demon on a wall.' The man who interpreted the phrase for me said that he understood its meaning fully but said that you would have to be of Finnish descent to appreciate its sentiment. I remember at the time being fascinated by the importance placed on the phrase by a 'demon' such as Darke and spent hours staring at the watch trying to break the code, as if it were the key to understanding the man. Such time was wasted.

As I looked inside the tin box meant for Tom Finnan, however, I realised that all of my mementos were worthless when compared to the treasure that I had kept undisturbed under my bed and had only now uncovered.

There, inside the box, was a camera with two nameplates attached to it. The first plate stated the name of the manufacturer, Ottewill Collis and Co, London. It was the second plate, however, which attracted my attention the most, for it read: Property of Sibelius Darke, Osborn Street, Whitechapel. Never had I dreamt that one of Darke's own cameras would have survived him. I had enquired after Darke memorabilia since arriving in London and had been told on countless occasions that nearly everything owned by Darke had been destroyed in the fire which had consumed his studio. To find a piece such as this together with – as I found on further investigation into the contents of the box – previously unseen photographic plates, was beyond my imaginings; a real and valuable treasure. I held the camera in my hand and considered its beauty. This was the tool of Sibelius Darke's trade, the man himself had held and used this very item and, for the first time in my long obsession, I felt a real connection to him. I lifted the camera up to my eye and chanced a look through the viewfinder.

I had never had cause or want to use a camera before. Other than their use by Darke, they did not interest me in the slightest. To my mind, they could not capture a moment, evoke emotion or look into the soul of the subject in the way that a beautifully constructed paint-ing or sketched drawing could. They had their place, I supposed, in recording and documenting a person or place, but that was all I thought them useful for. I had not yet seen a photograph that had really fired my imagination or filled me with interest as much as a quality piece of art could, and I knew for a certainty that they would never replace the much finer art form at which I excelled.

As I peered carefully into the wooden box, a sudden sense of ner-vous energy rippled through me. The beast himself had repeated this very action with *this* camera, and I felt his dark soul flood into me as I looked through the lens and saw the other side of my room inverted before me. A wave of tension coursed through my body and for a moment I felt quite dizzy. I put the camera down. Was it my imag-ination or had Sibelius Darke, child killer and cannibal, left a part of himself in this object? Did it sense my own hidden darkness and see a kindred spirit with which to join? The thought made me feel sick to my stomach which, combined with the head-spinning faintness, sent me lurching to my feet and running for the sink, retching in nausea. Once purged, I sank to the kitchen floor, bathed in sweat and riddled with a gnawing anxiousness. Thoughts rushed through my mind; memories of chocolate factories, of my bedroom and Victoria, of brothels with sweeping staircases, of bright hot metal and of a man dead in my wake, his face torn apart and his skull fragmented by my hand. Darke had not infected me with anything that was not already in place. I was as much of a killer, worse even, as I was heedless of the destruction that I had brought on those around me.

I wept.

I sobbed uncontrollably, wracking howls of penitence and humiliation, as the guilt and self-hatred of what I had done was finally revealed to me.

I do not know how long I sat there, but eventually I pushed myself to my feet and made my way back to the tin box, almost reluctant to see what further horrors it would bring me.

The rest of the contents of the box comprised various letters and notes written in Darke's hand. Normally these would have sent me into a frenzy of excitement at my discovery but, in truth, I had not the energy left within me, nor the lust for knowledge, to bring even the spark of a smile to my lips.

Underneath the letters was a photographic plate, which I withdrew and examined. The plate contained the image of a newborn child, seemingly dead and sitting upon the lap of a woman wearing a large cloth of black velvet over her head. I had seen pictures such as this before and was aware of the fashion among post-mortem portrait photographers to conceal the face of the mother when capturing the image of a recently deceased child. I brought the plate closer to me and studied it. At first glance there seemed to be nothing amiss, but as I looked more closely at the babe, and more notably at its face, I could see that all was not quite right. There was something about the eyes of the child that was unnerving to me. Normally in such pictures the eyes took on a glazed and rheumy appearance, a sign to all but the most ignorant of viewers that the subject of the photograph was quite dead. This child was different, though. There was something about the shadow under the eyes, the shine of the pupils and the furrow of the brow, a desperate malevolence, which made me feel as though this child had seen and tasted death – but had somehow returned and hungered for more. I found myself entranced by the image, drawn in to staring at this fey babe's eyes, unable to pull my gaze from them.

I do not know how long I held the plate in front of me, lost in time and place, and, if it had not been for the creeping fear which snaked its way up my spine and lit up my mind with terror, I feel sure that I would have become trapped within its power forever. The torment, however, the sheer dread and cold turmoil which the sight of the babe instilled within me – it built. A ball of anguish developed inside me, churning its way up from my stomach until it reached such an unbearable level that I found myself screaming out loud in shock and hurling the plate across the room, where it shattered on the far wall.

Cold, bilious sweat dripped into my eyes as I sat shaking and staring at the broken pieces of the plate, which even then held something of a magnetic hold over me. I reached for my brandy glass and drained it, the sharp bite of the alcohol cleansing my soul of the horror that I had witnessed. Was this the foul magic to which Darke had succumbed and had it directed him in his spree of murder? I continued to drink voraciously until the power of the spirit took over me and I slumped into unconsciousness.

***

I slept fitfully and full of torment. Many times I woke myself with loud cries and pitiful sobs. My dreams were full of the dead, the dead I had created, such as Hiram Osborne, his thin body plastered in brown tar as he leaned into my cowering form and spat words at me, his breath rasping into my face. 'Drown a man, will you boy?' he hissed. 'Strike a man and send him to the bottom. Is that how it is?'

Sweet plain Victoria stood at the end of my bed, dressed in a gown once white but now soiled with dark red blood. In her cupped hands she held something, and at first I could not make it out. I leaned in closer and saw that it was small, bloody and... raggedly breathing.

'Look at our boy, Sam. Look what that man did to our special boy. We would all have been so happy together, just as you promised we would. We could have been a family but you lied to me.'

I tossed and turned in my bed, my sheet a sweat-soaked shroud which suffocated and strangled, pulling itself tighter around me until I felt that I would disappear within it and leave nothing behind. I fought to wake myself from my nightmares, but I had neither the strength nor the power to escape; I was weak and slow, brought low by my crimes.

Next came the beautiful Isabelle, radiant still; her long red hair fell about her shoulders, her green eyes hypnotic and enticing, but her head lolled loosely, her neck twisted and lumped where the bones had been snapped as they had struck the stair risers time and time again.

'Did I try to hurt you? Did I not just try to bring you joy? And this is what you brought me to, a worthless whore, discarded and pushed aside.'

'I'm sorry,' I sobbed. 'It was an accident, you were in the way...'

But she had gone, replaced by what I knew to be Tandry, although he was unrecognisable to all but me. His face was a crumpled mess of bone and blood, no features to be found, just holes and red wet matter. Somehow he managed to speak, although there was no mouth and his voice was a gargled froth.

'You let out your anger, sir. Ha! Yes you did, let it out, all that pent-up desire to destroy. The boss would have made good use of you. Good use of you indeed, yes.'

A pain within my head stabbed and stabbed again, jolting me violently in my sleep, causing me to claw at my face to stop the blade from sinking in. I felt the agony of the final moments of Marcus Tandry, but still I could not wake.

It was, however, when the final ghost arrived before me that I knew that my hell was complete. The sight of it sent me screaming and choking in agony and only ended when my head hit something hard and I finally woke myself.

I was lying upon the floor, having fallen from the bed. The damp

sheet was still wrapped around me, but not tightly; there was no suf-
focation, no strangling grip upon my body. I shook it from me and
pushed myself to my feet, staggering into the kitchen and reaching for
a cup of water, which I drained noisily. I would not sleep again this
night, I said to myself. No amount of tiredness or alcohol would drag
me back into that hell. No, I would return to my bedroom and light
a candle, I would pin my eyes wide open if necessary, but I would see
the sun rising in the morning.

I poured myself another cup of water and stumbled back towards
my bedroom, picking up a book as I went to occupy my mind and
keep me from sleep.

'That is a great read, one of my favourites when I lived, I recall.'

I turned quickly, to see a tall man standing by the window, looking
out into the night beyond.

'Did I make you jump, Sam? I suppose that is my lot now, isn't
it? To scare and to bring fear. But then again, like you, I am an
accomplished killer. Allow me to introduce myself, in case you did
not recognise me.' He reached out a pale white hand towards me. 'My
name is Sibelius Darke.'

13

The Golden Woman

For a moment neither my father nor I spoke. I looked to the face of Harold, who appeared more than a little confused; his wide mouth, which not moments before had been full of threats of death, now hung open and dumbfounded.

It was Father who spoke first.

'Harold, untie the boy and leave us,' he said, his eyes not leaving mine.

'But, sir?' Harold protested. 'He killed Isabelle!'

'I am aware of the events within this house tonight, but I have given you a simple instruction. Please do not cause me further upset this evening by questioning, or worse still, disobeying my orders. Now do it!' It was obvious that he was a man who was not used to being defied, as Harold immediately leapt into action and loosened the binds securing my wrists. Without another look towards me the large man left us alone, closing the door behind him.

'It would seem,' said Father, 'that we have caught each other in rather difficult circumstances, have we not?'

I did not speak, I could not, but instead rubbed at my sore wrists and carefully touched my swollen face.

'Harold is a good man really,' he said, observing my injuries. 'It is obvious that you have upset him, for it is rare that he does such things nowadays. Tell me, why are you here, son? What, other than the obvious attractions, has brought you through these doors tonight?'

'You will laugh, dear Father.' I rubbed at my chin, my hand coming away stained with blood. 'It was work and nothing more. I came here in the vain hope of uncovering the type of men who profit from such places. If I had known that it was you all along, I would have saved myself the trouble and written my piece from home. I knew that you had ample opportunity to deal with 'fallen women' but I never for one moment thought that it was you who actually owned them.'

'I own nothing. I merely provide these women with a safe roof over their heads and protection from those who might take advantage of them. It would seem that my protection was not enough for poor Isabelle – good God, boy, you've killed a girl!'

'Why, yes I have. Do not look so shocked. Perhaps it is a family trait? At least my killing was an accident. I hear from Harold that I have quite some way to go in my career before I reach your heady heights.'

'You do not know what you are talking about!' He quietened his voice before continuing, 'I do what I do for a greater good. If you will let me, I will explain.'

'Oh no, Father, there is no need to waste your precious time on explaining anything; it is all perfectly clear to me. I can see the head-line now – "Respected Local Vicar is Whore-Monger and Villain"; now *that* is a story that would make my name.'

'Stop, boy!'

'I should think that I would rise very quickly, being known as the reporter who brought his own father down.'

'Stop!'

'Tell me, did Mother find out about your little sideline? Is that why you beat her, why you had her locked away?'

For all of his many faults, my father had never struck me before, but strike me he did then. I fell from the chair into a crumpled heap on the floor. My body could take no more and I did not try to get up again.

'You will not be reporting the events of this evening,' he said, standing over me. 'In fact, you may count yourself quite lucky that I don't send in Harold to make of you what he will. You will be taken to a safe place where you will stay until I have resolved the disorder that you created here tonight!'

He stamped on my chest then. A brutal crunch told me that at least one rib was broken and, as I groaned in pain, he left me, and the door was locked behind him.

***

The devil stood before me, his hand outstretched in greeting and I took it in my own. It was cold.

'I know who you are, Mr Darke,' I said. 'Won't you sit down? I would be most interested to speak to you.'

To be in the presence of the object of my obsession was not a little shocking to me, even if it was all a part of my imagination. Darke looked much the same as he had when he last appeared to me at the Devil's Bush in Pluckley. Then, he had been white and ghostly, ethereal even; and here, in the flesh as it were, he had retained the pallor of spirit form. His skin had the look of one who had never seen sunlight, his hair blond but closer to white than gold; it was as if nearly all the colour had been drained from his body, his only physical feature demonstrating any kind of hue being his bright blue eyes. It was no wonder, I thought, as my mind raced to make sense of this vision, that he was known in Whitechapel as 'the Pale Demon'. When combined with his height, his physical features gave him a truly inhuman appearance.

He laughed a little and settled himself down. 'I am aware of your little obsession. I see you even have one of my cameras.' He pointed to the tin box and contents that still sat in front of my fireplace. 'It was one of my particular favourites; in fact, I completed a good many jobs with it. Tell me, have you looked through the lens at all?'

'I did, and it is not an experience that I wish to revisit. There is something ungodly and evil about it. Much the same as you, it seems.'

Darke smiled and raised his hands to his chest in mock offence.

'Oh please, Mr Weaver, you do not really still believe that I am the dastardly killer the world would have you believe? Do you not know enough about the Dolorian Club to know that they have the power to twist and distort the truth?'

'I know that you were a member of that vile place and that you carried out murders at their behest.'

'Did I? Well, if that were true then I should be a villain of extraordinary proportions. Tell me, do I look like a killer and eater of children to you?'

'No, but I learnt long ago, from people close to me, that you cannot tell everything about a man from the face that he shows to the world.' I walked into the kitchen to retrieve my bottle of brandy. 'I am pouring myself a drink, would you like one?'

'Mm, yes please. Do you have any whisky?'

'Whisky? No, I can't stand the stuff.'

'Then brandy it is; I cannot remember the last time I tasted alcohol.'

I poured two large tumblers and seated myself opposite him at the table. 'Do the dead not have the opportunity to drink? My God, how miserable for you.' I took a small sip. 'So if you are not the killer that I supposed, then who is? You cannot expect me to believe the man who killed all of those children is still alive?'

'Oh no, of course not, Samuel. The thing that slaughtered the children is long since gone from the world. Do you know much of Finnish mythology?'

'A little, but only from those who I have spoken to about your killings.'

'I grew up steeped in the knowledge of it; my grandfather was a great storyteller.' He lifted the tumbler to his lips and tasted the brandy, savouring it. 'When I was young, Grandfather told me of a being called Surma who guarded the gates of Tuonela, the underworld. This was a task given to him by the great god Ukko and it is a role that he maintained without question. That is, until he was taken from his place of work and his spirit dragged into the world of the living, our world. Men did this; dark, twisted men who sought to use Surma's power to cause harm to the world. These men were led by Charles Earnshaw.'

'Earnshaw? I have heard of him, and of Surma, from a couple of sources, one being Beth Finnan.'

'Ah, dear Beth. I visit her on occasion, you know?'

'Yes, she told me; I thought her crazed. As were her words about Earnshaw.'

'Oh no, she spoke the truth about Earnshaw; he was the devil in human form. If it had not been for the assistance of Beth, I would never have uncovered the truth about the plans of Earnshaw and the Dolorian Club. Unfortunately she lost her mind in the process, unlike me – I only lost my life.'

'Burnt to a smouldering crisp, I hear,' I said, enjoying the moment. 'So you are totally innocent?'

'Innocent? Why yes, in a way. Any harm I caused was either purely unintentional or caused to those who deserved it. Beth and I discovered that Earnshaw and his cronies had somehow summoned the spirit of Surma and put it into a man, Arthur Downing to be precise; there it dwelled, taking Downing on a nightly rampage through the streets.'

'So why did you not take this information to the police? Have the man taken in and hanged?'

'Come now, Samuel. Surely you know the workings of the club well enough to be aware that their tendrils reach throughout society? The only way to stop the beast was to kill the man myself, which I attempted to do and failed. The man was already dead, Surma had passed on to another and Downing, aware of his terrible actions, took his own life.'

'Passed on?'

'Yes, the spirit passed through to another host and would have continued to do so if I had not stopped it.'

'And so you are saying that I should not think of you as a killer but as a hero?'

'I am no hero, just a man cursed by fate to be involved with the Dolorian Club's dealings. I decided that the only way to stop the killing was to destroy the club itself, which I thought I had done by killing Earnshaw and his men, burning their club to the ground, and trapping Surma within myself. I was successful on both accounts, hence my demise. Surma returned to the underworld – and the world of the living had a flesh-and-blood demon to blame, and blame me they obviously did.'

I took a moment to read the man. Here in front of me was someone who had become a singular obsession of mine, in the pursuit of which I had lied, cheated and stolen; and now, after all of this time and effort, here he was sharing a drink with me in the middle of the night, telling me that everything I knew about him was wrong. I was, in truth, a little let down: the man was totally plausible.

'What do you know of Falconer?' I asked, my brow furrowing.

'Falconer? Lord William Falconer? Oh yes, I know of him, he was a member of the club. He was even a client of mine once; dead mistress as I recall, there was even talk that he killed her himself. I never met the man but, from what I heard, he was not one to be crossed. Is he still doing the rounds?'

'You could say that. It seems that he is the man at the top now; the club runs from his house in Cavendish Square. I have had the displeasure of seeing him for myself on two occasions, the first in passing but the second was much more threatening and violent in nature. I had cause to think that he, and indeed the club, is involved in a string of murders, including that of a close lady friend of mine. I now know this to be true.'

I had decided that I was enjoying this discourse now. Even to dream of meeting the subject of your life's obsession was something to savour indeed. I hoped that, like some dreams, this particular one would last long into the night and that I would remember it when I woke.

'How many are dead?' he asked, leaning forwards.

'I am not entirely sure, as I do not think that they have all been reported. If my suspicions are correct, the killings started with the deaths of twelve women in a ritualistic fashion, not two miles away from here.'

'And the killer? Have they been seen?'

'Ha! I have even seen it myself.'

'It?'

'Yes, "it" – for I do not think that it was human, at least not in a way that any normal man would imagine. This was a woman made of pure gold.'

A twinkle came into his eye as I described to him my meeting with the killer, her speed and agility, and the brutal but exquisite manner in which she despatched her victims.

'This Golden Woman of yours, I think I may know what she is and where she came from,' said Darke, suddenly.

'You do?' I said, playing along with this figment of my imagination. 'Well then, please do tell, I'm dying to know.'

'And tell I will, Samuel, but first you must promise to do one favour for me, a favour which is at the heart of my visit to you this evening. It is why I tried to contact you in Pluckley. I was most disappointed when you and your friend fled at the sight of me.'

'Ah, Higgins. Yes, I am afraid we were rather shocked, and thought it some kind of hallucination. We had drunk quite a lot.'

'He is like that, your friend. I have tried to send messages through him before but he refuses to allow me in. I think I scare him.' He had a look of bemusement about him, as if puzzled by the notion that the ghost of a known killer appearing in dreams should not be deemed as commonplace as any other encounter.

'What messages?'

'The same ones that I bring to you, Mr Weaver: there is danger afoot, a stirring in the underworld, in which I now live. An old darkness has surfaced on the lips of those who have passed. There is talk that the Witch Queen herself has arisen and has links with the living world.'

I laughed aloud at his last statement, preposterous as it was. 'Witch Queen? Mr Darke, you really are the most enjoyable dream I have had in an age! You talk of such things as if they are real. Am I to start believing in fairies and goblins next? Does your Witch Queen command an army of trolls intent on taking over the world?'

'I know how this sounds to you, Samuel,' he said. 'You're a man unable to comprehend that the world around him may not be as he sees it. However, there are things in this world and the next which are difficult to explain and even more difficult to understand. Yes, there is a Witch Queen and yes, she does aspire to return to this plane. Where do you think that legends and myths come from, Sam? Do you think them all dreamt up by some lunatic? No! They are the stories which are handed down from generation to generation, becoming ever more magical at each telling, but the base for them is in fact, Sam!'

I could tell that I had angered the man; not a thing to do with a self-confessed killer, be he a figment in a dream or not, and I held my hands up in submission. If this 'ghost' were here to give me a message, and if that message involved some long-forgotten fairytale, then I should sit back and enjoy the story.

'I apologise, Mr Darke,' I said. 'As you have perceived, I am a cynical man, firmly grounded in the world that I can see, hear and touch. I have never been a lover of the make-believe. But, in deference to you,

I will say not another word until you have told your tale.' I poured us both another imaginary tumbler of brandy, looking forward to tasting the real thing when I woke.

His smile was brittle, but he continued all the same.

'As I have told you, the Dolorian Club has attempted to bring death and fear to the streets of the capital before, most notably the set of murders – including those of my father and my brother Nikolas – for which I was blamed and am still held accountable. I say again, I was not the culprit in those atrocities. The only deaths to which I will proudly hold up my hands and admit were those that occurred when I discovered the root of the evil and confronted it, resulting in the death of Charles Earnshaw and the fire at the club. As it seems you have discovered, I was not entirely successful in destroying this foul association; they have simply moved premises and started anew.'

As he spoke his eyes blazed with anger and I hoped that, when I finally did wake, I would remember all of what he said. For, even if it was a figment of my troubled imagination, such stories would surely be a useful and sensational addition to the Darke legend.

'Now, you say that this man Falconer is at the head of the club,' he continued. 'That his home is their base and his monies fund their schemes. I think that maybe you are right but I have come tonight to tell you that all of what you have seen so far – the ritualistic killings, the murders and the Golden Woman – has been carried out for a higher purpose; Falconer is in fact working at the behest of another.'

'Your Witch Queen?' I said.

'Not my queen, but yes, an ancient queen who is known by many names, but best known in Finnish legend as Louhi. She ruled over Pohjola, the frozen wastelands in the north of Finland, in ancient times. She was the daughter of Tuoni, the god of death, and reigned over her accursed land for many years. She had many daughters, and men would travel from far and wide across the ancient world to sue Louhi for their hands in marriage.

'Now Louhi was a cruel and conniving woman who would set each suitor an impossible task that they had to achieve before she would give her blessing to any marriage. One such suitor was the hero Väinämöinen, a bard who was challenged by Louhi to bring the master creator Seppo Ilmarinen to her, so that he might create her an object of power; with this object she intended to rule over all the lands.

'Seppo Ilmarinen plied his trade as a simple blacksmith but was in fact a god and master conjurer, able to create and form anything that he was bid. When Väinämöinen asked him to travel north with him to Pohjola, he initially refused, even after Väinämöinen told him that for his troubles he would receive the hand in marriage of the Maiden of Pohjola, Louhi's most beautiful daughter. Väinämöinen would not be dissuaded and tricked Ilmarinen into climbing a tree to collect the moonlight which shone upon its branches. Once he was high enough in the tree, the Bard sang a song of power, conjuring an almighty wind which blew Ilmarinen all the way to Pohjola.

'Although upset at Väinämöinen's trickery, Ilmarinen soon changed his mind upon meeting the Maiden and become entranced by her beauty. The Maiden was promised to Ilmarinen in return for the creation of a tool of power for Louhi.

'On the first day he created a crossbow made of gold, but within the weapon was an evil spirit which demanded a new victim each day. Seeing the misery that it would bring, Ilmarinen threw it back into the forge. On the second day he forged a beautiful ship but, once again, it was evil at heart and longed for battle; it too was cast back into the fire. The third day came and Ilmarinen made a cow of gold. It had a foul temper and sought to maim all those who came near it; the cow was melted also. In his frustration, Ilmarinen used his heavenly powers to bring the four winds of the earth to his forge to fan the flames. For three days the fire within the forge raged until finally the Sampo was created, a mighty tool indeed. The Sampo was a mill capable of creating grain, salt and gold, a device which would bring any who wielded it great power. Ilmarinen took the Sampo to Louhi, presented it before her and asked for his payment, the hand of the Maiden of Pohjola. This was granted by Louhi but refused by the Maiden, who held no love in her heart for Ilmarinen and would not leave her homeland. Ilmarinen was upset at being spurned and demanded that the Sampo be returned to him. Louhi refused, saying that her payment had been given and as such the deal was complete. In anger, Ilmarinen left Pohjola a bitter and angry man.'

'That is a very lovely story, Mr Darke,' I said. 'And I am sure that there is, as in all fairytales, a moral to it. How does any of this apply to me, though? Am I expected to try to win the hand of some ancient ice maiden also? I shall have to buy myself a considerably warmer overcoat if you expect me to travel to the frozen wastes of Finland.'

Darke chuckled a little and took a small sip of his drink. 'Oh, Mr Weaver,' he said. 'You have no patience, for I am coming to the part of the story which will be of interest to you. Did your father never read you stories as a child, or did you harry him along just to get to the end?'

With the mention of Father, I slumped back in my chair and bade him continue.

'Seppo Ilmarinen did find love; he married eventually and happily enjoyed a simple life on his farm, with his wife. That is… until she died a most horrible death at the hands of a cursed youth called Kullervo, another wonderful story, which I will not bother you with at this time for fear of sending you apoplectic with impatience.

'In his despair at her loss, and in fear of the loneliness that the death of a spouse can bring, he set about his forge once more and created for himself a golden…'

'Woman!'

'Yes, Mr Weaver, he created a woman made entirely of gold. However, she was cold and heartless and incapable of love; and Ilmarinen threw her, as he did with all of his failed projects, back into the forge.' Darke picked up his tumbler again and flung the rest of the drink down his throat. 'So there we have it, Mr Weaver, the golden bride of Seppo Ilmarinen is a woman not dissimilar to the one who currently stalks the streets of London, killing all in her path. The fears and whispers which I have heard regarding the return of Louhi, are, in fact, real. Somewhere she has found a man, someone in the employ of the Dolorian Club, who has been able to recreate the feats of Ilmarinen and forge life from metal through magic. This is the first part of a bigger plan, Samuel, I am sure of it. This conjurer that she has found will soon be set hard at work at bringing back Louhi and creating other such tools of power and destruction. These steps will not end until the Witch Queen has been given the power that she has craved for eternity.'

'But I thought she was already in possession of this 'Sampo'. Wasn't that meant to be some kind of all-powerful tool with which to rule the earth?'

'It was such a thing, but it was not in her possession for long. When Väinämöinen and Ilmarinen realised the evil of the Witch Queen Louhi, they decided that such a thing of great power should never be used by her. They stole it from her and, in the ensuing battle, it was smashed to pieces and Louhi vanquished forever.'

'Until now?'

'Until now, Mr Weaver. For I fear that she has made union with whoever the Dolorian Club has employed as their conjurer. She must be stopped.'

'But why do you come to me? I am not some ancient hero, ready to save the world from a new Dark Age. I am sure there are better men for the job.'

'I'm sorry to say that you are right, Samuel, you are far from the perfect hero, but there are limits to those I can speak to; it must be those who have a close bond with me or those with the power to converse with spirits. You are closer to me now than any other person still living, so it is you who I must come to for assistance. I have watched you for a long time, Samuel. I have seen into your past, and your possible future, and I know what you are capable of. My old friend Tom Finnan is near to exposing the club and all of its foul work, but he needs all the help he can muster. You know him; you also know what the Dolorian Club is capable of. You have the evidence to help Tom bring them down and halt the return of Louhi. Even if you do not have faith in yourself, Sam, please believe in the faith that I have in you. Use the knowledge that you have to destroy them.'

I settled back in my chair. For a dream, he was most convincing.

'Well thank you, Mr Darke,' I said, draining my tumbler for the last time. 'I fully expect to wake up at any moment, but it has been a pleasure to meet you at last. Tell me, what would you have me do?'

'Find the Golden Woman,' he urged. 'Find out where she resides when she is not at her work. Destroying her will disrupt their plans.'

'Destroy her? Did I forget to mention that the last time I saw her I loosed half a dozen bullets in her direction with no effect, whilst watching her cleave a man in two?'

'Ask yourself, then, how is it that you met this Golden Woman and lived to tell the tale?'

'Why, I do not know, Darke. I guessed it to be good luck.'

'The reason that she did not strike you down is because she recognised in you a cold killer's heart, just like hers. She sees herself in you, like a mirror, and that is why she did not harm you.'

'Now look here!' I said. 'I know my past, but that is not all I am.'

'I have no doubt that, deep within, you are a good man, but you have done terrible things, things that blacken the heart, things that cannot be undone easily. If you are the man that you say you are, then show the world this – the good you are capable of. You are a resourceful man, a man who has concentrated his abilities for his own end. A way of destroying the Golden Woman and her acolytes will come to you.'

'What comes after my heroic success over the unstoppable killer, then?'

'Use your evidence, use your contacts. Let the world know. You have the proof to do it, and in the right hands Falconer can be brought low. Do this for me and Tom, do it for your lady friend – for God's sake just do it for your own soul, man!'

I thought of the ledger and the copious notes I had made whilst investigating the club. If I knew who to trust, I could just possibly do it.

The sun was beginning to rise over the rooftops outside; the noise of the early risers began to sound from the street below. Sibelius Darke, the man over whom I had long obsessed, stood and walked over to his box camera where it lay on the floor in front of the mantel.

'This camera was always a favourite of mine; look after it for me, will you, Sam?' He reached down into the tin box and brought out a plate which he inserted into the back of the camera, before placing it on the mantelpiece so that the lens faced me. I watched him silently as he withdrew a length of cotton from his jacket pocket, one end of which he tied to a small metal ring on the edge of the lens cap. He carefully unwound the string and paced towards me, my face dumbfounded by his actions.

'What are you doing?' I asked.

'Be quiet, Sam. It is almost time to wake up.' He stood beside me and placed a long arm around my shoulder so that he faced towards the camera also. 'Now, look at the lens, there's a good fellow.'

He tugged the cotton sharply, an action which pulled the lens cap free from the lens.

'Goodbye, Mr Weaver,' he said.

All was blackness.

***

I felt cloth on my face and I realised that I was lying in bed, my blanket over my head. I slowly pulled it down, squinting as the morning sun shot arrows into my eyes. I had been right, my drunken imagination had got the better of me in my sleep; I had dreamt the whole thing.

I rolled myself upright and stood, walking slowly out of the bedroom. I could remember it all so clearly; so strange that a dream should stay with me. As I looked over to the mantelpiece I froze in my tracks. There, pointing to where we had stood in my dream, was the camera, the lens cap now replaced. It was not this that caused me the most unsettlement though, it was the item sitting next to it.

It was a fully developed photographic plate, the picture on it of myself and Sibelius Darke smiling broadly; and written in ink at the bottom were the words: 'Good Luck S.D.'

14

The Rush for Gold

The rain drummed against my bedroom window as I sat idly reading the newspaper. Mrs Coleman had made sure I had a copy of the *York Herald* every day since Father had brought me home, late in the night, a week earlier. The story we told was that I had been attacked and robbed by 'violent lowbrows' whilst out in York. She had never asked any more of the incident and I assumed that Father had strictly forbidden any conversation regarding the cause of my injuries.

Father's friend Dr Furnbridge had attended to me shortly after we arrived home; he told me that I had fractured my cheekbone and suffered a cracked rib or two. I was lucky, he said, that I had survived the night as he had seen too many young men like me beaten to death by those who lurked in the shadows of York. As he and Mrs Coleman fussed over me, helping me into my bed and tending to the weeping wounds upon my face, I silently watched the elderly man, all glasses and whiskers. As Furnbridge shone his dazzling light into my eyes and muttered about long-term damage to the brain, I wondered how much he knew of Father's secret other life. Perhaps he was even a regular patron of the house on Fossgate? I could see him, bumbling along the street and knocking gingerly upon the door, only to be greeted by Harold, who would spread his arms wide and beckon him in.

'Back again, good Doctor? I don't know where you get your stamina from. I shall ask Isabelle to arrange your usual room.'

Isabelle. I cursed my terrible luck for causing her downfall and bringing myself to this godforsaken point. During our carriage ride home, I had been assured by Father that any word from me to another living soul would not only bring about my own disappearance and death, but also that of my mother. He told the truth about this and I was never more afraid of any man either before or since. He had spent many years building his 'business' and he was not about to lose it to anyone, not even his own flesh and blood.

I had spoken little since getting home; how could I trust those close to me when I had been so wrong about Father? I had always wondered about the amount of time that Father had spent away from the home, his 'mission' to aid the fallen women of York and of course his cold and callous treatment of my mother.

Did she know, I wondered. Did everyone except me know that he was not a saintly parish vicar but a brutal gang leader, owner of brothels and torturer of those who stood in his way? Perhaps she did, and perhaps this was why he had her committed to the asylum, safely placed where he could ensure she was watched day and night, whilst never being believed by those who cared to listen.

In the following week of confinement I did not even venture out of my room. All meals were brought to me on a tray and I spent my days sitting by the window, looking out on the grey world outside and pondering my next move.

Father had contacted the *York Herald* to tell them of my 'attack' and the injuries that I had suffered. I saw with some dark humour how they ran a small story regarding my robbery on one of the inner pages, not three days afterwards. I was described as bravely fighting off my assailants, who fled.

Late every evening, once Mrs Coleman had gone to bed and Mr Morgan had returned to his small cottage at the end of the garden, Father would come to my room. I would not speak to him at first, would not reply when he asked after my injuries; eventually, however, sheer inquisitiveness caused me to make conversation with him. He would tell me little, of course, but that did not stop me: I would ask how long he had involved himself in such business, and was there good money to be made in the profits of sin? Did he partake of his own goods? The list of my questions was endless and he would not bite at the bait which I dangled in front of him. He would simply ignore me for a short moment, take a deep breath and start the conversation again, discussing the events in today's paper or some other insignificant matter. Each night he would tell me that once my injuries were sufficiently healed, he would arrange for suitable employment for me elsewhere, possibly in London at one of the larger newspapers. He even offered to purchase accommodation for me and send me an allowance each month to live on. It was then that I realised that all of the ire and fury which he had directed towards me on the night of Isabelle's death had been spent and he had realised that he could no more dispose of me, his own son, than he could bring harm to himself.

In those days, alone in my bedroom, I thought on his offers. Of course a move to London and employment on a national newspaper would be all I had ever dreamt of. I could see why he offered it; with me out of the picture, and Mother committed to an asylum, the risk of his being unmasked would be lessened.

Of course, I would not tell him how attractive his offer was to me; I would hold out until the last moment before agreeing to such plans. But it was as I sat there, alone each day, with only my own mind and conscience to guide me, that I decided that if I were to leave York to find my way in the world it would not be by Father's design, but my own.

***

I hid the picture of myself and Sibelius Darke in the chest under the floorboards where I kept all of my pieces of evidence, drawings and notes regarding my investigations. It was a strange addition to my collection, being the recording of myself standing happily next to a man long dead whose crimes I had long obsessed over.

As I returned the floorboard, there was a knock upon my door.

I opened the door to a young man in a well-worn suit and battered hat. His smile was a pleasant one and sat comfortably upon a clean-shaven face, adorned with quick, bright eyes.

'Mr Weaver? Are you Samuel Weaver, of *The Illustrated Police News*?' he asked, his voice as rough London as could be, with the faint clippings of one who was trying most carefully to sound a proper gent.

'I am he,' I returned, looking down the hallway and noticing that another man, much larger than my visitor at the door, stood at the top of the stairs. The large man smiled politely and touched the brim of his bowler.

'Wonderful,' the young man said. 'I am Langton, George Langton. I trust that you have heard of me?'

'You are the new... inspector?'

'I am indeed. May I come in and have a short word? I had been hoping to meet you "on the job" as it were, but it seems that my colleagues at the station are not so forgiving as I. It is only a quick word, sir. I am just here to introduce myself.' He lowered his voice slightly and leant in to me. 'I am also a great admirer of your work, sir – unlike many of my associates.'

I paused for a moment; was this one of Falconer's men, coming to warn me off again? He certainly looked harmless, but then again that would be how the Dolorian Club operated. I decided to listen to what the man had to say.

'Yes, of course. Come in, please.' I stepped back and allowed him to enter. 'Will your sergeant be joining us?'

'Who, Butler? No, no. I have asked him to keep his distance and keep an eye on the front door for me. I will explain all, I promise.'

I led Langton inside and bade him take a seat, which he did nervously, his eyes flicking to the door as I shut it behind him.

'As I said,' he began, 'I had hoped to see you out at work, but I gather that you are not exactly high up on the local police's list of favourites at the moment. I keep my own counsel of course. I am new to the area, from south of the river.' He shifted slightly in his seat, as if a little embarrassed, and I could not work out where the tension within him had its origin.

'Would you like a drink, Inspector?' I asked. 'Is it too early for a spirit for you?'

Langton raised his hands at once to me. 'No, no, Mr Weaver. I am afraid that it is always too early for me no matter what time of day it is. I do not drink, you see. One drop of alcohol and I'm bedridden for days; it would seem that I'm destined never to enjoy the treasures of intoxication.'

'Good lord, how terrible for you!' I exclaimed. 'My dear man, you have nothing but my greatest sympathies.'

He laughed out loud. 'For your sympathies I am grateful, but it is a cross which I bear with bravery and strength!' There was, of course, sarcasm in his voice and I decided that, on first impressions, I liked this man. The initial nervousness had begun to settle with him and he continued, 'As I said earlier, I am a great admirer of your work. Your pictures are quite remarkable, and I always await, with relish, any copy of the paper where you have had a hand in the cover. Do you do all of your drawings on site? I understand that my predecessor, Inspector Thomas, would often call on you when heading to the scene of a crime.'

'I do initial drawings, Inspector. But a great deal of the work I bring home and finish here. Tell me, did you know the Inspector?'

'No, I am afraid that I never met him, although I had heard of him of course; the man was a legend. In fact, if you do not mind me coming straight to the point, he indeed is the reason why I am visiting you today.'

'Really?' I answered. 'Why is this?'

'Well, I have taken his office you see, not that it is a place where he ever spent much time. From all accounts when he wasn't out on the job he was touring the pubs in the area.'

I smiled gently at the thought. 'He had his own way of keeping his beat.'

'Indeed, indeed. Well, you see I am much more of an office type, if you will. I am more about using my mind and studying evidence to solve crimes, if you see what I mean?'

'But of course.' I looked him up and down. Although not small, there was something light about Inspector Langton, something in the way he held himself, how he sat even, that marked him out as a man of thought and not action.

'It was in Inspector Thomas's office that I came across something a couple of days ago. Something well hidden, something that I am not sure he wanted found – a notebook.'

'That would indeed be something that Abe would have wanted hidden.' I coughed. 'I have never known him take notes at a scene. Even the thought of him owning a book is quite bizarre.'

'Well, notes he did take, copious amounts; the book in my possession is nearly full and has been kept for at least six years.'

'Notes on what?'

He shifted nervously in his seat once more and stood, walking over to the window and glancing out of it.

'I am sorry. I am not normally the nervous type but what I have read in his notes is most alarming. You see, after reading them I did not know who to speak to – other than yourself. The Inspector held you in great regard and you are mentioned in the book as someone to trust in this matter.'

'This matter being?' I asked.

'Murder, Mr Weaver, terrible and ritualistic murder planned and overseen by those who we are led to believe are respectable and free from sin. Tell me, sir, what do you know of the Dolorian Club?'

It was my turn to be struck with anxiety.

'I have heard the name,' I said cautiously. 'In fact, it was one of the last things that Abe said to me. He told me he was suspicious of this club. What does his notebook say? Have you brought it with you?'

'No. It is in a place of safety now. I am not sure who it is safe to speak to at the moment – other than you. Inspector Thomas seemed to believe that they were the force behind the recent killings of servant girls in the area. He even claims that they were involved in the murders committed by Sibelius Darke back in 1877. He has done a great deal of research into the club and its members, although a lot of it is pure conjecture. Do you have any information on them?'

'Not much,' I lied. 'Although I would be glad to use my sources to look into them, if you wish.'

Langton's face dropped, not in sadness but in relief, and I found myself wanting to believe that this was a man who I could trust.

'I would be most grateful,' he said. 'I hope that you are a man I can rely on. People who I feel I can trust are in short supply. I will not lie to you, Mr Weaver – I am scared; scared but committed to bringing these men down, if what Abe has written is true.' He stood then and held out his hand for me to shake; and shake it I did.

'One last thing, Inspector,' I said as I clasped his palm. 'Have there been any other murders since Thomas's death? I had a friend… Alice, she is dear to me and went missing recently. I feared that she may have gone the way of the other girls but got short shrift when I reported it to the police.'

'I'm afraid not, Mr Weaver. In the last couple of weeks there has only been one vicious murder and that was not a young girl, it was a man who ran a local employment agency.' I attempted to remain untouched by his words. 'It was a brutal attack indeed; the man's skull was smashed to pieces. Whoever did it would be a man to avoid.'

I laughed then; perhaps the wrong response, but I could not help it. 'Then I should watch out for a skull-smashing monster on the loose as well keep an eye out for particulars about this club that you and Abe seem so worried about.' To my relief he joined in with my laughter, although his was more of a nervous chuckle, while he jotted an address on a piece of paper, which he said was a safe place to send any information I found. As I waved him off and watched him walk away down the street with his sergeant, there was a small glimmer of hope sparkling within my mind. Perhaps I had found an ally at last.

***

It was with a refreshed and committed mind that I went about my business that morning. I now knew that somehow I had to find a way to stop the Golden Woman and that only by halting her parade of killings at Falconer's behest would I then be able to attempt to tackle the man and his organisation in the best way I knew how: by exposing their schemes in the national newspapers.

Mr Purkess, although cautious in some respects, would not be able to stop himself from putting such a high-profile story on his front page. However, if he did refuse me I had decided that I would go to *The Times* or the *Daily Telegraph*.

I took a room in the Portland Hotel that looked out upon Cavendish Square and set about observing the Dolorian Club from a safe and secure distance. This form of observation would not be as obvious as my previous attempt, and I made sure that I came into and went from the hotel through one of the side doors, out of sight of the club and any of its members.

My watches throughout the day yielded no new information; many of those whom I saw coming and going through the large doors I had already noted on my previous visits. I saw the doorman, Mávnos, on numerous occasions, as well as the torturers Dawes and Soames. I wished to bring those two terrible men to justice for the happy jollity with which they carried out their heinous work, perhaps even more than I did Falconer.

It was at night, though, that I kept my closest eye on the comings and goings, for if the Golden Woman was indeed based within those walls, it was in darkness and shadow that she would appear.

After over a week of tiresome watching I caught no sight of her at all and I began to wonder if this was time wasted, time that could have been spent trying to convince Mr Purkess to go forward with the information that I had already gathered. I sent a couple of notes to Inspector Langton to inform him of my surveillance. It was on the eighth night, however, that I saw a figure draped in a black cloak emerge from the cellar stairs below the main doors of the house. There was an easy glide to the figure's movements, a way that the cowl of the cloak was brought low over the face, which told me immediately that this was my quarry.

Gathering the only tool which I felt I could use against her, I rushed from the hotel room. As I burst from the building, I saw that she had not yet left the square, but was nearing the far corner and would soon be out of sight. Others walked the streets but did not give her a second look. I sped through the central gardens, jumping over gates and bundling past pedestrians. She was still in sight, head down and walking at pace along the pavement, avoiding the looks of those whom she passed and hiding her face from the light of the gas lamps, which surely would have reflected her golden features to all. Carriages rumbled past her at speed, their wheels bouncing off the cobbles as they hurried towards their destinations. I was catching her fast and hoped beyond hope that I could reach her before she slipped into the shadows and ran with all of the speed that I knew her to possess.

Closer now, I concentrated my hearing on my prey, focusing on the hard metallic clicks that her feet made as they struck the paving stones. I slowed my pace to a brisk walk and found that I was catching her still. The perspiration poured from my forehead and into my eyes as my earlier exertions took their toll on my body. I was not a man made to run; if she gathered speed I would not be able to catch her.

Closer still and, had I reached an outstretched hand towards her, I would have been able to grab at her cloak and unclothe her for all to see; surely then none would be able to deny the fact that the Golden Woman was real? Yet I resisted and kept my pace.

The sound of my heartbeat thudded in my ears, pounding louder until I could no longer hear the sound of either her or my own foot-steps; even the noise of the constant hackneys flying down the road was lost to me. I looked up and along the street, counting the gas lamps ahead. There were three left before there was a stretch of dark-ness; time was running out before me; I needed the light.

Head down, I passed the Golden Woman, resisting the urge to turn and look at her. My feet began to pick up speed a little and I passed one lamppost. I was desperate to glance over my shoulder, to see just how far I was ahead of her, but I knew that if done too early it could ruin everything. I reached the second lamppost and thought to make my move, but something stopped me. I cursed myself for my inde-cision. I had only one chance left. The lamppost approached and the muscles in my arm tensed around the object in my hands, thinking through the next set of moves which I would have to make. 'I must be smooth,' I thought, 'I must be steady.'

I reached the lamppost and swung round, bringing Sibelius Darke's camera up to my eyes and flipping the lens cap off from the front. I was a full ten feet in front of the Golden Woman – I could see her face through the lens. I held it steady, capturing her image, catching my prey.

She stopped.

I did not move, and held the camera as steady as I could in my shak-ing hands.

There was no expression in her face, but I could sense that she was unsure of what I was doing. My shaking hand brought the lens cap slowly back up to the camera and I replaced it with a soft click.

Slowly the Golden Woman stepped towards me; I did not move, I could not. As in Regent's Park on our last meeting, she brought her-self close to me, observing me intently, her smooth golden eyes inches from my own and I saw my reflection in her face. People walked past us and, despite not taking my eyes from her own, I could tell that we were being noticed. Would she attack me here, in front of all of these people, in clear sight of passing carriages, their passengers and drivers? Would she strike me down in plain sight? Even though I had survived our last meeting I knew that she was a creation, an automaton not in possession of human awareness and sensibilities, and I fully expected to feel her blade between my ribs. Once again, however, it did not come. Perhaps Darke was right and past sins were my saving grace.

In a moment of madness I reached out with my free hand and grabbed her cloak. Her head lowered quickly, seeing my action, but it was too late to stop me and I pulled hard, with all the strength I could muster.

The cloak, which was fastened only by a golden clasp at the neck, fell from her and suddenly all movement around me stopped as the Golden Woman was exposed and naked for all within sight to behold. She had the form of an unclothed female but without explicit detail, her skin smooth and without feature, her hair as if moulded from melted gold. She froze as if turned into a beautiful but immobile statue for a short but devastating moment, shining brightly in the lamplight and drawing the gaze of all around her. There was a moment's silence and all time seemed to come to a jarred and deadened stop. I stood before her, her unveiler, a camera in one hand, the black cloak of a killer in the other.

Without warning she sprang into action, darting away into the road and narrowly avoiding two horses as they thundered past, pulling a large black carriage. A woman screamed and soon her cries were echoed by all, as the shining form of the golden creature leapt across the road towards an alleyway at the side of one of the large houses on Margaret Street. Wrapping my camera in her cloak, I gave chase and found myself sprinting after her, dodging through the night traffic and the people who stood dumbstruck at what they had just witnessed.

I knew that I would be no match for her if she decided to turn and take me on, but I had her in my sights; I was reluctant to lose her and gave not a damn about my safety in pursuit of my goal.

I bounded into the alleyway just in time to see her at the other end, turning left. She was not moving as quickly as she had in Regent's Park and I warranted that her unclothing and exposure had made her confused. She had set out into the night to commit a murder but everything had changed and she was now vulnerable.

As I ran down the alley, I could hear the sound of a policeman's whistle up ahead, followed by further shouts and cries as more and more people saw her. I followed the noises that came in her wake and saw that we were entering Park Crescent, a place as busy as any in London no matter what time of day or night.

The Golden Woman found herself in the middle of the road, surrounded by an ever-growing crowd of people. Her head turned frantically, looking for some escape, some path away from the eyes of the mob. They kept their distance, though, and a wide circle formed, full of the scared and the angry, a crowd of those that realised that this supposed make-believe killer, invented by the press and discounted by the law, was in fact very much real. The clamour of the crowd grew and more policemen arrived, themselves not knowing what to do now. The Golden Woman was trapped.

Suddenly she stood bolt upright and spread her arms wide, an action which brought sudden silence to those around her. The silence continued as all eyes gazed upon her and wondered what her next move would be; no one other than myself had seen her before and no one knew what to expect next.

Slowly, as if subject to a terrible yet invisible fire, her hands and the ends of her arms began to melt. They melded and moulded themselves, lengthening and flattening, until her arms appeared nothing less than two thin but deadly swords.

Still the crowd stood dumbstruck; it was as if they did not see the danger that had now befallen them, as if they thought themselves immune to her deadly power.

Her head turned and she surveyed the circle of people around her and the buildings which stood behind them. Her gaze settled in one spot and, before anyone had a chance to do anything to get out of her way, she charged the crowd at unbelievable speed, her arms swinging and spinning with such deadly force that they clove a path, leaving a line of shattered and bloody bodies in her wake.

Screams rang through the air followed by gunshots, as those policemen who were armed attempted to stop her with bullets, unaware of the futility of such actions. The bullets which struck her ricocheted off into the crowd, bringing further injury.

As the Golden Woman reached the edge of the pavement she leapt towards the building and her hands changed to spiked claws as she flew, so that they punched through brick and stone to form handholds for her to climb. Swiftly she began her ascent, smashing hole upon hole into the brickwork and rising towards the rooftop's edge.

Cries came from the police – to get men up to the roof, to cut her off – and men quickly ran into the buildings to climb the stairs to the top.

She scaled the building like a large golden spider, her head flicking from one side to the other as she made her path up, pausing frequently to survey her attackers. I knew that her face, if it were able to give expression, would be one of panic and fear.

Lights appeared on the tops of the buildings: men with torches stood on the edges, looking down at her as she scuttled up the wall towards them. She saw them and paused, desperately looking for another escape route, looking for a way to disappear from sight; there was none. She continued to climb but, as she reached the top and tried to clamber over the edge, the men attacked her with anything to hand. Some used iron bars to strike her, others hurled half bricks towards her.

Her hands changed to blades once more, slicing out at her attackers. But they were too many. Again and again they struck her until eventually one of her hands slipped from its grip on the parapet of the building. One of the men grabbed at the arm, seizing hold of it, and she pulled at him, sending him toppling over the edge and screaming into the baying crowd below. Another of her arms was seized, this time by two men who pushed at her, trying to send her down. This they managed and she fell backwards, dragging men with her. The crowd below saw what was going to happen and stumbled backwards, clearing a space on the pavement.

She fell.

I watched her and the two men, her last victims, as they plummeted towards the ground, the men crying in fear, knowing that their time was done; but from her there was no sound, no change in expression, no look of terror at her demise. She hit the ground first, the sound ringing through the air as metal struck stone and she shattered into pieces. The men landed on top of her, their bodies breaking and bleeding over the splintered lumps of gold that had once formed the shape of a beautiful woman.

For a moment there was silence as the crowd, and I, stood and stared at the blood and gold which littered the ground. I do not know who moved first, but I knew that I followed quickly. I dived at the broken mess, grabbing a lump of gold and stuffing it under my arm where I held her cloak and my camera. The crowd descended into frenzy, each trying to get a piece of her, not caring for the broken men who were cast aside in their lust for gold. I did not stay to watch; I walked slowly away back to the Portland Hotel, where I gathered my things and, hailing a passing carriage, went back to my rooms on Amberley Road. As I sat in the carriage and unrolled her cloak, I found that I held before me a perfectly formed hand. The hand of a golden killer, summoned to do the devil's work.

***

A half hour later I got home and slowly climbed the stairs to my rooms on the third floor. As I reached the top and looked down the corridor, I noted that a dim light shone out from beneath my door. The light was creeping and flickering across the crusted floorboards as if it were alive. I knew immediately that my fire had been lit; I was used to such a sight when coming home to Alice and Benjamin.

I paused for a moment, wondering what evil lay within. Was it Dawes and Soames returned to finish the job?

I thought of Alice and of how she had been taken from me and in that brief moment I also saw the image of my mother flash through my mind. I saw her face the last time that I visited her, so pale and lost, and remembered her violent removal and incarceration on the orders of my father. A knot of pain formed in the pit of my stomach, sending tendrils of anxiety through my body. My hand shook as I reached out for the door handle. So this was where I would meet my end.

As my fingers touched the cold metal, however, these pangs diminished and the ball of tension within me dissolved into a wave of calm. There was not the will nor the strength left within me to fight any more. All that I had held dear, little though it was, had been lost to me, taken by dark and irrepressible forces which could not be met. I turned the handle and calmly stepped inside to see a figure sitting in the high-backed cushioned chair next to the fire.

The high wings of the armchair shrouded the figure's face in darkness but I could tell that it was a man, well dressed and holding a half-empty bottle of brandy in his hand. He leaned forwards as I entered, the soft dancing glow of the flames illuminating his face.

'Hullo, old boy,' croaked the man. 'I'm afraid I have helped myself to your brandy supply. You really need to hide it better; any fool could have found it.'

I placed the bundle, still wrapped in the black cloak, upon the sideboard and lunged forward in relief, thrusting an outstretched hand towards my friend.

'Higgins! Good God man, you are a sight for sore eyes!' I shook his hand vigorously and it was then that I noted the sadness in his face. It sagged in weariness and he wore the stubble of more than one day's growth. His complexion was pale and damp, his cheeks sallow, and I thought then that he looked for all the world like a man with consumption. He sighed and sank back into the darkness of the chair. 'You look terrible,' I said. 'Are you sick?'

'I fear I may be ailing, Sam. But it is not a sickness that is recognised by any medical man. Things have been bad for me since our night together in Pluckley and our interaction with the spirit world. I have been plagued by terrible dreams and visions, haunted and chased; there is no escape for me, not even through my usual means.' He lifted the bottle to his lips.

I drew up a chair opposite him and sat. 'It would seem that we have both been cursed since that night, Edward. I could tell you stories of murder and death that I have witnessed that would make fine additions to your tour. But first you must explain your presence here. Is there something with which you feel I might help?'

His eyes raised towards me and he held out the bottle for me, which I took, gulping a swig.

'Do you remember the spirit that appeared above the Devil's Bush? The one that tried to speak to us?'

'Why of course, how could I forget...' I made to interrupt, to tell him about my meeting with Darke, but he continued.

'Well, it seems he is the insistent sort and, after you left, he attempted to visit my dreams on a nightly basis; it was all that I could do to resist him. I took to not sleeping, to try to save myself from his scourge, but lack of sleep can turn a man to madness, Sam, really it can.' He took the bottle back from me – it was nearly empty. 'I even confided in Tom at the Black Horse,' he continued. 'I told him that I was being plagued by the spirit that had wished to speak to him at the séance, but that I could sense the evil within it and would not let it in.'

'How did Tom react?' I asked.

'He became excited, Sam, very excited. He even asked that we go ahead with the séance; he said that he wished to speak to him. I could not allow it, though; I could not let this beast take over my body. I have told you before, Sam, that I do not revel in my so-called gift. If I did I could be a rich man by now, tending to the desperate needs of those who wish to speak to the loved and lost. No, it is not for me.'

'And is it this that has brought you to such a state of distress and undoing?' I asked, genuinely concerned for the welfare of my friend.

'Gods no, man. It takes more than a ghoulish visitor in the night to get to me. It was what Tom confided in me that has made me such a wreck.' He took another long swig of brandy, checking the bottle as he lowered it to see the paltry amount that remained. 'I am afraid I have emptied your house of booze.'

'You underestimate me, Higgins. Even you could not dry my house so easily.' I stood and made my way to my bedroom, picking up the cloak as I did so. Closing the bedroom door behind me, I moved the bed to one side before lifting the floorboards and pulling out a wide chest, within which I kept all of my notes, pictures and items of interest concerning Sibelius Darke, and subsequently the Dolorian Club.

Therein I carefully placed the hand. I knew that I could trust Higgins with everything that I knew about the Golden Woman murders but, for some reason, I wished to keep the hand to myself; it was not only an item of value because of the metal of which it was made, but a memento of the murders, and I knew that its value would be unlimited once the truth of this whole affair came to light.

After ensuring that the chest was safely hidden under the bed once more, I opened my bedside cabinets, wherein lay another bottle of brandy; one which I kept in case of emergency. The visit of Higgins to my home was indeed a suitable example of this.

'I apologise for the delay, Edward,' I said, passing a new bottle to him, the label of which he examined briefly before hungrily pulling on the stopper. 'Pray continue with your story, I am listening.'

Higgins withdrew a cigarette case from the inside of his jacket and lit himself a stick before dropping into the storytelling manner which he employed to such good use.

***

'It was late one evening and the Black Horse was beginning to clear. It had been a good night for me; I had taken a small group from London around many ghostly spots of interest, some that you saw and a few others besides. They had been most appreciative, paid well and even put some money behind the bar to pay for my beverages.

'Miss Finnan was in fine spirits for a change and had not hurried me along after ringing the bell and I was looking forward to a rare bit of after-hours drinking. According to Anne, Tom had been out since just after lunch on one of his secretive jaunts which had become much more frequent of late. I noticed that I was the only customer left and had decided to chance my arm and ask for another, when Tom came blustering in, full of bother and fret. Anne asked him what was wrong, and it was clear that she was unused to seeing him like this. He brushed her concerns away, however, and, seeing me, said that he was glad that I was still there and that he needed to have a private word; Anne took the hint and left us.

'I was a little nervous as I wondered whether he would attempt to persuade me to commune with the devil in my dreams again, but decided to give the man my time – as long as the booze kept flowing. Thankfully it did. Tom stepped behind the bar and brought out a bottle of Grant's Morella, which he knew I could never resist. He poured us both a good measure and opened his mouth to speak; however, I stopped him before a word could pass his lips.

"If you plan to have me infested with some sort of demon spirit from the otherworld then you are wasting your time, Tom," I said, quickly picking up my drink before he could snatch it back.

"Nothing of the sort, Edward," he said, smiling. "You have made your beliefs perfectly clear and I would not force a man to undertake such an action. I have another proposition for you, one which comes after an explanation of sorts. An explanation as to where I disappear to during the day and to the nature of my presence in this village."

"Well, I must say that I had wondered what you have been up to, Tom. I assumed it was some religious task, seeing as you spend so much time in the company of Mr Williams, the verger. I have even gone so far as to quiz the verger myself, but found him to be aggravatingly unhelpful."

'Tom laughed at this comment and told me that Mr Williams was a good friend and most certainly a man to be trusted. I drained my glass and was overjoyed when Tom filled it once more.

"As you may know, I lived and worked in Whitechapel before coming here," Tom said. "Anne and I ran a pub called the Princess Alice; my daughter lived with us also. Tell me, Edward," he said cautiously, toying with the rim of his glass. "Have you ever heard of Sibelius Darke?"

"Why of course," I said. "There is not a man in England surely who does not know of his terrible crimes and how he terrorised London. I just wish he had visited Pluckley so that I could include him in my tour. You didn't know him, did you?"

"I did, Edward. I knew him very well, since he was a child in fact. He was like a son to me and his brother was betrothed to my daughter Bethany."

"But didn't he murder his brother and father in cold blood?"

"That is what people have been led to believe, but it is not true. Nor did he commit the child murders that he was accused of."

"'But was he not seen striding out of his club as it was engulfed in flames? Had he not walked the halls and rooms shooting dead any club members in his path?"

"'That he did do… but I can speak for him for those crimes. You see, it was not he who committed the child killings and those of his brother and father. They were carried out by some kind of otherworldly beast that inhabited a human form and killed upon the instruction of its master."

"'What?" I exclaimed, thinking that Tom must have spent the day drinking in the sort of quantities I thought familiar only to me.

"'Darke's club controlled the beast and bade it kill," said Tom. "When Sibelius discovered the truth, he destroyed the club and later vanquished the beast, dying himself in the process."

"'But what has this got to do with you and your move to Pluckley?" I asked, proffering my glass for another refill.

"'The effects of the murders upon my daughter, Bethany, were terrible; she lost her mind through the trauma of losing both her betrothed, Nikolas Darke, and subsequently his brother Sibelius, whom she had grown close to. She saw some awful things when aiding Sibelius to discover the truth. She witnessed the murder of children and even came face to face with the demonic spirit itself. It was all too much and she retreated into herself. In the end, Anne and I had no choice but to commit her to a safe place, while I carried out my own revenge for the loss of Sibelius and the damage to Bethany's mind."

'I could not help but smile.

"'It may seem to be humorous to you, Edward," he continued. "I understand that I am not everyone's idea of an avenging angel, but I was angered by the course of events. I had lost my dearest friend and my daughter; someone had to be to blame."

"'But you said that Darke had killed them all?" I said.

"'Not all. He had taken many lives when he had burnt the club to the ground, but it is a large organisation connected to many influential individuals and, of course, not every member was there during the fire. In fact, many of the more leading members were absent at the time. Of the inner circle who led the organisation, only Charles Earnshaw died." Tom paused for a moment and finally took a small sip. "I followed the story in the newspapers," he continued. "I scanned them daily for word of the club. Soon all of the rats came scurrying from the woodwork, stating publicly how terrible Darke had been to try to damage such an important institution, not just a club but a fellowship of men committed to the furtherance of our country.

'"One man came forward who had donated his house in London as a new base for the club, a place where they could start afresh and continue striving towards the values that they held dear; that man was Lord William Falconer. I decided to concentrate my efforts on the man, find out all I could, but he is a living mystery; on one side is the man about town, often seen at the music halls and society gatherings of London, but on the other, he would often disappear for weeks on end, with no one knowing or being willing to admit where he went. I discovered that his country home lay here, not three miles away at Surrenden Manor. According to some, he had won it in a card game."

'Tom told me then how he and Anne had visited Pluckley to come and see the house for himself. They had even stayed at the Black Horse, when it was owned and occupied by the previous landlord. It seems he had some money put away and he offered to buy the Black Horse for more than it was worth in order to obtain it; the landlord agreed.

'Tom and his sister moved in shortly afterwards, first selling their pub in Whitechapel, and Tom spent his days going off to investigate the big house and find out all he could about its occupier, noting down all visitors. He ingratiated himself with the servants, many of whom either lived or day-tripped into the village. Finally, after listening to the many ghost stories concerning Pluckley and the surrounding area, he heard tell of a secret passage which led from St Nicholas's Church straight to Surrenden Manor. Working with Mr Williams, the verger, he journeyed through this passage to conduct surveillance on the house and its inhabitants.

'He has discovered some terrible things, Samuel; terrible, terrible things; stories of ritual murder and of offerings to some dark power. It is enough to turn your hair white, truly it is. But now that he has the information he requires, he has sent me to you, Sam. He knows who you are, of the job you do, and who you work for; he wants you to expose Falconer. I fear for him, though, I really do. Surely it is only a matter of time before this Falconer fellow finds him out and then God only knows what will befall him – or anyone connected with him, me included. We are all in terrible danger, Sam, and you have the tools that Tom needs to bring us to safety, you and your newspaper. Will you come back to Pluckley with me and meet with him?'

***

I had listened closely and carefully to Edward's tale, to the pleading tone of his voice when he asked me to return with him, but all the time my mind had been spinning in thought. Suddenly there was clarity in my mind; firstly, regarding the stag's head painted on the wall at Boston Place and the subsequent appearance of these forms on the gateposts of Surrenden; secondly, concerning Tom's mysterious disappearance when I had tried to follow him during my day in the village; and lastly the absolute truth that Falconer was indeed the villain that I knew him to be.

For the first time in so very long I felt that I was not alone in my fight; a friend, Higgins, had appeared this night and I now knew that Tom had as much reason to hate the Dolorian Club and its members as I did for their part in Alice's death. I raised my bottle to old Edward then.

'Of course I will return with you,' I said. 'Like Tom, I already have much evidence against Falconer and his fellows, and together I am sure that we will have enough to bring them down. I have even met this so-called lord in person, Edward; the man is a beast who must be stopped before he takes any more innocent lives.'

'You have met Lord Falconer?' Edward exclaimed. 'You are a braver man than I gave credit, Samuel. If what Tom said of him is true then you are lucky to still be alive.'

'I think he toyed with me. He enjoys watching people suffer and, by his actions towards me, he gained greater enjoyment through observing my mental pain. It is of no matter, though; we have him now and will bring about his downfall together. However, I must pay a visit to my employer George Purkess tomorrow, first thing; I will not tell him much, merely that he can hold his front page for this week until I return from Pluckley. I know that Falconer's club has widespread interests and connections throughout London, but I am sure of Mr Purkess; he is a man whom I would trust above all others. Once I have seen him, we will travel back to Pluckley, where Tom and I will compare our evidence and destroy Falconer once and for all.'

For the first time since Alice's disappearance I wore a smile on my face. While Edward and I sat for a while drinking and talking, he described to me how even inside the manor house there were secret tunnels and passageways, which were used by Tom and the verger Williams to keep watch on the club members' activities when they were in residence. However, they had still not seen Falconer himself, as he had always remained obscured from the various spyholes.

I told him of Alice and Benjamin and of how I had been happy in their company; of how I had, for the first time, dreamt of living as a family with someone, and of how those dreams were dashed by Falconer. I rambled on, telling him of the Golden Woman and the murders of the servant girls and explained how, this very night, she had been destroyed.

I do not know how long I spoke, but when I had finished telling my story, I realised that Edward Higgins was long gone in the chair, a half-empty bottle of brandy still clutched to his sleeping body.

15

A Most Disreputable Party

I stood before the hearth, watching the flames as they danced and caught on the coals, carefully placed there by Mrs Coleman shortly after daybreak. The fireplace had a brass surround which was polished to within an inch of its life on a weekly basis by her, too. On one side stood a coal bucket, also brass, which, thanks to Morgan, I had never seen empty in any of the nineteen years that I had lived. The fire was dwindling and I took the poker from the stand, feeling the weight of it, before idly poking at the coals, stirring them into life.

The carriage to take me to York Station had been arranged for eleven and I had ventured out of my bedroom and down the stairs early to the dining room to breakfast. Mrs Coleman, who had served up an insurmountably large plateful for me, was now upstairs putting the finishing touches to my suitcases; she had been told by Father that I should be packed for a long trip and that he did not expect me to return for some time.

Father had arranged rooms for me in Amberley Road, Paddington. I was assured by Father that, whilst small, they would fully meet my needs and would be the ideal starting point for my new life. I would be met at King's Cross Station by a colleague of Father's (I did not dare to think in what capacity, as he could have been anything from an archbishop to a brutal gang enforcer). Once met, I would be escorted to my rooms and given the keys, whereupon the associate would then leave me and continue his own business, be that preparing a liturgy or planning a murder.

The rest, Father informed me, was entirely up to me; if I wanted a position on one of the London papers badly enough, then I would have to use my own skills of persuasion. He did, however, add that there would be a monthly allowance available for me to access if I wished; this I understood to be Father's way of ensuring that, even if I were unsuccessful in finding work, I would not return to York to ask for money.

It was a little after nine when I heard a carriage pull up outside. It was far too early for my ride to the station, so I assumed that it was Father, come back from one of his morning calls to ensure I was indeed leaving. I continued to prod the coals as the door to the drawing room opened behind me and he entered.

'All is set, then,' he said. 'Your carriage should be here in a little over an hour. I take it all your bags are packed?'

'Yes, thank you, Father,' I replied. 'Your thoughtfulness and care for my well-being are quite overwhelming.' The tip of the poker nudged one of the new coals into the centre of the fire and its edges began to sizzle slightly as the heat took hold. I left the poker pressed into the coals.

'You know that you can write to me? It would be good to know of your exploits in the capital city. A life in London is all quite exciting; really, I am jealous of this adventure of yours.'

I still had not turned to face him and continued to stare deep into the flames.

'Well, please feel free to go in my stead if you wish. Far be it for me to deny you the opportunity for excitement – although it would seem that nothing much denies you from engaging in your pleasures. My future life looks positively dull in comparison.'

I heard the rustle of his clothing as he stepped towards me; still I would not turn to look at him. The tip of the poker began to glow red and I could feel the heat of the fire running up the metal and into my hand.

'One day I hope that we can mend this. Perhaps we will restore what we have lost.' I could not see him, but I felt sure that he held out an arm towards me, his hand hovering just inches from my shoulder.

'Restore what we have lost? Tell me, Father, what is it that we lost along the way? Was it Mother?'

'Let us not bring your mother into this. I did what I did for the good of us all – you do not know the full story.'

'And nor do I wish to. I know enough now. I have had enough of your tawdry lies!' The poker was bright red now and my right hand began to burn, the pain tingling in my fingers, making me want to drop it; I did not, though. 'Did you come to say goodbye, or sorry? Whichever it is, get it over with.'

'Son, I...'

I felt the weight of his hand upon my shoulder and I swung around, the poker striking him on the left side of his face. He dropped to the floor, smashing into the small drawing-room table, the glass lamp sitting on it moments before hitting the floor and shattering into a thousand pieces. I stood over him, poker in hand, waiting for him to try to rise to his feet; he did not move.

I watched him cautiously, looking for any sense of movement from him.

A light wispy gasp from his lips told me that he still lived and I raised my hand ready to strike once more. There was a large red welt appearing on his temple. His chest rose and fell in the slightest of manners and I knew that he would wake at any second. I put the tip of the poker back into the fire, resting it on the grate, and calmly took a seat, my eyes not once leaving Father.

I glanced up at the clock once more; there was time still.

For a five full minutes I sat and watched him. Here was the man who had imprisoned my mother; here was the man who had lied to me his whole life; here was the man who had taken everything.

Still he did not wake.

Slowly I got to my feet and picked up the woollen cloth which sat by the coal bucket. Wrapping it around my hand I retrieved the poker from the fire. Its end glowed bright as I stood over Father.

With the outside of my boot I nudged his shoulder; no response. I pushed a little harder with my foot, rolling him onto his back. How helpless he was. Any more time wasted and I would lose the heat; it had to be now. .

Holding the handle of the poker with both hands I brought it swiftly down. His shirt caught fire and his flesh sizzled as the poker slid into his chest and through his heart. For a terrifying moment he brought his arms and legs up to meet me, but there was no going back now and a gush of smoke billowed up to meet me, filling my nostrils.

Feeling the tip of the poker hit the floor below, I withdrew it quickly. A perfect hole had been created through my father and, at last, the job was done. There was no expression on his face; I did not know what I expected to see there, but I knew that, at that moment, I felt almost a little disappointment that he had not suffered more in his passing. His shirt still smouldered; I stamped it out.

A sound from behind in the doorway caused me to turn suddenly. Mrs Coleman was standing there, my suitcase in her hand.

'Is it done now?' she asked.

'It is; Father and I enjoyed a truly heart-warming moment,' I said, carefully returning the still-warm poker to the ornate and beautifully polished brass stand. 'How long will it be before my carriage arrives?'

'Time enough to clear this mess up,' she said, placing my suitcase on the floor, her broad smile sitting lovingly upon her face.

***

I awoke early, my head throbbing in pain from the evening's brandy. I thought of my visitor and listened out for any sign that he was awake; there was none and so, rolling from my bed, I padded through to the living room where I found Higgins still asleep in the armchair. He had not moved an inch, it seemed, and I observed him closely for a short while, just to ensure that he was still breathing. When he jumped a little and muttered in his sleep, I jerked back. Content that he had not expired in the night, I decided to leave him for a bit to continue to sleep it off.

It was as I was walking to the kitchen to put on some coffee that I noticed a letter that had been slipped under my door; it was from George Purkess. It would seem that the events of the previous evening in Park Crescent were now the talk of London and, due to the late hour when the demise of the Golden Woman had occurred, none of the dailies had as yet managed to put anything in print about it. Mr Purkess was worried that they would steal a march on him and his paper by taking the Golden Woman – 'his own story' – from him.

I glanced at Higgins once more, still sleeping, and decided to leave him a note, telling him I would be returned before midday and that our journey back to Pluckley would begin straight afterwards.

Assured that he still slept and that the note was attached to the first thing he would check upon waking – the brandy bottle – I set off.

The carriage ride to the office was quick and I was soon standing before Henry Cope, who wore a smile at my arrival which unnerved me completely.

'Weaver, you are prompt indeed, for I only sent the boy with the message not an hour ago. Exciting times. I suppose you will have heard about the events of last night in Park Crescent?'

'Heard, Mr Cope?' I replied. 'I was there myself, sir. Quite remarkable really, and altogether reassuring to know that I, and indeed Mr Purkess, by allowing me to publish, were perfectly correct in our claims of a Golden Woman. Tell me, is he in? I would very much like to see him and tell all.'

'Why yes, of course; he has been anxious to get hold of you since the news reached his club last night. It is amazing how quickly these things spread about town. Although I suppose Cavendish Square is quite close to where it all happened.'

I made to move towards the staircase which led to Mr Purkess's office but stopped in my tracks.

'Cavendish Square, you say. Is that where his club is?'

'Yes, I suppose that there would be no reason for you to know which club he belonged to, but it is not something that he has ever hidden. Why would he?'

I shrugged my shoulders nonchalantly. 'No reason, I suppose. I shall go straight up.'

'Marvellous,' beamed Cope. 'I shall go out to fetch coffees for you myself.'

I made to climb the stairs. Surely nowhere was now safe for me? Other than Tom Finnan and Higgins, I could not vouch for a soul any more. I stopped on the second stair and turned quickly. Cope was still watching, a broad grin plastered on his face.

'Problem?' he asked.

'No, Mr Cope, no problem at all. It's just that, before I go to see Mr Purkess, would it be possible to borrow some paper and a pen of some description? I just want to make sure that I have recorded all the facts of last night and have them clear in my mind before I speak to the old boy.'

Cope fetched me what I had asked for and said that he would return presently with the coffees. I watched him scuttle out of the door before settling down at his desk to write.

I did not, of course, jot down any notes, but instead wrote a short scribbled message for Inspector Langton. I gave the note to one of the boys who regularly sat in the reception awaiting running jobs and, pressing half a crown into his hand, whispered its destination, promising that the man receiving the message would provide the same to him should he deliver it swiftly enough. Without a word, the boy stuffed the note into his pocket and ran from the offices.

I looked once more at the stairs and wondered whether I would gain anything from ascending them and seeing Purkess one more time. My foot resting on the first step, I looked around and noted that all eyes of the office were upon me, almost threatening in their gaze.

I turned and made for the door, calling over my shoulder to anyone who would listen, 'Tell Mr Purkess I shall return this afternoon; I have a pressing engagement!'

***

The train journey was uneventful, and, in an attempt to lift the gloom and sense of threat which seemed to hang over us, Higgins and I attempted to scare the wits from each other with our most gruesome tales. These invariably involved stories of ghosts and the underworld from Higgins and of terrible murder, blood and depravity from myself. Despite my recent brushes with the supernatural, I remained convinced that it was brutal reality and the terrors that come from within the human soul which send the most chills through the spine.

As much as I enjoyed Higgins's storytelling, I knew that I was correct in my opinion – and that my very good friend would never even be able to contemplate the types of scenes which I had witnessed and attended in the past. I pictured the look that would be on his face if he were to stand behind me, watching me quickly sketch the body of a small child hacked to pieces by their drunken father; I doubted he could bear to stay more than a minute. I thought of the words that I had told Abe Thomas: 'Some people are meant for this.' And it was true, for it took a particular type of individual to be able to cut themselves off from their emotions enough to do paid work when the dead lay before them.

Unlike the weather on my last visit to Pluckley, there was not an inch of clear sky to be seen overhead as the train pulled into the station. Grey, stormy clouds fought for space above us, moving swiftly as the harsh winds pushed them about, sending them rumbling into one another. Of rain, however, there was no sign, not even the slim portent of such; the afternoon was instead dry and drawn tight.

We stepped from the train onto the empty platform and I wondered whether anyone, other than myself and Higgins, had set foot in this place since I left here in the summer. As I expected, the station clock read twenty minutes past eight and I told myself that it was not worth even looking at my watch or asking for the time for the duration of my stay here.

'Are we walking to the village, old man?' I asked.

'No, Sam, I have arranged for a carriage to take us to the Black Horse,' Higgins replied, looking along the lane for any sign of life. 'Once there I must return to my cottage for a short while. Tom is expecting you and there will be much to talk about before my return.' Although his face was dour he attempted to lighten the tone by adding, 'Perhaps you can have a large drink or two ready for me on my return; something to strengthen the nerves.' His eyes flashed nervously at me, as if searching for any hint of happiness that might break through the overwhelming sense of oppression which hung in the air.

'Of course.' I forced a smile.

He smiled and pointed towards the gate of the station, where a small horse-drawn carriage awaited us, next to the Dering Arms. The driver, seeing us approach, stepped down from his seat and, without saying a word, nodded towards Higgins and opened the door for us.

'How do you have access to such a carriage in the middle of nowhere?' I joked as we took our seats.

Edward looked a little embarrassed by my comment and would

only reply, 'I know people, Samuel. You would be amazed. There is a lot to be gained from being the jovial drunkard who is a friend to all.'

I smiled at this comment; I had honestly known no better nor friendlier man in my lifetime and could not imagine anyone refusing a request of his. We spent the short journey up the lane to the Black Horse looking out over the rolling fields, and my attention was drawn once to more to the houses which, as during my last visit, betrayed no trace of inhabitation or their occupants.

'Tell me, Edward,' I said, as we ambled past a deserted farm. 'Where does everyone in this village actually live? The only place where I have seen any of the residents is in Tom's pub. Surely they must return home or go out to work at some point?'

'Oh they are there,' he replied, staring out over the fields.

We lapsed into silence as, on a hill in the distance, we saw Surrenden Manor. Somehow it looked more imposing and deathly now: a dark scar on the landscape casting a shadow over everything in its view. If what Higgins had told me was correct about the place, combined with my own knowledge of the ritual murders carried out by the Dolorian Club at Boston Place and in the streets of London, then it surely was a place to be feared; and yet here we were heading.

We neared the end of the lane and turned left, the church and Tom's pub coming into view. There was no smoke coming from the chimney of the Black Horse and I wondered whether it was even open, as there seemed to be no sign of life. As the carriage pulled up outside, I jumped down with my small bag, turning to wave Edward off as the wheels started turning once more.

'I shall be a short while, Sam!' Higgins called from the window. 'Don't do anything rash without me. Just sit and hear what Finnan has to say!'

I watched the carriage as it disappeared from sight, before trying the door of the pub; it was locked. I thought to check my watch, but knew it to be a pointless task. There was no light coming from inside and I could see no sign of activity. I returned to the door, rapping hard on the wood.

'Mr Finnan, are you in there?' I called. 'It is Sam Weaver!' Nothing; I knocked again and stepped back to look up at the windows on the first floor. As my eyes travelled upwards I caught a glimpse of the movement of a curtain.

'Tom!' I called again. 'It is Samuel Weaver; Higgins has brought me to see you, as you asked!' The curtain twitched again and I saw Anne Finnan's face appear, pale and ghostly. 'Miss Finnan, it is Samuel Weaver, do you remember me? I stayed here in the summer... Is your brother in?'

She struggled with the window momentarily before forcing it open and leaning out. 'Go away!' she called. 'Tom is not here and we're shut. I shall not open up again until he returns!'

'When will he return? He sent Edward Higgins to fetch me from London; it is a matter of some urgency. Can you not let me in to wait until he returns?'

Her face was thunderous and she pulled the window closed with a slam. I was beginning to wonder if she had decided to ignore me, when I heard a bustling from inside and the locks of the pub door were pulled clear, the door opening slightly. Anne's face appeared from the darkness.

'I don't know when he will be back... or if,' she said.

'What do you mean? Can I come in?'

The door was opened just enough so that I could squeeze inside. Once she had bolted it shut behind me, she broke down.

'I do not know where he has gone,' she sobbed. 'He left yesterday, before the pub was due to open. He seemed very agitated about something. When I asked him what was going on, he said that he couldn't tell me all of it, as it would put me further in danger. He said that I should close up behind him and not open the door again until he returned here. Where is Edward? You say he brought you back to see Tom?'

'Edward has returned to his cottage – he will be here shortly.' I placed my hands on Anne's shoulders in an effort to calm her. 'Do you really have no idea where he is, Anne? It is very important; Tom was correct, there is great danger and I fear he may have done something rash.'

The tears fell from Anne's eyes at my words and she pushed herself into my chest, sobbing. 'The verger, Mr Williams, came to see him in

the morning; he seemed flustered and the pair of them talked for quite
a while. After Mr Williams left, Tom immediately called me down
from upstairs. He told me that I should not open the pub nor answer
the door. I watched him as he went; he walked off towards the church.
I am so scared for him, Mr Weaver. There was a look in his eyes, the
like of which I have never seen before, so much anger. I have not slept
all night for worry.'

'Worry no longer, Anne,' I said, holding her tightly to me. 'Edward
and I are here now and we will bring him back, I promise.'

A sudden rap on the door caused us both to jump in fright.

'Anyone home? I'm dying for a drink if there's one going,' came
the voice of Higgins from outside.

'Anne, fetch me a bottle of brandy and lock the door again behind
me,' I said. 'Edward and I will return with Tom, trust me.'

I unbolted the door as Anne fetched a bottle from behind the bar.
As I opened it, I saw Higgins standing there, a look of confusion on
his face.

'What's going on? Where's Tom?' he asked.

'I shall explain on the way,' I said. 'Remember what I said, Anne.
Do not open the door until our return.'

She nodded and, when I had joined Higgins outside, slammed
the door shut. Higgins's face was the picture of bewilderment, only
altered when I uncorked the bottle.

'Here, Edward,' I said. 'Have a drink – you will need it, we are
going to church.'

***

The door to the church was locked also and I began to get the
impression that the entire village was shut away behind bolted doors.
This did nothing to reduce the fears I had regarding what had made
Tom become so agitated before he disappeared. Something must have
changed to make Tom act so. He would have known that Higgins
would be returning to the village with me by his side and I wondered
what he had been told by the verger that could be so important.

I banged hard on the door, but with no reply I found myself walking around the church and peering through the windows as I had

226

done before on my last visit. There seemed to be no sign of movement within and I thought of the secret passageway leading to Surrenden Manor. If both Tom and the verger had travelled through this passageway then they could be a full two miles away from here, under the ground.

'Any sign of them?' asked Higgins, who had remained at the door to the vestry and was a full quarter way through the bottle of brandy.

'None,' I said thoughtfully. 'Tell me, Edward, are you a religious man?'

He smiled a little before replying. 'I would think, Sam, that everything that I have heard of or seen in Pluckley would make me the most religious man in the land but no, religion is and will always be a mystery to me; all that kneeling and faith in the invisible, it stretches even my imagination too far. Why do you ask?'

I took the bottle from him and took a swig before passing it back.

'Oh, I didn't want to offend you, old man, that's all,' I said as I took a step back and kicked at the door hard. The wood around the lock splintered and the door gave way, swinging inwards; I stepped into the church followed by my dumbstruck companion.

There was indeed no one to be seen inside and I strode forwards to look in the vestry, which was also empty.

'Higgins,' I said, as we approached the doorway to the crypt, 'how are you with the dark?'

His face blanched and I could see that we would soon be coming to the point where I would be on my own. We descended.

Candles were lighted in the crypt, causing the tombs of the Dering family to cast large shadows upon the wall. The soft glow from the candles revealed what I knew would be there. On the wall underneath one of the arches, beneath the yellow shield with the black cross belonging to the House of Dering, a doorway now stood – a doorway which I had not seen on my last visit. As I neared it I could see that a piece of false wall had been pushed aside at the entrance to a tunnel. The passageway was dimly lit by candles in sconces, heading down into the depths as the tunnel dropped steeply deep into the earth. Behind me, Higgins cleared his throat.

'I've been thinking, Sam,' he said, looking at the floor. 'Perhaps it would be better if one of us stayed here at the entrance, to guard the rear, so to speak. I would hate for us to disappear in that godforsaken place without anyone being left behind to raise the alarm if we didn't return.'

I smiled at my friend, taking one more sip of his brandy, and I clapped him on the shoulder.

'Very good, Edward. I was thinking the very same thing myself. I shall head into here and see if there is any sign of Tom or the verger. If by the time I reach the manor I have not found them, I will return immediately. How far do you think it is from here? One and a half, maybe two miles?'

'Two, I would think.'

'Perfect. Then shall we say that if I do not return within two hours then you are to return to the Black Horse immediately and call for assistance? Contact the local police, it doesn't matter too much what you say, as long as they come to the manor looking for me. Tell them that an intruder is heading to Surrenden intent on burning it down or something; that should bring out enough of them.'

'Damn me for a coward, Sam,' Higgins said, taking the stopper out of the bottle once more.

'Do not give it a second thought, my friend,' I said. 'We both have a role to play here, Edward. Yours will be as important as mine should things not go our way. I shall see you shortly.' Head down, I stepped into the passageway and began walking.

The tunnel was bricked and seemed sturdy enough; I picked up one of the larger candles and carried it with me as I went. The walls were damp and running with water in places, which made the floor puddle at some points and muddy in others. Lighted candles were set into the wall at twenty-feet intervals and I could see the wax from many candles past, melted and covering the sections of the wall where the small alcoves stood. There was no sound other than that of my own footsteps and I began to feel not a little nervous the farther I travelled into the darkness. There was a damp, mildewed smell to the passage and a cloying heat which only made my nervous perspiration worse the further I walked.

After about fifteen minutes of walking I saw ahead of me a widening of the passageway into what looked like a small room. It was well lit and I heard a small noise as I approached. I slowed to a creep, extinguishing my candle, and began to edge along the moist wall.

I stopped as I reached the entrance, my back pressed hard into the side of the tunnel, my breathing deep and controlled. There was certainly someone up ahead. Cautiously I peered around the corner and found the verger, Mr Williams, sitting hunched over a desk; he had not heard me approach. I stepped into the room.

Williams immediately jumped out of his seat and swung towards me with a letter opener brandished in his hand.

'Who are you?' he cried. 'Tell me now or I will use this; I am on the edge!' The short man's dark suit was heavily caked in the mud of the walls.

I raised my hands in submission.

'Please calm down, Mr Williams,' I said. 'I mean you no harm. I am Samuel Weaver, a friend of Tom Finnan.'

'Weaver, you say.' He pushed his glasses a little farther up his nose and studied me intently, the letter opener still raised in his hand. 'Tom never mentioned you. How am I to know who you are?'

I took a step towards him, causing him to start and jump backwards.

'Edward Higgins brought me to Pluckley at the request of Tom. I know of your business here in this tunnel and of where it leads; I am here to help.'

'Higgins? Edward Higgins? Where is he? If he brought you here then where is he now?' The blade in his hand dropped a little.

'Edward is back in the crypt awaiting my return. Now, where is Tom?'

'I do not know. That is, I fear he has been taken. Tom and I have been travelling this tunnel for a long time now, watching the manor, recording the comings and goings. We have never seen Falconer himself; although we have heard his voice, he has always remained obscured from view. Two nights ago, whilst at the end of the tunnel, watching through the eyehole which shows the drawing room, I saw two men discussing an forthcoming party – something significant was being planned, a visit from royalty. I left immediately and returned to the village to find Tom. He became most animated and said that we should return to the manor through the passageway to find out more. He said that help would be coming to us soon, but that it was important to gather as much information as we could. Are you that help?'

'Yes, I am. I am a newspaper correspondent. He asked me to come so that he could tell me all and we could expose the Lord of Surrenden Manor and all under his governance. Now where is Tom?'

Williams looked downwards, his expression one of fear.

'Well, there's the thing, you see. Tom told me to stay here and wait for him, but that was hours ago. When at first he did not return, I made my way along the corridor towards the manor again – and that is when I heard his cries.' Williams stopped for a moment, gathering himself. 'I should have kept on going and tried to help him, but I ran; God help me, I ran from him when he needed me most.'

'But why did you not return to the church, to the village, raise help?'

'I did, but as I neared the crypt I heard the voices of men, and I knew that I was trapped here. Was there no one in the church when you arrived? No sign of any intruders?'

'No, it is safe to return now I think, but I must carry on and find out what has happened to Tom.' I took the little man by the shoulder. 'Go back to the church and tell Higgins what you have told me. Tell him that I am headed for the manor and to raise the alarm as planned. Hopefully we will not be too late to save Tom. Now go!'

Williams scuttled off along the corridor, muttering to himself nervously as he went. Here was a man surely taken to the very edge of madness and despair by this affair, and I pitied him.

***

I continued down the corridor for what seemed like a lifetime, holding my candle out in front of me. Each drip of water, each echo of my own footsteps caused me to step warily through the darkness. I imagined that Williams had now met with Edward in the crypt and that they were currently heading off to get help from somewhere. The nearest town to Pluckley, however, was Ashford and I knew it this was over four miles away. I could only hope that the 'people' that

Higgins knew, and their carriage, would be able to take my friend there to bring back assistance. I did not know what I would do in the meantime; perhaps if I could at least find out if Finnan was still alive then that would be a start.

The passageway continued to wind until at last it began to slope upwards to what I hoped would be the surface, and Surrenden Manor. As I rose, the ground became firmer underfoot and the walls appeared to dry out somewhat until I came to an oaken door.

I pressed my ear against the door, listening for any kind of sound on the other side; there was none. I slowly turned the handle, peering through the crack as the door opened. I saw what appeared to be a meeting point in a corridor of some sort. There were four exits, not including the one that I had arrived by, and each led off in a different direction. Higgins had told me that rather than just leading to one place in Surrenden Manor, the secret passageways led to concealed doorways and viewing points throughout the house, hidden within false walls and behind bookcases. It was through these viewing points that I supposed Tom and the verger had maintained a constant watch over the manor and its inhabitants, apparently keeping copious notes on the comings and goings, and of the terror which had been performed here.

I decided to remain on the ground floor to start my search and took the path to my left. I trod carefully so as not to make any noise and, seeing that there was light ahead coming from the holes in the walls which spied into the rooms, I blew out my candle. It was as the candle was snuffed that I heard my first noises from inside the house; it was the sound of men talking.

I crept forwards to the first viewing point and hesitantly peered through. This was the drawing room that Williams had spoken of. Now sitting in the room, as far as I could see from my vantage point, were a number of men dressed in evening wear, lounging on plush couches, drinking and smoking cigars. Their conversations were many and mostly carried out in quiet mumbles. Occasionally I would hear the odd word. It was nothing of import: discussions on articles seen in the newspapers, a sudden impromptu laugh or guffaw.

It was no different from any other drawing room in any stately home or gentlemen's club throughout the country.

I have to say that I was a little disappointed in this; it was not as if I wished to hear tales of human sacrifice and worship of long-dead foreign witches but I had expected something a little out of the ordinary.

As I looked around the room I found that I recognised some of the gentlemen present; I had sketched them as they came and went at Falconer's home in Cavendish Square. For me this familiarity was further proof of how these supposed pillars of modern society were as corrupt and foul as I had imagined. They had come here, to Falconer's country home, for a party, the true nature of which I did not dare to consider. Judges, senior policemen, lawyers and medical men, the cream of British society, were all gathered here to revel in their murderous schemes.

There were large double doors in the far corner of the drawing room, by the side of which stood two tall men in the livery of house staff. Young women in grey woollen maids' uniforms wandered about the room, refilling glasses and lighting cigars for the men; I had seen these uniforms before, for they were the clothes worn by the staff sent to Falconer by Marcus Tandry. The anger within me surged.

The double doors opened and a familiar figure came into sight: Mávnos, the doorman from Falconer's Cavendish Square home, entered slowly, dressed in a cloak of white fur and a headpiece adorned with large teeth. Despite his height he held his head high and carried himself as if he were the Lord of the Manor himself. As if to play to this charade, there was immediate silence and all eyes in the room settled upon him.

'Gentlemen, thank you for coming this evening – a night that will live long in our memories,' he said. 'I have received word that Lord Falconer is on his way but has been slightly delayed. He sent a message to say that we should start dinner without him and that he will be joining us once we have dined and our ceremony is set to begin.' There was not a murmur within the room; he held their gaze as by magic of some kind. 'If you will please join me in the dining room, I have been assured by the cook that tonight's meal will be one to remember.' He turned sharply and walked back through the doors. Only when he had disappeared from sight did any noise return to the room as the men drained their glasses, put out their cigars and followed him through to dine.

The doorway was to the left of the room, the same direction that the passageway followed, and so I continued walking until I came to the next thin viewing slot. Before I even reached it, however, I could hear the hubbub of the men as they entered the room and witnessed the dining table; there were cheers and laughter from the gentlemen and I rushed to look through and see what all of the noise was about. As I peered through my very worst fears were realised.

The table was long, long enough for over thirty men to sit around it. It was dressed in a bright white tablecloth and adorned with silver cutlery, chinaware plates and crystal wine goblets. Along the dark red walls of the room hung large paintings of what I can only imagine to be the parents, grandparents and great-grandparents of the Falconer line, all dressed and posed as if they were royalty and all looking down their noses at the diners as they took their places around the table. The ceiling of the room was high, with a fresco painting upon the plasterwork of the clouds of heaven, lined with angels all looking down and weeping as they gazed upon the world below them – and weep they should. At the ceiling's centre hung a large chandelier, the lowest piece of which was a curved knife cut of pure crystal which pointed down at the table's centrepiece.

Mávnos stood at the head of the table and waited for the men as they moved their seats back and stood uniformly around the table. They lapsed into silence as they saw him waiting, their arms hanging by their sides, their heads bowing as if in prayer. In the centre of the table lay a bound and gagged Tom Finnan, struggling to free himself from his bonds, his eyes wild in terror.

'Gentlemen!' called Mávnos, picking up a large knife from the table before him. 'Before dinner is served, let us, the Domini Mortum, the Lords of Death, in deference to our ancient mother, begin this evening's proceedings!' He held the knife aloft as if holding a glass to raise a toast; the men around the table followed suit, each picking up a knife of their own and raising it to point to the centre of the ceiling.

'Gentlemen!' he cried. 'The Queen!'

'The Queen!' they returned and together, in an act of dark union and cruel allegiance, they each thrust a blade into Tom's body and cheered.

I could not help it, but I cried out then and banged my fist against the wall. I did not care if they heard or saw me – they could not do this without complaint.

It would seem that the noise I created was not the surprise that I had hoped it would be; for as my anger burst free and my tears flowed, I was seized on either side by two men who had crept along the passageway behind me. I struggled and fought, but it was to no avail; the wall panel in front of me slid to one side and I was marched into the room to the further cheers of this corrupt gathering.

'It would seem, gentlemen,' called Mávnos, as the rowdy mob around him grew ecstatic in their frenzy, 'that our guest of honour has arrived at last. Welcome, Samuel Weaver! We thought that you would never make it to the party!'

I was struck hard on the back of my head and, to the sounds of the laughter and undiluted joy of the gentlemen in the room, sent spinning into unconsciousness.

16

A Death at Surrenden Manor

I bent down to help Mr Morgan pick up Father's body from the floor of the drawing room.

'Don't you worry yourself with this, young sir,' he grumbled. 'I am not yet as old and weak as you would have me believe, you know.' He put both of his arms under the body and stood, until he was cradling the flesh that had once been my father in his arms as if it were a large child.

'Damn!' I said as I looked down at the rug where it had lain just moments before and noticed that there was a small burn mixed among the intricate pattern. 'Perhaps I was little too forceful in my actions. I am sorry, Ma, I seem to have left a mark.'

'Don't you worry yourself,' she said. 'I can soon mend it so the mark is not so noticeable. That's my job; you've done yours right enough.'

I looked at the pair of them and in that moment I felt nothing but love.

'Thank you both for this. I am in your debt forever. I could never have wished for better people to guide me through my youth. You have been truer parents to me than my own ever were.'

Mrs Coleman rushed towards me and took me in her arms. 'You are a wonderful boy!' she cried. 'And you deserved better. Ever since you told me how you suspected he was responsible for what happened to Victoria, it has been playing devilishly on my mind. The more I thought of him and his ways, the more I knew that it was he who had put her into that position; delivery boy indeed! Your father was a bad one and we will all be better off without him. So let us be thankful that we have each other.' She wiped her eyes before righting herself once more. 'Now, this will not do! We have much to do before you leave, sir.' She turned to the gardener. 'Mr Morgan, don't you be standing there like a great clod. Take that thing out to the orchard and make sure it's buried deep. We don't want it to be found – ever.'

'The hole is already dug, Harriet. We did it together las' night, didn't we, boy?' He smiled at me and carried the body out of the room, to a door at the back where a wheelbarrow waited.

'Now then,' Mrs Coleman said, looking me up and down. 'Has everything been arranged as we planned? I don't want to have any nasty surprises to deal with when you've gone.'

'Of course, Ma,' I said. 'The carriage driver who brought Father back this morning has been well paid. If asked he will say that he took him to the train station this morning, where Father boarded a train to Liverpool. Later this morning, you will find a letter from Father in his study, stating that he has decided to leave to start his own mission in the islands of the South Seas and does not expect to return soon; tickets for such a journey have been bought and paid for. You will give this letter to Father's solicitor, Mr Bainbridge, who will take over the affairs of Father's estate, namely the continued payment of yours and Mr Morgan's salaries until Father's return. I have spoken to Mr Bainbridge myself and made sure that if any questions arise regarding Father, he shall find his own name on the cover of all the newspapers as a visitor and investor in brothels. Mr Bainbridge will also take over Father's other business affairs himself and as such will become a very powerful and wealthy man because of Father's downfall. Everybody benefits from today.

'The house will remain in Father's name until such time as it is decided that he is no longer able to return – I will ensure that news reaches England at some point in the future of Father's untimely death whilst ministering to the newly Christian peoples of the world.

'Mother will be collected from The Retreat Hospital at the soonest opportunity and be returned to her home, where she will be cared for by Mr Morgan and yourself. Finally, as for me, I shall leave today, as planned, to start my new life in London, where I am away from any doubt or suspicion regarding Father's hasty disappearance. I shall write, of course, but I shall probably not return unless forced – it is time to start afresh for me.'

Mrs Coleman smiled at me gently. 'Oh Arthur, we are both so very proud. You are like a son to me. If only it had been you that Victoria gave her attentions to.'

I held up my hand to her. 'Arthur no more, Ma. From now on, and for all of our safety, I shall make my name as Samuel Weaver. It is fitting for me, in my new adventure, to leave Arthur Lambert behind in York.'

Within the hour the carriage arrived to take me to the station. Mrs Coleman and Mr Morgan stood on the steps of the house and waved me off as I went. Something within told me that this would be the start of a great adventure and, sure enough, the following day I found myself in the offices of *The Illustrated Police News* arguing with Henry Cope and introducing myself to Mr George Purkess for the first time.

***

A splitting pain in my head awoke me and, as I tried to lift my hand to my head to rub it, I realised that I was shackled. The room was quite dark and my eyes struggled to adjust, the only light coming from a barred grill in the top of the door, catching the dust motes in the hazy atmosphere. It was as I looked over that I saw, sitting on a cot bed on the far side of the room, the silhouette of a man. He heard my movements and spoke.

'What a mess, what a state, what a terrible place we have put ourselves in, Samuel. How did we get here? We must be fools.' He leant forwards so that the light from the grill illuminated his face.

'Oh God, Higgins! Not you as well?' I said. 'I had hoped that you would be out there somewhere, fetching assistance. What happened to you, Edward? Did the verger, Mr Williams, not get to you?'

'Williams? No, I did not see the man.'

'I am so sorry, Edward. It seems that I have led you to destruction. I wish I had never started all of this now. Perhaps Williams made it out, though? Perhaps help is on its way?'

Higgins laughed then and I took it to be the laughter of a man facing his end.

'What is it?' I asked. 'What is so funny, my friend?'

'You led me here, Sam?' he laughed. '*You* led *me* here? Please do not tell me that you still believe that. Oh goodness, what a joke this is, Samuel! What a perfect and most ideal joke this all is. Do you not see it yet? Do you not see?' He stood from the bed so that he looked down upon me, his face still a smile, his eyes glistening. He was not shackled as I was. 'You did not lead me anywhere. You have not led me anywhere at all; it is *you* who have been led. I really thought that you were better than this, really I did.'

'But what do you mean?' I tried to stand, but the chains kept me sitting upon the floor.

'Samuel Weaver, you are a disappointment to me. If you weren't so valuable to my cause I would walk out of this door and leave you to slowly die. Tell me, Sam, what is my name?'

'Edward Higgins, of course.'

'Is it, Sam? Is it?'

'Why yes, what kind of game is this? What are you playing at?'

'I'm afraid, my friend, that the time for games is now over. From here on in, it is just terrible reality for you. Think about it for a moment; use that cunning brain of yours. *What is my name?*'

I froze, staring at the man standing above me.

'Lord William Falconer,' I muttered, hardly wanting to believe the words that came from my lips. 'Your name is Lord William Falconer.'

'Good man! Good man!' he cried, clapping his hands together in glee. 'At last the boy has got it. Really, Samuel, I obviously had you down for a much more devious and twisted mind than you obviously own. Has it really taken this long? Really?'

Memories came flooding back to me then. Of how both men were said to go missing for days on end; of our chance meeting that night at the Egyptian Hall; of how he had appeared in Pluckley shortly after Surrenden Manor was taken under new ownership. I was such a fool.

'But I met Lord Falconer,' I exclaimed. 'I saw him twice, didn't I? If you are Lord William Falconer, then who was *he*? I don't understand. Why did you pretend to be my friend? Why did you bring me here?'

He smiled at my rush of questions and slowly sat down again on the bed, withdrawing his cigarette case from his pocket, before taking out a stick and lighting it.

'Well, initially it was for sport, of course, but then it became something much more fun,' he said. 'As to my other self, you are, of course,

referring to another of my good friends – Freddie, a man of the theatre. Oh how he loved playing that role for me. According to Mr
Soames and Mr Dawes he was very impressive, a true actor; which, of
course, is what he is. I found him on the stage at the Alhambra about
a year ago – such a talented man, if a little guilty of overacting when
he gets carried away. I really would have expected you to see through
him, Sam. The man cannot put on an accent to save his life!'

He laughed and ran his fingers through his hair, before settling back
on the small cot bed, leaning against the wall and kicking his legs
out in front of him. He continued, 'I have watched you for a long
time, Samuel, since shortly after your arrival in London in fact. You
were not such a good reporter that you hid the fact that you were
obsessed with Sibelius Darke. I have people on the ground, Samuel,
people who let me know when my business is being looked into –
and subtlety is not a skill that comes easily to you. When I heard that
you were heading down to Pluckley, I couldn't believe my luck. It
was too good a chance to miss, Sam, really it was. I must say, though,
that I found your company very entertaining – you are a good man
to have around, if only for a drink. When you returned to London
and continued to dig, I thought to have you killed immediately, but
then I remembered dear Freddie and decided to continue my play for
a little longer. It really is such a shame that you set yourself against
me; we could have worked so well together, you and I.' The smile on
his face was so wide that I thought that it would crack his cheeks as
he spoke. 'Tell me, Samuel. Did you ever work out why the girls in
Boston Place lost their hearts?'

'I assumed that it was just some kind of ritual murder, something to
do with your Golden Woman.'

'Correct, most correct. Good man! But what was it for, though?
Why those women, in particular? Any ideas? What did they have in
common?'

'They all worked for the service agency. And they all killed their
own children.'

'They did indeed, Sam. They did indeed. And there is good reason
for this. For just as the hearts and souls of the innocent and pure are
powerful tools in magic, so the heart of a killer is a much more pow-

erful thing. Taking the life of another, especially one dear to you, it
blackens that fragile muscle inside your chest; it fills it with a darkness
that will never leave and which can be used to create power, Sam, terrible and great power. I have always been entranced by magic, Sam;
ever since I was a small boy. Do you know anything of the tragedy of
my upbringing?'

'I know that you were orphaned at a young age and that your parents died on the Southern Cape. What of it?'

'Ah well, when my parents died I was heartbroken – what small
boy wouldn't be? I grieved for years until finally, after becoming a
man, I decided to travel to the Cape, to find out more about their
demise. Africa is a wonderful place, Samuel. I cannot tell you how
much it opened my eyes to the world which surrounds us; a world
of magic and forces which can be harnessed, if you have the right
tools. I did not find out anything new about my parents' death that
I hadn't already been told, but it was on my travels that I first met
Master Mávnos, a fellow traveller from the far north of Europe, and
a magician and conjurer of quite extraordinary proportions. He was
travelling in Africa to learn new skills, especially those concerning the
creation of life. We became close friends and journeyed together; it
was he who opened my eyes, and it is from him that I learnt each
culture possesses its own particular magic, which can be harnessed for
certain uses.

'We travelled into Asia and the plains of Mongolia, working our
way back west through the countries of Europe until we returned to
the home of Mávnos, the Sammi lands near the Arctic Circle. It is a
remarkable place, Sam. I would encourage you to go there but I'm
afraid your future is rather somewhat curtailed now. It was here that
Mávnos finally told me of the ancient Sammi queen. Now I am a
fickle man, I admit this. My mind wanders and my allegiances dance
about like a flighty young girl, desperately seeking something perfect
in the world. It was then that I found it, in Louhi.

'Here was a beautiful and powerful woman, someone to admire,
someone to follow and to love. I became entranced by the stories of
her, something which Mávnos saw in me. And so, when he told me
that there was a way we could bring his queen back, I charged him

with making it possible; with bringing together the elements required to bring my own true queen back to life. Now that is real magic, Sam. That is real power, the power of life over death, the power of the gods.'

'The type of magic required to create a living woman made of gold?' I offered.

'Exactly, Sam. You really are picking this up at a pace now, you know. Now, The Fellowship – what was left of my club once that fool Darke had taken a match to it – we set up the agency on the Marylebone Road to attract the type of girls we needed. Once on board, we used my man Mávnos to have a little talk to them and to persuade them that it would be in their best interests to take the life of one dear to them. He is a very clever man, Mávnos, most persuasive when he needs to be. When the girls had carried out their task they were taken to a special place, where they were kept until we had the required number.'

'Twelve.'

'Twelve, indeed. And so, once ready, these twelve willing participants took part in a ceremony whereupon their blackened hearts were given voluntarily for the greater cause – and to bring our Golden Woman to life.'

'She left footprints on the floor of the room.'

'She did indeed; that is where she took her first steps for us. So now we had our 'perfect' killer and we let her out on the streets at night to do her work. The girls she killed were all employed by the agency and sent out into the dark for our own golden girl to hunt and kill. It was some sport for her – and we really hoped that she would take to it better.'

'In terms of what you needed, did she not do a good job?' I asked, my mind a blur.

'Well she did, but, you see, the problem with an automaton is that they will only do directly what you ask them to. There was no finesse, no enjoyment in her work. She killed and placed them as instructed, even using the railway spikes which we provided for her by the sackful, but she was a little… cold. There was no fire in her belly, no lust. In many ways her downfall, and the way you brought it about, were a blessing to us. It got rid of her and brought a truth to us that we had previously not considered.'

'Which is?'

'The fact that a killing machine is all very well, but you can never really beat getting a man to do the work for you. And I believe that you may be that man.'

'Me? You must be joking with me, Edward – or is it William? If you think that I will do your bidding, then you will be very much mistaken.'

'Oh, there is no mistake. You are a killer after all, aren't you, Sam? Poor Mr Tandry was in a terrible mess when we found him. From the look of his face, you have quite a rage inside you – a rage which can be put to better use.'

I thought then of the others that I had killed: of Hiram Osborne drowned in chocolate; of sweet Victoria spurned and sent to the butcher's knife; of Isabelle lying at the bottom of the staircase; and finally of my father, a burning poker thrust through his chest before being buried in an unmarked grave at the foot of an apple tree. If only Falconer knew of these killings his glee would be even greater.

'I will not,' I said. 'You cannot make me do your bidding; I am not some poor servant girl, weak and ready to be persuaded.'

'Oh, those girls were not weak; my man Mávnos has... skills. You will be a wonderful addition to our armoury, but first we require something from you. We have a host for our queen, a fitting body for her to take once the soul has been cleansed from it and the shell made ready for Louhi's arrival. But to bring our queen to us we require a token, something that you hold within you.'

'Look at me. I am chained to a wall – what could you possibly take from me? And it doesn't matter anyway; I have already made moves to expose you. At this moment, the police will be looking through all of my work and finding all the evidence they need to bring you down.'

'The police?' He laughed. 'The police? Please, Samuel, do I have to explain to you how influential I am? There is not a station in London in which I do not have eyes and ears, and there is not a policeman I cannot own.'

I thought of George Langton; was he one of Falconer's men? Had I been fooled by him as well?

'We shall see,' I said. 'Now, is that all, or do you wish to taunt me further?'

'No, that is all for now, Samuel. I will be seeing you later, though. We are all desperate to see our star act perform for us tonight.' He stood from the cot bed and knocked on the door. Bolts were moved on the outside and it was opened. A tall, thin man wearing spectacles entered the room, carrying a metal tray. He placed the tray on the cot and took from it a glass syringe, before turning to me.

'We will be back for you shortly, Samuel,' Falconer said, looking down on me. 'You will enjoy your role as our new weapon. But for now, and as a parting gift from a friend, I think it is best if you sleep for the next part of the procedure. Honestly, I have seen it performed on those awake and it is not something that I would see you suffer.'

He left then and, as I struggled to get away from the man with the syringe, the needle was stuck into my arm and the plunger depressed. I fell into a dark sleep.

***

A searing red glare burned through my head, waking me from my drugged state. Slowly I opened my eyes, squinting at the shock of the light as it struck my pupils. My vision was hazy, but I could tell that I had been moved and was no longer in the cell. I tried to lift my hands to rub at my face, to bring more lucidity, more awareness; they would not move, however, and nor would my legs. Stiff leather bindings were holding me down and I knew then that I had been strapped to a table; to an altar.

I moved my head to look around me and saw that I was not alone. I was in a large room of red-painted brick and around the room, lining the walls, stood men in golden cowls. A few yards away from me stood a plinth similar to the one I lay on. There was another person laid on that altar, but they were covered in a black silk sheet; from the shape and size I guessed it to be a woman. By the wall, past where my feet were bound, were two large chairs; they too were covered in black silk, and they were at present empty.

My arms and chest burned as if stuck with a thousand needles and I looked down at myself as best I could. The top part of my body had been shaved and I only wore a pair of short grey trousers which came to the knee. It was not my state of undress that most shocked me, however; far from it. It was what covered the skin of my chest and arms; for, as with the women who'd lain nailed to the floor in Boston Place, my skin had been carved: neat intricate cuts of many shapes and sizes. There were spirals and circles, triangles and lettering; carvings of such detail that they reminded me of the hieroglyphics that I had once seen on a visit to the British Museum soon after my arrival in London. There were other symbols there too which were similar to Chinese writing: swooping arcs and carefully placed dots, each marked in my own blood on my skin. It would seem that the whole of the upper half of my body was covered in the marks. I was reminded of the last time that I had visited the circus, where I had seen a man tattooed from head to toe. I was not covered in ink, however, but in cuts that would become scars – if I were to live beyond this point.

The heavy perfume of opium hung in the air, its smoke cloying and grabbing at my senses, desperately trying to enter my body and spread further confusion. I coughed and spluttered in an attempt to free myself from it but could not fight and it numbed my mind, painting pictures in front of my eyes, corrupting my thoughts.

I called out to the men standing around the room – desperate, pleading words – but they stood like marble sentinels, waiting. Their faces remained impassive, despite the cries and insults that I screamed at them.

Suddenly I was aware of another presence in the room, of someone appearing at my side. It was the man Mávnos. He was dressed in a long golden tunic marked with bright silver and red decoration; there were patches of patterned fur upon his shoulders and large black feathers woven into his bright white hair. He smiled down at me.

'Soon,' he mouthed.

The sound of a door opening behind my head made me aware that someone else had entered. They walked past me and took their place on one of the silk-draped chairs; it was Falconer. He too was dressed in ceremonial robes, brightly decorated and beautifully sewn; he looked every bit a king.

I called to him, but he too did not respond. This moment was too important for petty squabbles now; he was too close to achieving his dream, I thought.

Finally, Falconer stood and spoke to the room.

'Loyal guardians, men of Dolor, Domini Mortum; we have come to this place tonight to bring death and rebirth. The death will be of this man, chosen for his task and providing us with the organ of life. Yet death is not the end; death is never the end. He will give to us but he will live on; he will provide, and continue to give, for his work here has only just begun. Stubborn and unconforming he may be, but in the end he will follow the path set for him.'

As he spoke the cowled men around the room nodded their heads in deference. Their master spoke and they listened like children, awestruck and full of wonder at their great work.

'And by his side,' he continued, 'here lies our Queen, soon to be reborn in this world through the gift of life, given gladly.'

At the stroke of Falconer's hand, a man stepped forward from the wall and took hold of the black sheet covering the woman. With a sharp tug, it fell from her and she was revealed to me.

It was Alice.

I screamed then. I screamed in pain and in anger. I cried and howled, cursed and struggled, but to no avail.

Alice's head turned towards me. She was in a drugged state, her eyes milky and glazed, unable to fully focus. I saw that she was not bound to the altar and I called out her name, hoping to draw her out from her daze, to spur her into action, but it was not to be. Her mouth began to move, a hoarse whisper as she tried to form words, but such was her state that I recognised only one utterance before her eyes closed and she was lost to me: 'Benjamin.'

I began to shout again, pulling at my restraints, desperately trying to free myself to save us both, but the straps holding me down had no give in them. It was over for us.

Mávnos smiled beside me and brought his dagger into view. It was long and sharp, curved and wicked, and held above my chest. He began to chant under his breath; words that I did not understand in a harsh clicking tongue that I had not heard before.

'We are entering a new age!' said Falconer, his arms spread wide. 'An age where our Queen, Louhi, will take control once more! And what better way to bring Louhi to the world and begin her journey back to power than by giving her the black heart of the killer who loved her host. It is almost poetic. Master Mávnos, bring it out!'

I did not feel the blade enter my chest. I did not feel the slice as it opened me up, nor the hand of Mávnos as he reached inside and clasped my heart within his hand. When he withdrew it from my body I only felt a slight tug as it came free; I saw it beating in his hand and I screamed, I screamed until my voice was hoarse and my lungs could breathe no more; I screamed until death took me, finally.

17

And in the End

Darkness.

At first I wondered whether all of those stories that Father expounded were true: whether there was indeed a heaven and hell, and I had been sent to the eternal damnation of the latter. It was as my eyes became accustomed to what little light there was, that I realised this was not hell as anyone would imagine it to be, but that I was indeed back in my cell at Surrenden Manor where I was laid upon the cot bed.

My hands reached up and carefully touched my arms, and the scars carved upon them, symbols which I was now destined to keep. It was as I felt my chest, though, that I came across the wound left by Mávnos where he had cut into me with his blade. There was a line running down from the base of my throat to my navel, a line which had been stitched together with coarse thread. The skin had been joined again and would, in time, repair itself until only a long scar remained.

But what of my heart? Did I not see it pulled from my body and held up above me? I was sure that I did, or perhaps it was just the opium affecting my senses and fooling my eyes. My right hand settled on my chest in an attempt to feel the gentle and steady beat of my heart, surely still within me. There was no such sensation. I moved my hand desperately to the left and then back to the right of my chest, but I could feel no rhythm. I felt down my arm, to my wrist, touching it with my fingertips for sign of a pulse; there was none. Finally I touched at my throat: it was cold, no precious blood flowing through it from my heart, for the heart was no longer there.

How could this be possible? How could I still live? I thought on the Golden Woman; if Mávnos could summon life from inanimate gold, then what was skin and bone to such a magician? It would be child's play.

I tried to sit up, but my body felt numb, without strength, immobile. So this was indeed hell; trapped in a lifeless body for all eternity. I lay and stared at the darkness of the ceiling, trying to sit up every now and then; until slowly, over a period so long I cannot give it a value, movement returned to me.

I raised myself slowly, my body stiff – as stiff as a corpse, I thought. The darkness in the room remained and there was no sound of life outside, no voices or footsteps; I had been put in the cell and abandoned. Over the next few hours I managed to stand and finally to walk, although I would have resembled a newborn foal to anyone willing to watch.

Still no one came.

My movements became more fluid, less rigid and forced, and I found myself returning to some kind of normality. Why had I been left here? Where were Falconer and Mávnos, come to view their new creation? I was alone here; left to die perhaps, although I knew that my time of death had passed.

I do not know how long I remained there. I did not hunger nor thirst; what use is food and water to a dead man? It would matter not if the air ran out in my cell; what use was air to a man who did not need to breathe? I was in limbo.

After a period of time too long to count, I heard footsteps approach. Bolts were pulled open and the door pulled wide, letting in a shaft of cold yellow light.

A figure appeared in the doorway.

His face was still in darkness and I leaned forwards to see him, thereby illuminating my own face.

'Good Lord, Samuel Weaver. I thought you were a dead man!' exclaimed Inspector Langton, as he rushed forwards and took me by the arms, helping me to my feet.

'How the devil have you survived in here for so long – and what has happened to your arms? Your chest? You look like they certainly put you through the ringer.'

'It is a long story, Inspector, and one which I will tell gladly, but first please tell me, how long have I been shut away?'

He stood back from me for a moment and looked me up and down.

'You mean you do not know? Gods, man, it has been nearly two months since you sent me that message and came to Surrenden. The house has stood empty for most of that time.'

'Empty?'

'Yes, sir. When I received your note I gathered as many men as I could and we travelled down in force to come and assist you. From your files, and the notes left by Abe Thomas, I knew that I would have enough to seek a warrant to search the place, although it proved a hard job finding someone not in Falconer's pay who was willing to provide one. By the time we had the means to come, they had got wind of our arrival and cleared out in a great hurry. We did not get here until late the next day, after your note. When we arrived, the house had been abandoned and there was no one left. Well, no one except you it seems.

'It worried me that we had never found you, either alive or dead. I have been coming back here as often as I can to search the house. I saw in your notes how there were many hidden and secret passageways within the house. I hoped to be able to find you in one; but I never expected to find you alive. How did you do it, man?'

I thought for a moment. So Falconer had fled, forced to leave me behind. How that must have galled him! It would seem that a role as his new weapon would not be mine after all. There was, however, the small matter of my death. Now was probably not the best time to announce my demise to Langton; would there ever be a good time?

'I was left with a store of food – not much, but it has kept me going. Tell me where is Falconer? Was he caught?'

'I'm afraid not, sir. He is long gone, last seen boarding a ship at Southampton and heading to New York in the company of a young woman and a short, white-haired man. His Cavendish Square house has been cleared out too – it is an empty shell. No one saw them leave, of course. Many others have disappeared also, high-up, prominent figures; you would be surprised at who was involved in their operation.'

'Oh, it would take a lot to shock me,' I said, allowing myself a smile. 'Tell me, did the verger, Mr Williams, come through?'

'I'm afraid not, Mr Weaver. He was found dead in the church, his throat cut.'

The anger within me burned but I did not show it. There would be a time in the future to take revenge, but it was not now. The amiable George Langton led me from my cell and, after suitable clothing was found to cover my scars, I was taken back to London.

***

It has been three years since the events at Surrenden Manor and my death and rebirth. In that time much has happened. I have returned to York, to the Rectory, where I now live with Mrs Coleman, Mr Morgan, my mother and you, Benjamin. I have written these words above, so that you may know the truth about how you came to live here, and of how your sister disappeared from our lives. As you now know, her body still lives, out there somewhere, but it is just a shell: your sister does not exist within this world.

As you know, my father's estate is now in my hands and, in the future, it will be yours to own; when this future is, I shall tell you shortly. You are growing up into a brave young man. You have dealt with the wound inflicted upon you on that terrible day in Amberley Road with great grace and courage, and it has not stopped you from developing into a bright and intelligent boy. When I told you that your sister had disappeared and was lost to us, you kept a firm face and did not cry. This is why I have trusted you with my secrets; this is why you must now know what became of our dear Alice.

I hope that you will understand the things that I have done and will not think ill of me. A man could have no finer son than you – and I am proud to call you such. Mrs Coleman and Mr Morgan think dearly of you and they will always be there to protect you, as they did with me. My mother, in her own way, thinks greatly of you also; and, although she lives a solitary life, I know that she watches you in the gardens from her window and takes joy in seeing you flourish.

My body is beginning to fail me, Benjamin. I have felt it coming for some time. The time of my death has long since passed. My body, once kept alive by dark magic, is starting to decay and I fear that soon I will be able to hide it no longer. My limbs are wrapped with bandages to hold them together and, despite the quantities of cologne in which I douse myself, the stench of death grows ever stronger about me.

It is for this reason that I will be leaving our house, never to return. I have made arrangements with my solicitor to pass all of the estate over to you upon your eighteenth birthday, and until that time you will remain under the legal care of Mrs Coleman and Mr Morgan. I am glad to say that your future wealth is as secure as I can possibly make it. The sales of my book about the Dolorian Fellowship are strong and should provide you with a steady income for the foreseeable future.

I do not mean to return, but I have a goal in mind. Somewhere out in the world there are three people whom I must find.

One is a man who I once called my friend, but who turned out to be my most terrible adversary.

The second, a woman whom I once loved, but who is now lost, her body inhabited by a most horrifying danger to the world.

And the third is the man who holds the power to keep my own long-dead body alive to me.

I doubt I shall return to stain your life any further; I have always been a curse on those around me and now I must suffer the consequences of my mistakes.

As I said to you at the beginning of my story, there is no heaven and there is no hell, not in the sense that all God-fearing men and women upon this earth believe. However, we all make choices in our lives and we all must pay for our actions.

There is goodness and glory, as well as sin and defeat; I made choices, many of them bad, but towards the end I think I made the right ones and stood against what I saw as evil in the world.

Yet we are judged by fate and it seems that my wrongs outweigh my rights, and I must live in penance and suffering for the rest of my days.

However long that may be.

For death is not the end.

Patrons

Caspar Addyman
Pat Alexander
Lulu Allison
James Ambrose
Lesley Anker
An Anonymous Donor
Sandra Armor
Tim Atkinson
John Auckland
Duncan Bailey
Jason Ballinger
Neil Bates
Naomi Beaumont
John Bradley
Catherine Bramley
Charlotte Brittain
Marie Catchpole
Cazzikstan Cazzikstan
Ann Chaddock
Chris Chamberlain
Anthony Cole
Julia Coleman
Sean Collins
Ian Colville
Karen Cornforth
Tamsen Courtenay
Grant Cousins
Harriet Cunningham
Melissa Davies
Kate Day
Jenny Doughty
Alys Earl

Jennie Ensor
Christine Farrell
Bethany Finnan
Drew Fleming
Chris Fletcher
Anita Frith
Angela Frost
Jenny Fuller
Laurie Garrison
Nick Gerrard
Beth Goodliff
Sarah Greenley
Geoffrey Gudgion
Emma Guinness
Kelly Harrison
Archie Harrison
Jake Harrison
Baylea Hart
Michelle Harvey
Maximilian Hawker
Mike Hawtin
Jess Hebron
Martin Heeley
Sandy Herbert
Rob Herdman
Neil Herring
Rhian Heulwen Price
Julie Heyes
John Patrick Higgins
Sean Holliday
Jenny Holmes
Jade Hutchinson
Rhiannon Ifans
David Jacobs
Oli Jacobs
Kwemmeh James

Sez Jennings
Samantha Jennings
Elena Kaufman
Lisa Keenan
Shona Kinsella
Julia Kite
Sonya Lano
Natalie Lazenby
Nikki Livingstone-Rothwell
Amanda Lloyd Jennings
Jeni Loosley
Anna Lyaruu
Helen Mason
Kirsty McCue
Fiona McDonough
Pete McGrath
Eimear McKenzie
Bethany McLean
Mike McPeake
Erinna Mettler
Lucy Moffatt
Carlo Navato
Jan Newton
Naomi Noad
Claire Norman
Mark Norton
Paul O'Connell
Par Olsson
Colin Chuck Owston
Sarah Patmore
Ray Pentland
Janet Phillips
Debs Pinkney
Steve Plews
Rebecca Read
Sue Reubens

Oliver Reynolds
Jamie Richardson
Katherine Risi
Auriel Roe
Alex Rose
Claire Rowntree
Terry Rutherford
Fiona Scott
Sue Sharpe
Chris Sharples
Caroline Shepherdson
Anusha Simha
Ian Skewis
Debbie Smith
Wendy Stead
Ellen Steele
Becky Stephenson
Bobby Stevenson
Ruth Sudlow
David Tasker.
Trevor Taylor
Karen Taylor
Andrew Tees
Sarah Thompson
Deborah Thompson
Jodie Thorne
Sadie Thorne
Aaron Thorne
Katy Thorne
Andy Tomkins
Ann Watson
Kathryn Weatherburn
Jessica White
Robert Wilcock
Suzie Wilde
Caroline Wilkie

Derek Wilson
Candice Wilson